W9-AAO-049

MR.
SHAKESPEARE'S
Bastard

A novel

RICHARD B. WRIGHT

A PHYLLIS BRUCE BOOK

HarperCollins*PublishersLtd*

A Phyllis Bruce Book, published by
HarperCollins Publishers Ltd.

Originally published in a hardcover edition
by HarperCollins Publishers Ltd: 2010
This trade paperback edition: 2011

HarperCollins books may be purchased for educational, business,
or sales promotional use through our Special Markets Department.

HarperCollins Publishers Ltd
2 Bloor Street East, 20th Floor
Toronto, Ontario, Canada
M4W 1A8

www.harpercollins.ca

Library and Archives Canada Cataloguing in Publication

Wright, Richard B., 1937–
Mr. Shakespeare's bastard / Richard B. Wright.

"A Phyllis Bruce book."

ISBN 978-1-55468-836-4

I. Title.
PS8595.R6M78 2011   C813'.54   C2011-903740-8

Printed and bound in the United States
RRD 9 8 7 6 5 4 3 2 1

For my wife, Phyllis,
and for our newest grandchild, Nathan

My father, methinks I see my father.
O! where, my lord?
In my mind's eye, Horatio.
HAMLET [I, ii]

EASTON HOUSE

1658

CHARLOTTE LEFT FOR OXFORD this morning. This was irritating because she had promised that today she would begin to take down my words. The pen and inkhorn and the book with its ivory-coloured blank pages and marbled cover, Charlotte's Christmas present to me, are on the writing table in the library. I put them there myself yesterday morning in anticipation. So I was short with her as she said goodbye today, bending to kiss my cheek as I sat at breakfast. As usual, she was late and in a hurry, the hired coach already waiting in the courtyard. It was barely light and our new serving girl, Emily, was taking the baggage outdoors and looking none too pleased about it either. But then, she is already showing signs of insolence. I have to think about this, but I may soon give her notice.

"It's only a week, Linny," Charlotte whispered. "I'll begin your story when I return. I promise."

But she has promised many times before, and always it seems there is something to distract her: tea at a neighbour's house, a meeting with her church group, a gathering for cards. Now an engagement broken off, yet again; a friend in Oxford is in distress and must be consoled. Charlotte heard the news only yesterday. Surely I could understand how she was needed in the circumstances? I didn't say as much, but I would have been more sympathetic had this not been the third or perhaps even the fourth time her friend's engagement has been called off, either by the young lady or by the unfortunate young man who may have to spend the rest of his life in her company. My own feeling is that matters will be mended yet again within a fortnight. For the moment, however, there is drama in the lives of Charlotte and her friend, with tears and muffins and tea and endless pillow chatter in the night. I pity the young woman's mother more than anyone.

This dependence on Charlotte is maddening. Despite my years of hard work, she can yet prove unreliable; even now in her twenty-fourth year she can behave like a schoolgirl. At Christmastime she told me that in the spring she would set aside the mornings for me until we finished what I have to say about my father, the poet Shakespeare: how he entered my mother's life and later my own. Now it is April and so far I have nothing but her empty promises.

Even as she left this morning she promised, "We shall get to it next week, Linny. I owe it to you—I really do—and I'm looking forward to hearing it all."

She does owe me, too, because I have raised her from the moment the midwife pulled her from her dying mother. Still, always something gets in the way.

I would, of course, transcribe all this myself, but I have left it too late and this cursed membrane across my eyes has set me adrift in a world of wavering cloudiness that blurs faces and familiar objects: the edges of tables now snag my hips and chair legs bruise my shins. I have to be mindful on stairs. As for words on a page, they are but clusters of letters swimming before my eyes. A lifetime of reading by candlelight must now be paid for, and if I am to live much longer, I expect I shall end my days as blind as justice.

Yet not for a moment do I regret those years of reading. I have read nearly all my life. In my fifth year I could recite the letters of the alphabet from my hornbook. Then I began to see how these letters could be put together to form words that could name the plants and creatures of this world and describe our very thoughts and feelings. Soon I was reading Aesop's fables and the *Book of Ancient Riddles*, *The Hundred Merry Tales* and others like them. Reading was important, for it meant we could become acquainted early with the word of God. Mam and I lived with her brother and his wife, Uncle Jack and Aunt Sarah, and they were pious folk, my aunt especially disdainful of pleasure in any form. In our house was not a top to spin nor hobbyhorse to ride, and as I grew older my reading was confined to religious books. Before I was seven, I could write the words of the Lord's Prayer and the Ten Commandments. By then I was also absorbed by the gruesome deaths of Protestants as recorded in Foxe's *Book of Martyrs*; I knew by heart passages from the big Geneva Bible which sat on the sideboard in the dining room of our house in Worsley. I loved the copperplate illustrations of Jonah in the whale's belly and Daniel in the lion's den. But it was the words with their magical power to put pictures inside my head that truly excited me.

After my mother's death and my time in London, the details of which I shall duly relate, I returned to Oxfordshire and was interviewed here at Easton House for a position as nursemaid. It was arranged by my uncle, a draper by trade, well known for his probity and goodwill. I was then in my fifteenth year and Mrs. Easton was carrying her first child, Walter. Sometimes when I look now at Mr. Walter coming into the house from the fields or the markets at Woodstock or Oxford and sitting down to his dinner, I find it hard to believe that he was once a little boy perched on the window seat of the nursery listening to one of my tales.

For a long time Easton House has been a quiet place, and now with Charlotte away, the house seems even quieter and emptier. After a long and brutal winter, it is milder and below stairs Emily is cleaning the fire grates. I told her to be sure to open the windows to freshen the air in the rooms as she worked. I have to tell her everything, go through each step of a particular job or she will not do it properly. It is irksome, and though I like the girl well enough, she taxes what little patience I now have left. She is not so much lazy as indifferent, her manner suggesting that she would just as leave be somewhere else. No doubt she is waiting for a young man to claim her, take her away from the drudgery of dirty fire grates and cobwebbed ceiling corners, though I am equally certain that she lacks the imagination to foresee another kind of tedium within the staleness of married life. Still, she is a plump little morsel and I dare say already knows a thing or two about the ways of the young in darkened hallways or leafy bowers. Men must find appealing the merry enticement in those soft brown eyes that always seek forgiveness when you remind her of something she has forgotten to do. Now she is rattling those grates and raking out the ashes, eager, I am sure, to be done with it and sit down in the kitchen with a cup of tea and tell Mrs. Sproule the latest village gossip. There will be dust on the furniture and Emily will forget unless I remind her, but then I too may forget, and of course I can no longer see dust as well as I used to.

Mr. Walter seldom notices anything in the house, let alone dust on a table or chair. He could as easily eat his meals on an overturned box in the stables, so little regard has he for the niceties of household living. This has grown on him over the years and now his mind is ever on the price of oats or hay or barley, or the weather and its uncertainties. And there's no wife to complicate his single-minded way of thinking. But he is a kind man and a good farmer, well regarded in the shire. His reputation for honesty and fair dealing saved us from ruin in the late civil war. I am certain of it. The Eastons and those of us in their service supported the King's party, and while other like-minded people had their fields trampled and goods looted by Cromwell's armies, they left us alone.

I recall an evening a few weeks before the war began. A friend and neighbour, Mr. Murdoch, visited Easton House to talk with Mr. Walter. They discussed the weather and their crops, but as Murdoch was leaving, they stopped at the front door, and I overheard their parting words, for I was behind an open doorway.

Murdoch said, "And when the time comes, Walter, how will you be placed?"

Mr. Walter replied, "Conscience binds me to the King, Zachary."

"And I to Parliament, Walter," Murdoch said.

"I know that," said Mr. Walter, "and I pray to God we may remain friends whatever happens."

"I pray so too, Walter," said Murdoch, and I watched them shake hands by the front door.

After the war, the Easton lands were not sequestered, and I am sure that it was Murdoch's doing, for he had influential friends in Parliament. Then too we lost our precious Nicky at the Battle of Naseby, and there was sympathy throughout the shire for Mr. Walter and Charlotte, since Nicky was well liked with many friends on both sides of that war. It will be thirteen years this June 14 since we lost him, and Charlotte will have a difficult day as she always does; she was only eleven when her stepbrother was killed and she was deeply affected, loving him as only a young girl can love an older brother, which is to say purely and with complete adulation. I remember how she lay in bed for weeks, thin and pale and sick at heart. In her misery one day she told me that she had taken a vow never to love another. Of course, over time her grief has abated, but the fourteenth of June will forever remain a sad day in her life.

The racket Emily is making with those grates is getting on my nerves and I can imagine the dust she is raising. Upon her return, Charlotte may notice it and she will enact a little scene by looking down on a side table and writing in the dust "Oh dear!" or some other pale expression of reproach. Then she will call for Emily, who will look at the words and break forth in tears. Charlotte will comfort her and Emily will promise to do better, because she wants to please Miss Charlotte, who is a lady and dresses beautifully. All this is really my responsibility and if I did my job properly, I wouldn't have to endure these needlessly melo-dramatic displays of remonstrance and forgiveness. But the truth is I am well past it now and I expect I will feel relief only when I am told as much.

I am fairly certain there has already been talk about this between Charlotte and Mr. Walter. On Christmas Day, he asked to see me in the hall. Charlotte had gone to the library to write her annual letters to her two half-sisters, who have lived in America these twenty-eight years past. Charlotte, of course, has never laid eyes on them, but they are still her sisters and she likes to let them know what is going on at Easton House. They in turn write about their lives in Massachusetts, a place I can scarcely bring myself to imagine, though both Mary and Catherine and their husbands and children seem to have made prosperous and happy lives for themselves out there. I can hardly recall now what they looked like. They will always be two young women who left us with their new husbands, and I suppose I will always see them as two girls whom I told stories to and minded forty years ago. They always reply to Char-lotte's letters and tell her of life in the New World. So while Charlotte was in the library, Mr. Walter sat by the fire with a glass of brandy, which he seldom touches, preferring, as I do, ale. I told myself that it was Christmas and so he felt like a glass of brandy, though I was not sure that together with the heavy meal it would necessarily agree with him.

He has gout now, and brandy is no friend to gout. Besides, his colour was high and he had undone the buttons of his waistcoat. Mr. Walter is a large man and hefty in both front and beam, no longer young at fifty-five. And that day he looked ill at ease, though I thought at the time that unless he was unwell, there was no need to be discomfited, for while beyond the window it was bitter cold, we were well placed, warm by the fire with a good dinner inside us. I had cleared the dishes for Mrs. Sproule, another old party who no longer moves as sprightly as she once did, and as she constantly reminds me, "I am the cook and not a maid-servant." This is true. It is not her job to serve. Where was Emily? We must have given her—yes, I remember now—we had given her Christmas Day to be with her family. She had told me her mother was ill and this could well have been untrue, but what does it matter anyway. I had served the dinner to Mr. Walter and Charlotte and it was then that Mr. Walter asked me to share a glass of brandy with him.

That was unusual, but I could tell that he had some-thing to say to me, and was having difficulty. No surprise in that, for he does not like dealing with situations which may involve personal feelings. It is well known that he has no difficulty in matters of business and is reputed to be a shrewd trader in cattle, sheep and grain. In personal matters, how-ever, he is uneasy, though amiable and kind-hearted to a fault, those last two qualities inherited from his mother, a woman as well-natured and benevolent as you would find on this earth, as different from the old squire as cheese to chalk. I guessed on Christmas Day that Mr. Walter wanted to discuss my position as housekeeper at Easton House, but I didn't say anything at first. Early on, I discovered that in service you must never presume to know what your employer is thinking; you must constantly feign ignorance and say little unless asked. So I sipped the brandy and waited. I had drunk two glasses of ale with my dinner and so was feeling merry enough, though watchful all the same.

Mr. Walter stared out the window at the bare trees and the grey sky. He may have remarked on the possibility of snow by nightfall and I may have replied that I thought it too cold to snow, but I don't really remember. At length, however, he said quite unexpectedly that I was never to worry about a place to stay. "Your home will always be here, Linny," he said. "Don't ever fret about that." The truth is I never *had* fretted about it, had never entertained the idea of the Eastons putting me out on the road after my long years of service. I have known such things to happen and in this very shire, but not, I believed, in the house of Walter Easton. It was comforting, however, to hear his words, and I smiled and thanked him. Then he asked me how I was feeling. Charlotte, it seems, had mentioned my failing eyesight.

"We are all getting up there," he said, and laughed as if our aging was some coarse jest played upon us by Providence, which for all I know may be true. I often think so with certainty when I suffer pains from the gravel in my kidneys. But I told Mr. Walter my health was tolerable, though far from what it once was. It might soon be time to rest from my labours. He seemed pleased to hear it.

"Good, good, good," he said, and offered more brandy, which I took. We both sat back in quiet and looked out upon the grey afternoon, content enough in our own ways. What I gathered from this meeting was that plans were afoot to replace me, but that I would have my room and small comforts and remain with the family. This to me was the best course, for in truth Easton House itself now seems exhausted in spirit, and I am no longer much interested in setting tasks for girls like Emily Backhurst. I feel I am entitled to some rest in my seventieth year.

At one time there were thirteen of us living under this roof, and in those days I earned every penny of my wages. When the first four children were young, and the squire and Mrs. Easton alive, there were eight of us in service to the family: the housekeeper at the time, a Mrs. Smith; the cook who preceded Mrs. Sproule and a cook's maid; a manservant, Harvey; two housemaids; a gardener; and myself, nursemaid to the children in those early days. That makes fourteen, but the gardener lived in one of the labourers' cottages. There were parties and dances, Christmas masques and harvest festivals. Noise and laughter and tears in darkened corners with the girls in love; in brief, the clamour and confusion and sometimes gaiety of life itself. And then, within a few years, it all came asunder.

The two girls, Mary and Catherine, born two years apart after Mr. Walter, and inseparable, were taken from us by a pair of gospellers, the Lawford brothers, Cyrus and John, who came up from Bristol in the summer of 1629 to stay with a well-to-do aunt in Oxford. The story was they were seeking money from her to pay expenses for travel and settlement in America, where they hoped to go the following spring on an expedition organized by one John Winslow. He and his followers were discontented with religious life in England at the time, and hoped to build a more zealous community of believers in the New World. That, at least, is what the brothers always talked about when they visited Easton House. The girls had met them at a religious meeting in Oxford, possibly at the aunt's house, I am not certain. But the four young people were soon courting, and it became clear that both girls were smitten by these pious fellows with their plain black dress and severe manner. They were handsome enough, I suppose, if your taste runs to tall, sallow-skinned young men with bushy eyebrows mouthing Scripture a good deal of the time. I didn't much like them, but then, I could see how they were going to take the girls from us. I could understand their appeal for Mary, who had always been serious-minded, but Catherine? Such a gay, lighthearted girl who had always loved dancing and parties. Yet what do we truly know of even those who are close to us?

That October the two couples were married in St. Cuthbert's and left at once for Bristol, where they spent the winter, returning to Easton House in March for a brief visit before travelling down to Southampton and embarking for Massachusetts Bay. By then Catherine was pregnant and Mrs. Easton already stricken by thoughts of all she would miss in her daughters' lives. I remember the day they left, Catherine saying at the front door, "We'll meet again in Heaven, Mother." And poor Mrs. Easton in tears. Then they were gone, the coach disappearing down the avenue between the elm trees to the Oxford road.

Nicholas was only fifteen at the time, and how he missed his sisters. But the genuine loss was Mrs. Easton's, who despite the prospect of a reunion in Heaven seemed broken in body and spirit by the loss of her girls. With the passing weeks [it seemed to rain most days, as I recall] she grew increasingly forlorn and an ague took hold of her and would not let go. The doctor bled her, to no good effect, and she continued to weaken. I myself attended to her chills and fevers, but by the end of April she too was gone. She had been a sweet, accommodating presence in the household and a woman who, I believe, gave quiet counsel to her husband and kept him on a steady course.

The squire took his wife's death badly and for a long while succumbed to drink. Mr. Walter, only then in his twenties, had to manage the estate mostly on his own: collect the rents, plan the seeding and harvesting, oversee the labourers, buy and sell animals. But he learned, and quickly too. Those were hard times for him, with indifferent crops and falling prices, saddled with a father who was often drunk by the noon-hour bell; and there were older men at the markets eager to outwit the young man. I give Mr. Walter full credit, for he never lost his head, though I am sure that firm but kind temperament he had drawn from his mother was sorely tested.

In time the squire came to his senses and we were all grateful to see him sober and working again alongside his eldest son. Then, to our surprise and chagrin, he did something entirely foolish for a man of fifty-eight years. A case can be made that a well-to-do widower like Henry Easton needed a wife; men like him need women to keep their feet on solid ground—though I doubted he would ever again find one as strong and capable as his first. And in fact he made an imprudent choice. Or should I say his loins and not his head made the choice—for he began to court a Miss Pentworth from Islip who was visiting friends near Woodstock. He met

her at a neighbour's wedding, where I was told by one in service to the household that the young woman in a sky blue
taffeta gown was radiance itself, all blonde curls and blue
eyes, a pale golden beauty and no argument from anyone
about that. But she was barely twenty years old. Some said
she claimed to be a year or two older, but this same person
in the household told me that Anne Pentworth was barely
nineteen.

The squire was enchanted by her beauty, though as far
as I could see she had nothing else to offer. A high, prancing
laugh accompanied her everywhere and she seemed happiest
while talking and giggling among her young friends about
gowns and shoes. Or so I observed when she visited Easton
House. I think the girl's father was behind it all, eyeing
the squire's lands even as he walked about with his hands
behind him, smiling at old Henry, who looked as attentive
as a schoolboy with his master. A sight to behold, for this
man Pentworth, who would become the squire's father-in-
law, was at least ten years younger. Nor do I believe Abel
Pentworth had anything but promissory notes to his name.
I was told he ran a small shop in Islip, but to me he had the
furtive look of a man forever in debt. It was ludicrous; the
squire was clearly not in his right mind, though it would
have been folly to approach him about a change in course.
He was under the spell of that young woman's beauty, a state
described by my father in *A Midsummer-Night's Dream*

when he puts into the mouth of Theseus the best descrip-
tion of lovesickness in the language:

> *Lovers and madmen have such seething brains,*
> *Such shaping fantasies, that apprehend*
> *More than cool reason ever comprehends.*

My father, of course, was referring to the young lovers
in a forest near Athens. But how graver the malady when it
afflicts an older man with a much younger woman. As poor
Nicholas said to me on the eve of the wedding. "Dear God,
Linny, she's only a year or two older than I am—and must I
now address this witless young thing as 'Mother'?"

Within the year the squire got a child upon her, but the
poor woman was small and the birth difficult. I remember
her yet being worn down by those long, effortful hours, her
light hair splayed across the pillow, the sweat on her upper
lip, the desperate howling as I helped the midwife work
the child from her mother's exhausted body. Anne held
her daughter but briefly, then closed her eyes forever. The
squire was below, but his young wife's cries had driven him
to the brandy again, and he could only pace about and curse.

When I went down with the news, he was staring into
the fire and asked me if the child would live. I said she would
if we got in a wet nurse, a woman in one of the cottages
would do, and the maidservant had already gone to fetch

her. The old man's back was to me and when I asked him for a name he waved me away. "You give the child a name, Aerlene," he said, and so I did and called her Charlotte Anne. Two days later we buried her mother in the churchyard of St. Cuthbert's.

The squire didn't take to the child. It was unnatural and unfair, but I believe he couldn't help himself. Perhaps he had truly loved that young woman and this child's life was a constant reproach to him. Whatever the reason, he became a silent and disappointed old man, watchful and suspicious, his mind often muddled with drink, scarcely bothering to look upon his child in her cradle. He soon gave up on everything, and Charlotte was barely a year old when Henry Easton died in his sleep. I found him early one morning slumped in his chair in the drawing room, where he had been all night drinking brandy.

Charlotte has no memory of her father and when as a child she used to ask about him, I embroidered my tale for her benefit, relating how much her father had fussed over her as a baby. His death, I told her, had been in bed, where he had quietly gone to sleep.

So for the past several years, there have been just Charlotte and Mr. Walter and Mrs. Sproule and myself living in Easton House. Emily lives in the village and comes and goes each day; the gardener, Johnson, son of old John who was here when I first arrived, lives in the cottage his father once inhabited. As I have said, the two older girls, Mary and Catherine, live in Massachusetts and send us their Christmas letters each year. Both have prospered in their new circumstances and I marvel as I read their accounts of life in America. In the early days, I pictured them living on the edge of vast forests amid savages, but in their letters over the years they write of fine homes on streets with shops and churches and the general pleasantries of town living. Boston, it seems, is much like London, though I gather not nearly as large. Mary's husband, Cyrus Lawford, died a few years ago and she is remarried to a clergyman. But reading their letters is like receiving news from another planet and the girls I once told stories to and whose tears I used to dry with my apron now seem like strangers. Their long-ago journey, thousands of miles across the ocean, seems almost unimaginable to those of us here in Worsley, where people seldom stray farther than Oxford, nine miles away. The well-to-do may go as far as Bath or Bristol and sometimes to London, but most of us stay put.

My mother was hardly well-to-do but she went to London once, and there she met my father, and next week when my little amanuensis returns, I hope to record as best I can what Mam told me about her life.

I must first, however, amend an error in my foregoing account of Easton House and its history. The amendment came to me in the midst of one of my thrice-nightly pisses.

The man who led that expedition to America, the voyage that carried our girls away from us forever, was not called Winslow. His name was Winthrop. John Winthrop. Is it not strange how a word or a name, snagged on some impediment beneath the current of our memories, becomes unloosed and rises to the surface, where we reclaim it? And this may happen at the oddest times. At three o'clock in the morning, for instance, crouched over a chamber pot.

MAM'S STORY

FROM AN EARLY AGE I wondered who my father was. Other children had fathers. Who and where was mine? Mam and I lived in Worsley with Aunt Sarah and Uncle Jack, who owned a draper's shop in Woodstock, a mile away. He walked there to his work each weekday and Mam walked with him, for she measured and sewed linen in the back of his shop behind a curtain. As a small child, I waved goodbye to them each morning as they set forth. At first I thought Uncle Jack was my father, for unlike his wife, who was cold and distant, Uncle Jack treated me kindly and sometimes brought home treats, making me swear not to tell Aunt Sarah.

One day when I was likely no more than three, I watched Mam leave with my uncle and then asked Aunt Sarah if Mam was married to Uncle Jack and if he was my father. And if that were so, why did I call him "Uncle" and how did Aunt Sarah come by her name? My aunt was a tall, spare woman, handsome in her own severe way. When I think of it, she could, at least in looks, have been a sister to the Lawford brothers. I don't believe I ever saw her smile above once or twice in her life. Her entire recreation was preparing for Heaven; she read her Bible aloud each day—the raising of Lazarus was a favourite—and I can still recite that passage from John's gospel word for word, since I listened to it so often as a child. When, however, I asked my questions that particular day, I remember how her face grew dark with anger. She told me that Uncle Jack was most certainly not my father and it was foolish of me to think so. She and my uncle had not been blessed with children and had taken Mam and me into their house out of Christian charity. As for me, I was, as she put it, base-born. I don't recall being especially upset by these revelations, nor did I bother even to ask after the meaning of *base-born*. I imagine I was far too young to be anything other than puzzled by it all. Still, I carried the memory of how my questions that day had somehow offended Aunt Sarah, making her face grow dark, and so I was careful thereafter not to broach the subject of my father again.

Instead I went to Mam and from time to time pestered her with questions. Who was my father? How had she met him? Why had he not married her and lived with us like other fathers? Was he still living or was he looking down on us from Heaven?

In those early years Mam was not direct with me and would often say one thing and then another. My father had been a soldier but was killed fighting the Spanish, who were threatening the Queen's realm. How I liked the sound of that phrase, *the Queen's realm*! I had no idea where Mam found it, most likely from a storybook, for it didn't sound in the least like her. Then some weeks later, I would ask again and she would have forgotten her story about the soldier and launch a tale in which my father was a seaman who had sailed with Drake against the Armada in the very year I was born, and had died later in a shipwreck off the Canaries. Making up such stories was of a piece with Mam's oddness. As I would learn in time, she was seen by others not only as an unwed mother who sewed in her brother's shop, but also as a woman who kept to herself. Mam believed in all manner of fanciful things: imps and fairies, changelings and hobgoblins. As a child I would watch her tap a forefinger three times against the side of her nose at the sight of a pied-coloured horse, or upon hearing the first clap of thunder from an oncoming storm. Not that unusual among country people, you might think, but with Mam it was like a religion, a way of seeing into the world. At the same time she was a believing Christian. But she could not resist the enchantment she found in the natural world. Walking in the woods and meadows on the edge of the village she talked sometimes to birds and hedgehogs, voles and coneys; she sought the whereabouts of the little people near the roots of oak trees or under toadstools. In all its phases, the moon was both everlasting mystery and companion.

When I was very young and walked along beside her, I myself thought these things quite wondrous and asked endless questions about the pixies and fairy folk. But as I grew older I began to see it all as nonsense. Yet Mam persisted in believing in the efficacy of spells and magic, and she was conversant about trees and flowers. It is little wonder that she loved *A Midsummer-Night's Dream* and had me read it to her six times during the final year of her life. She told me that the sixth reading was a good omen, six being the double of three, which itself, she said, is a number possessed of magical properties. I was twelve years old then and, as she said, twelve is the double of six, another good sign that she might recover. But nothing, neither simples nor signs, could change her wasting away that awful year.

I have an image of my mother which I will carry to my own deathbed. I could not have been four years old and she had taken me with her to visit Goody Figgs, an old woman who lived in a hut in the woods near the river where she drew water each day for her potions. I was frightened of her and on my only visit stood at the doorway of her dark little home, peering in at the plants and herbs hanging from the rafters, the small fire in the grate, the hides of animals drying on benches. I would go no farther and Mam could not persuade me otherwise. Many accounted Goody Figgs a witch, though others found her useful, especially unmarried women whose courses had run dry. Years later, Goody's hut was burned to the ground by young men drunk on May Day ale and bravado. I have always believed they were inflamed by the sermons of Obadiah Littlejohn, the rector of St. Cuthbert's at the time. Fortunately, the old woman was not at home. She vanished into the woods, never to be seen in the neighbourhood again. Some said later she was living in the Royal Park at Woodstock, but I always doubted the story, as I never believed the gamekeepers would allow it. But Mam was fascinated by Goody Figgs, and on the day I went with her, I played alone and watched them together on the edge of a wood gathering simples, a pretty woman and an old hag. I remember my mother rising from the grass now and then to stretch her back, and holding her hand to shield her eyes against the sunlight as she looked for me. Then she would wave and I would wave back. A warm-hearted creature, Mam, but innocent in the ways of the world and far too trusting.

She called me Aerlene, a name no one in the village, including my aunt and uncle, had ever heard. Mam told me she got the name from an old book of Anglo-Saxon tales which she had read as a child. Aerlene means *elf-like* and she called me so because at birth I was early and small with a large head covered with black hair. "You reminded me of a little elf as soon as I saw you," she said. Apparently my birth had been more than the usual ordeal for new mothers. "What a time I had bringing you into this world," Mam used to say. And more than once, especially when she was vexed with me, "That head of yours nearly tore me apart. I could have perished from the pain." As if it were my fault!

She told this story so many times that I grew weary of it and said to her once—I might have been six at the time— "I don't know why you bother to put *little* in front of *elf*. Are not all elves little by their very nature?"

"Oh," she said, "haven't we become a smarty boots?"

"And what if I have?" I said. "Have you not made me so with words and reading?"

She laughed at that, for she was never angry long. Mam herself seldom read anything; she merely encouraged it in me because she thought I was plain and unlikely to find a mate. When she first taught me my letters, she was quick to tell me why. "You will never be a beauty, little elf," she said, "and so you must learn, and reading books will help you." What a thing to say to a child! And I thought as much even then. Like many handsome people, Mam lacked discernment regarding the feelings of those less favoured by nature in appearance. And, of course, she had long forgotten my little lesson in redundancy.

But it is true that my head is large and my brow imposing, which some claim betokens intelligence. When I was in my fifteenth year and first laid eyes upon my father on Silver Street in London, I took note at once of the brow I had inherited, though in fairness I must say that it suited a grown man's countenance better than a young girl's. As a child I was often mocked. Not only for being a bastard, but also for my appearance. But I soon learned to give as good as I received. When other children out of spite hurled stones at me, I sprayed them with words I found in little books Aunt Sarah bought from peddlers with titles such as *News Out of Heaven, A Potation for Lent, The Sick Man's Salve.* Words were my weapons and they sometimes discouraged jeering. Children called me Little Miss Big Tongue. So childhood—those years the elderly mistakenly recall most fondly—seemed to me only a time to pass through as quickly as possible.

At the beginning of my twelfth year, Mam promised to unfold the truth about my father but said I must wait for my birthday, for by then I would be old enough to understand. An entire year! I thought. How cruel. And I think I must have sulked a good deal in the ensuing months. I had always been an inward-looking child interested only in words on a page, though by then I was tired of reading accounts of Protestants roasted to death by Queen Mary's Papists, or tracts promoting wholesome habits that would ensure an afterlife. So my sulking and ill humour that year often led to encounters with Aunt Sarah, who had always despaired of my salvation. And these led to thrashings, mostly when Mam was away at my uncle's shop. I never mentioned them to her and I took particular pride in enduring those leather-strap beatings without tears. I was a hard little nut to crack and no mistake.

At the same time, I was worried about my mother, and that may have contributed to my surliness. There was something wrong with her that summer. It was not easily discernible; you had to look for it, and I was looking for it, observing with the passing weeks a thinning out of colour in her face, a sharpening of her features. One morning on her way to work she suddenly fell to the ground in a faint there on the flagstone pathway from the front door. I saw the collapse, her head narrowly missing a stone when she fell. Uncle Jack carried her indoors and upstairs to bed. She soon recovered and made a fuss about not wanting a doctor, laughing away her clumsiness. That evening, I overheard my aunt telling Uncle Jack that his sister's problems were merely vaporous; she had reached that time when the parts are undergoing change in accordance with God's design for women in this life. Perhaps so, I thought, for Mam at the time was about forty years in age.

Then, a fortnight before my twelfth birthday, a Saturday in July, Mam returned with Uncle Jack from Oxford. It was my uncle's habit to visit Oxford market every other Saturday to inspect the linen goods on display and enjoy the gossip of his trade with fellow vendors. He always took Mam along; he saw it, I suppose, as an outing for his sister.

While my uncle had a pint of ale with friends in the Hounds and Hare, Mam was free to roam about, perhaps attending to an errand for my aunt or looking for a trinket for me. On her return that Saturday, however, her gaunt face was flushed; she seemed agitated, but pleasantly so, and eagerly drawing me aside, she whispered that we should go to the stone bench in the garden, where we talked often together safely out of Aunt Sarah's hearing.

There she told me about wandering in Oxford market and happening upon the bookstalls—and what did I think she saw there? I told her perhaps a storybook that might please me, but she only smiled and took my hands and briefly held them.

"Your twelfth birthday is only a fortnight off," she said, "so there is no good reason now to wait, for truly I cannot keep this to myself another minute." And with that she withdrew from beneath her apron a copy of *A Midsummer-Night's Dream* by William Shakespeare. I read those very words on the title page.

"A storybook, then?" I asked. "Or poems?"

"A playbook," said Mam, "already enacted in a London playhouse. The bookseller told me it's only lately printed. And this play was written by your father, Aerlene."

I believe that at the time I was as puzzled as I was pleased. "But how would you come to know a man who writes plays?" I asked.

"He was only young when I knew him," Mam said. "An apprentice player living in London. In a place called Shoreditch. A country person like myself. He always said he wanted to write poetry. I will tell you how we came to meet in good time. But look now, I have another by him." And she showed me a copy of *Romeo and Juliet*.

"But his name is not on this," I said. "How do you know he wrote it?"

"The bookseller told me," she said. "A kind man and a great reader of poetry by the sound of him. He told me this *Romeo and Juliet* is a good tale, if a sad one, with fine verses in it. Mr. Shakespeare, he said, has written many plays. The bookseller hasn't seen them performed on the stage, but he has read them and he said I would enjoy this *Romeo and Juliet* as well as *A Midsummer-Night's Dream*, because Mr. Shakespeare is now accounted the finest playwright in London. His plays, he believed, have even been performed before the Queen. I got both plays for ten pence, for the *Romeo and Juliet* has been used, but *A Midsummer-Night's Dream* is new. I scanned it at the bookstall. It takes place in a forest with fairy folk and lovers and fine descriptions of flowers. We used to talk about the countryside, your father and I. He was homesick for it then, poor fellow. And now a gentleman and poet. I am so happy for him."

"Calm yourself, Mam," I said. "Your face is on fire."

"Well, what of that?" she said, squeezing my hand.

"This is your father's work, Aerlene. Your father was no idle porter. No, nor ploughman neither, though many hereabouts believe so." And drawing nearer she said, "But listen to me, child. These books must be our secret. If your aunt finds out there'll be the devil to pay, for she accounts such books wicked and she will not have them in her house. In London, I recall your father saying how the Puritans were always trying to close down the playhouses. Will—your father—used to make sport of their long faces and sombre dress."

My father, a poet and a gentleman? Was that not worth waiting for all those years? I wanted to know more about him, but Mam said, "I'm tired, Aerlene. All that traipsing about this morning and now this news. I should lie down for a bit. We'll read these plays, you and I. I like the sound of *A Midsummer-Night's Dream* and you can read the other. And then we'll exchange. I know you'll read yours half again as fast as I will mine, so be patient with me. And keep your copy well hidden from your aunt. You must promise me."

And so I have done until now, some eight and fifty years.

A T LAST WE HAVE begun. On Saturday afternoon Charlotte returned from Oxford and yesterday following church she told me that she was ready to begin today. And so she has, sitting at the escritoire this morning dipping quill into inkhorn and transcribing my words, as alert and attentive as I could hope for. Since returning from Oxford, Charlotte has been exceedingly good-humoured, and I think I know the cause of her cheer.

After we finished this morning, she told me she had met the new rector of St. Cuthbert's, Mr. Thwaites, at a gathering in Oxford which she attended with her friend, who seems to have a wide circle of acquaintanceship there. I would let Charlotte go no further without an inquiry about her poor friend's broken engagement, but she only smiled brightly. "Oh, that's quite mended now, Linny."

I told her I was relieved to hear it, but she was too eager

to talk about Mr. Thwaites to notice my admittedly regrettable snideness.

"We had a most pleasant conversation, Mr. Thwaites and I," she said. "He is no Puritan, Linny, but a fine-tempered man and well educated too. His college was St. John's. We spoke together a full hour. He said at one point that he had noticed me at his first service at St. Cuthbert's." And with that she blushed, which I thought becoming.

"You should come to service to hear him, Linny. His homilies are moderate and well argued. He is no Little-john." So at least she remembered Obadiah Littlejohn, who had delivered his stormy admonitions across the pulpit of St. Cuthbert's for fifty years—a hate-filled gospeller who called Mam a fornicator and would not deliver her funeral rites in the church. I was in my thirteenth year, and though I would continue to attend church for some years thereafter, I paid little heed to the preacher's words. Little-john's successor, Hainsworth, was another firebrand, but now we have Mr. Thwaites, who according to Charlotte is a vast improvement. Perhaps—but it is of no interest to me, beyond my observing the new rector's effect on Charlotte. It struck me listening to her this morning that she may be taken with him. Then, just as I was absorbing that notion, she said something that truly made me start.

"Mr. Thwaites," she said, "is a great admirer of Shake-speare's plays."

"Charlotte," I said, "please assure me that in your con-versation with Mr. Thwaites last week you did not mention anything about me and what we are about in this room. *Please* assure me of that." The tone of my remarks drained some colour from her face.

"Oh no, Linny," she cried. "No, no, no. It just arose in conversation. We were talking of reading. Mr. Thwaites, it turns out, is a great one for reading. Far greater than I. He told me he is an admirer of good poetry and cited Shake-speare as an example of his taste."

"And you are certain that you didn't mention what we are about here?"

"No, certainly not. This is our secret." Still, I thought I could detect, if only faintly, the quaver in a nervous liar's voice.

"I'll not be mocked for this, Charlotte," I said. "You know that."

"Of course I do."

But I could see Charlotte rushing headlong into con-versation with the rector, and in her giddy fashion blurting something that might prove novel to his ears and make her more interesting.

"*Why, yes, Mr. Thwaites. Speaking of Shakespeare, our ancient housekeeper, Miss Ward, is his daughter born out of wedlock, and in her dotage she has asked me to record an account of how her mother met the poet in London."*

Or worse. *"Speaking of Shakespeare, our ancient house-keeper, Miss Ward, poor old soul, claims to be Shakespeare's daughter born out of wedlock, and in her dotage she has asked me to . . ."* and et cetera.

I *have* wondered from time to time whether Charlotte believes me. When I first told her about my father at Christmas I thought I saw in her smile a trace of doubt. I imagined her wanting to say, even if she didn't, *Why, goodness me, Linny. The poet Shakespeare, your father? That is indeed a story. Why, it must be your best one yet.* At the time it made me wonder if I might well be paying for a lifetime of telling stories to the Easton children. Like the boy who cried wolf, had I, as family storyteller, become one who is never truly believed?

FROM MY FIRST READING on that warm summer evening in the year 1600 I loved *Romeo and Juliet,* though I wished Juliet had fallen in love with Mercutio, who seemed to me less pallid and far wittier than Romeo. I was excited too that like me, Juliet was born on Lammas Eve, and I saw in that a good omen, though of what I couldn't say. Mam was ever in search of omens, so when I told her, I expected her to be pleased. Instead she only scoffed.

"There is many a child brought forth on Lammas Eve," said Mam, who didn't care for the play. Some very pretty verses, she said, but the story was too sad. "I could not abide the scene where the girl awakens from the friar's potion to find her lover dead. I'll not look at it again, nor have it read to me either. I want you to read the other to me in the evenings, as I don't feel well and have need of distraction." Mam was then at the beginning of her long decline and often out of sorts. I vowed to be patient in her distress, but didn't always succeed.

Then one afternoon she said, "It is time for me to tell you things, Aerlene, but you must try hard not to think ill of your mother. I have brought suffering and shame to this house and this parish, and your aunt has good reason to despise me. Your uncle's good heart has been our blessing. Without him, you and I would long ago have been out on the roads among the poor and wretched of the earth. And God alone knows what might have become of us. So always remember our debt to him."

I said I would and it wasn't difficult, for I dearly loved Uncle Jack.

Mam then said, "From the beginning I had terrible judgment in men. I admit that freely. Even with your father I was heedless, though I thought at the time I was barren." She laughed, but it sounded more scornful than pleasant. "What a jest on me when I found myself with child."

I didn't like the sound of that, for after all, was I not what remained of the "jest"? But I let it pass, for I knew her rough way with feelings.

Mam told me she was pretty but headstrong, and when she was eighteen she fell in love with one Richard Wilkes, a porter, who was ten years older, a dissolute, shiftless, untrustworthy widower whose wife, it was said, had been worn away from ill treatment at his hands.

"Oh, I was warned by many," Mam said, "but there was no telling me anything at eighteen. I loved Wilkes and that's all there was to it. Your uncle begged me not to marry him, but it was all in vain. I was in love, and what do the young know of love? I will tell you, Aerlene, for who knows—one day you may be struck yourself. To the young, *love* is just a word for wanting to touch another's flesh and have yours touched in turn. That's all love is to the young."

I listened attentively while she told me how she used to look out the unshuttered window of her brother's shop on a Saturday morning and watch this handsome rogue lounging about the market square with other idlers. He worked once at the Freeman's Inn but was let go for quarrelling with a patron. So they courted, Mam and Wilkes, and she foolishly allowed him entry and was soon missing her courses. When she announced her condition, Uncle Jack and Aunt Sarah were unsurprisingly appalled, but there was nothing for it but marriage. She loved him, she said. She would make a better man of him. Nobody but she knew how really good he was beneath the swagger and the drink. On the morning of her wedding, Uncle Jack sat at the dining room table and cried piteously.

"There was Jack," Mam said, "as I came down the stairs in my wedding dress. He was weeping while Aunt Sarah stood by him and pointed her finger at me.

"'The village is laughing at you,' she said, 'and you will rue this day, Missy.'

"'I do not think so,' I said. 'Richard loves me and has promised to look after me. He is a changed man.'

"'A changed man, is he?' said Aunt Sarah. 'I wonder if his poor wife once thought likewise before he beat her half to death each night.'"

What happened next was a change not in Wilkes's character but in his fortune. Scarcely a fortnight after the wedding, Wilkes, who had barely drawn a sober breath since the ceremony, was killed in a drunken quarrel in a laneway behind the Three Crows on the Woodstock road, his head crushed by a large stone. The assailant, a stranger, fled into the night, never to be seen again. A week after Wilkes was in the ground, Mam miscarried. But never was a miscarriage greeted with more rejoicing in a Christian household. Uncle Jack killed a capon and roasted it himself in honour of there being no longer a remnant of Richard Wilkes on this earth. He fed his young sister spoonfuls of chicken broth to strengthen her while his wife offered prayers of thanksgiving. Even neighbours felt happy for them; after all, the Wards were good, respectable people and the poor girl had been spared a life of misfortune, freed from a scoundrel by the blow of a stranger in the night. There were some pious souls, Mam said, who believed the stranger had been an agent of the Almighty Himself.

After Wilkes's death, Mam told me, that she suffered through weeks of her sister-in-law's ministrations, scoldings and calls to prayer for guidance in leading a pure life. Mam told me all this with a little smile, which I took to mean that her heart was not really attuned to piety. Yet she did her best. "I became," she said, "quite God-fearing in my own way. At least to all appearances. I did try. I am no heathen despite what you may think." [I told her I had never considered her a heathen.] But neither could she find God in St. Cuthbert's with its whitewashed walls covering the images of the old religion, austere now with its plain windows and English prayer books.

"So," she said, "I continued to look for Him in the trees and in the passing clouds and in the dark night wind when I walked. He *is* supposed to be everywhere, isn't He?"

And each afternoon as she had promised Aunt Sarah, she opened the big Bible, and sitting at the dining room table, just as in time I myself would, she turned the pages and stared at the words. "I found it arduous," she said, "all those names. I kept getting them confused, and if I must speak truth, I didn't care all that much about the tribulations of the Israelites and their constant quarrels with neighbours. The stories about Jesus were more interesting, but I couldn't abide St. Paul with his scolding of the Ephesians and the Thessalonians, whoever they were."

In time Mam returned to her brother's shop and sold drapery and linens, ignoring the whispers of women but offering bashful smiles to their husbands. She simply could not resist the smile of a well-formed man. Yet now she was forbidden them. Her marriage to Wilkes had ruined her prospects for another husband. Many young men in the village may have dreamt of her naked and in heat with them, but there would be no question of marrying, because she had already displayed her poor judgment. She told me then how lonely she was in those years when she was in her twenties, ripe and full of yearning. How on her walks through Worsley woods she would imagine things. "I longed," she told me, "for a man's touch on my skin. I could not help myself. An embrace. A kiss. Sometimes I would press my lips against the inner flesh of my arm, just above the wrist. I would imagine a man doing this to me. Oh, don't think ill of me, child."

I didn't think ill of her and told her so. On the contrary, I was fascinated by her story, by her willingness to share longings that I myself felt stirring within. In my mind I could see Mam walking along those lanes or seeking out a glade in which to lie upon her back, holding a hand across her eyes against the sunlight, touching herself and dreaming of a lover. I knew by then it was only nature, and one day I too would feel that way.

"I felt all this commotion within," she told me, "so I would walk out into the night and find comfort in the darkness with the sound of the wind in the trees. I was never afraid, though I could hear small animals about, badgers and hedgehogs. Sometimes I came upon Goody Figgs, but I was used to her secret ways and she to mine. Goody seemed to like me, or at least she tolerated me, for she was a strange and quiet old woman.

"And so the years passed," she said, "and then I got into trouble with another man. I should have known better, for I was no longer a young girl but in my twenties when I met Henry Chapman one evening along the pathway on the edge of Worsley woods. I saw him walking towards me," said Mam, smiling at the recollection of what became a happy but brief interlude in her life. Henry was a farm labourer and he had been working that day in a field. He was coming towards her with a mattock on his shoulder, and he was whistling. He couldn't have been more than eighteen, she said, a fine-looking boy. "I had seen him a few times in the village on Saturdays with his father and brothers, looking at the cattle or sheep. Henry was the youngest of a large family that worked on the Easton estate, and he was thought to be simple-minded. I soon came to understand, however, that he was not hindered in intelligence, but merely dumb. That is to say he had no language whatsoever and had been so affected since birth. Yet he understood things well enough, and when we became acquainted, we found ways to understand each other. He would listen to my words, for there was nothing wrong with his hearing, and he would nod in assent or shake his head in disagreement. A sweet, sweet young man, Henry, and his only misfortune was shyness around strangers because he couldn't speak.

"That first evening as he passed, he touched his cap in greeting, affecting not the least surprise at seeing me on that woodland path. But a few paces on I turned to watch him stop and pick a bellflower daisy, which he then brought back to me. I must have smiled as I took it, but it seemed the most natural thing in the world to be handed a flower by this young man, whom I knew by name only. And not a word between us as he touched his cap again and, turning, went on his way with that mattock over his shoulder. He had the deepest blue eyes of any man I had ever seen, and in recollection it seems only yesterday evening that I saw Henry Chapman for the first time on that path.

"And so each day after supper I went out walking, hoping he would appear. And sometimes he did and other times he didn't, depending on the field he was working. He mostly worked alone, chopping at weeds, but now and then he would work alongside one or two of his brothers and I would see them coming along together, and then I would crouch behind a tree. I think he sensed that I was watching him, because he was always looking about and smiling. Sometimes people like Henry are taken for mad because they smile for what seems to be no reason, yet perhaps they notice pleasing things that others don't. I believe we were playing a kind of lovers' game with each other, a game without words that both of us had fashioned.

"This went on for weeks, well into August, and then one evening he appeared by himself carrying a brace of wood pigeons. We stopped together there on the pathway and he handed the birds to me. They were trussed at the feet by a vine, and I took them and kissed his cheek. He touched his face where I had kissed him and smiled and then went on his way. I didn't know what to do with the pigeons. It seemed a pity to cast them off, yet I couldn't tell the truth about the gift, not to my sister-in-law, who would instantly see mischief—and given my history, who could blame her? So I said I found them on my walk, and your aunt, whose thriftiness was next only to cleanliness and godliness, was glad enough and baked them in a pie.

"I was so taken with this youth, Aerlene. It wasn't proper in a woman of my years to be so caught up with one so young, but I could no more help it than I could help breathing. I was like a schoolgirl in my hunger. All manner of lustful imaginings coursed through my head, and if God was listening at all, He knew how I tried to make them go away. I prayed. I stopped going out in the evenings and instead read the Bible. St. Paul's letters to all those people, the Galacians, and the Thessalonians and the Ethiops. It didn't matter. It was all gibberish. I could think only of undressing Henry Chapman in the woods. I pictured every detail, and then it came to pass.

"On an afternoon when I ventured out again, I met him. He was out walking and dressed in Sunday clothes after church. I think he was looking for me. I couldn't say for certain, but there he was smiling at me as I came around the pathway where I often used to hide when I saw him with his brothers. And that afternoon, I unclothed the boy just as I had done in fantasies. Removed his clothes there in a glade far off the path where I had led him by the hand without resistance. Henry had never been touched by a woman in the way of lovemaking, had never been kissed, for I asked him later and he shook his head. Imagine this strong young man with feelings never expressed. And so I took him into my arms and taught him how to love me there in that sunlit glade with the trees above us and the wind in their branches throwing dappled light across his skin, his arms brown to the elbow and then his body so white. So I taught him how to love me, though not all at once, for such things take time and patience. As Goody Figgs used to say, 'You can't heat a pot with one strike of the flint.' You need to build the fire, and so it is with lovemaking, Aerlene, and I hope you are fortunate enough to learn this from a good man one day. With Henry I had to be patient, for he was like a child with a new plaything and had to be taught. But in time he learned and then it seemed we could scarcely keep our hands and lips from each other. Lust is a form of madness and the preachers may be right to rail against it, much good it may do them, for I don't believe we can stop what other animals do by nature, which is to mate.

"I didn't even care whether I had a child by Henry Chapman, so much had that madness overcome me, though looking back, no doubt I believed that with all my problems after Wilkes, I couldn't bring forth a child, so I was content to let that boy pour his seed into me. And so he did, and I was borne away with pleasure as we met in our glade in the evenings of late summer or on Sunday afternoons, twenty minutes after your aunt had finished her prayer of thanksgiving for another dinner sent from God. This boy, this farmhand from the Easton estate, was all I could think of day and night. In your uncle's shop through the week, as I measured or cut lengths from the bolts of cloth, in church on Sunday mornings, only hours away from meeting him, hearing but not listening to the preacher's words, God save me, thinking only of Henry's weight upon me and him deep inside me, the smell of his sweat. His breath was sweet, for he chewed parsley. He brought handfuls of it in his smock for us, bless him." She stopped for a moment. "I heard it said once that Henry now lives up near Chipping Norton. He married a widow with children of her own. It must be ten years ago I heard that."

I listened to all this as if it were a story from some book. I wanted to know then how she was found out, because people are always found out in such tales.

"Well, you get careless, Aerlene," Mam said. "When you are in love, nothing matters but being with the one you love. Your father wrote about that in his *Romeo and Juliet* and it cost those two young people their lives. As I've said, I couldn't bear the ending of that play, but I suppose there was truth in it. Nothing else matters when you are in love except being with the one you love," she repeated. "As you will find out one day." She gave me an absent-minded hug as though she only half-believed her words. "At least I hope you will, my little imp," she added.

Mam was always using such redundant endearments with me, and she never seemed to understand how much I hated them. How much I hated to be reminded by her how little space I took up in the world. How little of me there was, and how small and unimportant and ugly I felt. How tired I was of always looking up at others.

So to change the subject, I asked again, "So how *were* you found out?"

"Someone saw us," Mam said. "Who can say? Wandering children? A couple courting and out for a Sunday walk? Oh, to this day to think of others looking upon us at our ardent lovemaking. The cries I made. Yes, yes, we were careless, as are all lovers from time to time. And so the mischievous tongues began to wag. 'There was Lizzie Ward, naked and lying in the woods with that simpleton Henry Chapman. Can you believe it?' It's how most folks are, isn't it? By nightfall it was all over the village and into the ears of your aunt and uncle. Poor Jack. After that business with Wilkes he must have thought I was cured of the lovesickness, and now here I was again with a man who for all Jack knew had no more sense than a child. And I a grown woman. What was I thinking? Well, I *wasn't* thinking. Thinking had nothing to do with it. Some can be denied and others can't and that's the truth, Aerlene, and I was one who couldn't. 'A weak vessel,' as your aunt called me more than once. True enough. I couldn't deny it. How can you help the way you are? Prayer, as my brother and his wife suggested? Perhaps. Prayers seem to work for some, but not for me, though I knew it was wrong and I felt sorry for Jack. I had put him to so much trouble, poor fellow.

"It caused a fuss in the village, I can tell you that. The story grew with each telling: Henry and me lying in ditches. Running around the woods naked with flowers in our hair. Goody Figgs was behind it all. She was instructing me in witchcraft. We were practising sorcery on a simple-minded young man who didn't know any better. Oh, the names I was called, Aerlene, are not fit to repeat. I couldn't show my face in your uncle's shop again because all of Woodstock knew the story too, and your aunt wouldn't hear of it. 'Who would buy a spool of thread from the likes of her?' she would say to your uncle at dinner. I was suffered to eat at her table, but she wouldn't look at me and she wouldn't speak to me. 'You put her back in that shop, Jack,' she said, 'and trade will go elsewhere. You mark my words.'

"You know yourself, Aerlene, what a sweet, obliging fellow your uncle is and always has been, and he loved me dearly and couldn't help it, God bless him, but he could not go past his wife's words. He knew she was right about the shop. They had to make their livelihood, and their business would surely suffer as long as I was behind the counter. Lying in bed at night I felt entirely undone by everything, and over and over again I wondered why I had lain with that poor boy. Given myself over to pleasure like that with scarcely a thought for others. I knew such things never last and always bear a cost, yet I hadn't stopped until we were found out. In the early morning hours of sleeplessness you always think the worst, and sometimes I wondered if perhaps what some said of me was true after all; perhaps Goody Figgs, who often read my hands or sold me potions for a penny, had cast a spell over me. Perhaps I myself was now a witch ensnaring young, innocent men like Henry Chapman. At such times I thought of throwing myself in the river, for I knew a pool where the water lay still and deep beneath the willow trees. Yet I knew it was a grievous sin even to think about that and it frightened me whenever I walked by that pool in the river. I thought too of running away—but where would I go? I had little money, for Jack paid me no wages, only a few pennies now and then to spend on myself at Christmas and other festive times. He called it 'holiday money,' but it wasn't much. But even had I money, where would I go? How long would a woman last by herself on the road among the company she would meet there?

"You may well believe, Aerlene, that there were many in the village who wished me gone. Wanted me turned out like that to consort with vagrants. There were so many about in those days, rufflers and masterless men, many not right in their heads, pilfering what they could find, stealing onions from gardens and bedding left out to dry on hedgerows. And women with them too, thin and ragged with shifty eyes, beaten and treated little better than dogs. I often saw such people passing through the village, escorted by the constable and cursing him as they left, turning in the road to laugh at him and dancing a jig, making filthy signs with their hands. I once saw a man open his breeches and wave his soldier in mockery as he left. And I would then be among such fellows. Better off in the river, I used to think.

"For a while after Henry and I were discovered, young men would come from the taverns and throw stones at the house, making sounds like tomcats in heat. 'Come out, then, Lizzie, we'll away to the woods,' or 'They say you're the devil's maid, Lizzie. Will you come forth and seduce us? We've plenty here for you.' My aunt would soon be at the door, unafraid and facing them in her nightdress. I could hear her below on the front doorstep and see the dark figures scattering away and laughing. Sometimes, when I walked towards the river or the woods, children would follow, calling me names and throwing stones. But I could soon outwit them in the woods, and they were too frightened of Goody to venture far.

"I went to her hut one day and she was waiting as though expecting me. Nothing ever surprised her or changed the features of her strange old face. She had heard about me and Henry Chapman. She said nothing about it, but I could tell she knew. She invited me in and served me some concoction, which made me feel light-headed. Then she read my left hand, tracing the lines in my palm with her gnarled fingers. She told me I was going on a journey, but couldn't say where—only that it would happen if I was patient. I was not to worry but to wait, and I would find a new life somewhere else. Where that was she couldn't say, but I would go within the year.

"One evening a couple came to the door. I saw them from my window walking towards our house dressed in their Sunday clothes, looking ill at ease, the man large like Henry but with a worn face on him, and his wife small with sharp features. I didn't of course know who they were until after they knocked at the door and I heard the words they spoke to my aunt. The words that burned my face as I listened by the open window above them. 'Shame on her. A grown woman and a widow. Carrying on like that in the woods with a boy who is not right in the head and doesn't know any better. She should be stocked. I intend a word with the constable.' I couldn't hear it all. I think I may have clapped my hands across my ears. I gathered, however, that they were looking for money. Your aunt and uncle were shop owners. We weren't poor and I suppose the Chapmans thought they could be recompensed for the damage to their son's reputation. But your aunt was having none of it. Say what you like about Sarah, she was not one easily to be threatened; she would stand up to anyone and anything, fearless as a Tartar if you inflamed her. So she soon put the run to the poor Chapmans. Told them they had no business with her and her husband. Looking down I could see as I listened how the poor old man had snatched the cap from his head as soon as his wife had knocked upon the door. And then, listening to Sarah's words flail him and his wife, he looked as if he wanted to be anywhere else but there. I could see the slouch in his shoulders as the words took hold. 'Keep your feeble-minded son at home, where he won't bother others. Now be off with you or I'll see the constable and have him charge you with trespass.' They looked bewildered and somehow shrunken in those ill-fitting Sunday clothes. Words like *trespass* strike fear in the hearts of the poor, who want as little as possible to do with the law. I shall never forget standing at my window that evening watching the old couple retreat along the road, the woman turning to her husband and waving her arms at him. Scolding him for saying nothing. The poor man was still carrying his cap, fearful, I imagine, that they would get into trouble with the squire over this. I could see Henry's walk in his father and I remember thinking how much trouble I had caused so many because of my foolish longings. I wanted only to hide in my room and forget about living.

"Over that autumn and winter, I moved like a ghost through this house trying to avoid your aunt, enduring the silent meals. I found in a drawer—God alone knows how it got there in this house—an old, musty-smelling book of Anglo-Saxon tales. I judge it might once have belonged to Jack as a child. And I read those tales over and over. In one of the stories was a young girl called Aerlene, and she had many adventures and married a Norse chieftain and settled strife in this land long ago, and that is where I got your name.

"I fell into a melancholy, adrift in my mind, no longer caring one way or another what happened to me, eating little. I wouldn't go downstairs for meals and I grew weak with an ague, dreaming in my fevers of lying with tavern ruffians and other meaner sorts of men, sleeping in ditches, chased from towns and villages. Your uncle attended to me when he came home in the evenings, bringing me soup and stewed medlars. He nursed me back from my sickness, did

Jack, and all this time not a word of Christian comfort from your aunt, who never set foot in my room. I remember telling Jack that I was only a stranger in our house now and I wanted to die and leave them at peace, and he told me to stop such thoughts. He said, 'Lizzie, you must pray to God, Who will forgive you. You are always in my prayers and Sarah prays for you too but she is too proud to admit it. She will come around in time. You must give her time, for she is not as we are.'

"Perhaps he was right, for unbeknownst to me, Sarah had written her sister in London. And one day in late March of the following year, your uncle came to my room and he was holding a letter and smiling. Tapping the letter against my arm, he said, 'We have news, Lizzie. News from London, and it concerns you.'

"'Me?' I said. 'What have I to do with a place like London?'

"He told me the letter was from Sarah's younger sister, Eliza. She lived in London with her husband, Philip Boyer, who owned a milliner's shop and was accounted prosperous. Boyer was a Protestant Frenchman, a Huguenot as they are called, who had fled Paris some fifteen years before, following a massacre of Protestants by the Papists. Jack had brought me a cup of warm sweet wine. 'Drink this now,' he said, 'and get well, for the letter has wonderful news. Your sister-in-law wrote to them some weeks ago about find-

ing a position for you in their shop. She didn't show me
that letter, but I don't imagine she mentioned your recent
troubles, only your widowhood and need for work. I am sure
she wrote of how well you tended the counter of our shop.
And so here is her reply. Lizzie, her husband has a fine business not far from the great cathedral of St. Paul's, which I
saw once as a child forty years ago and have never forgotten.
It is a chance for you to begin again. I will be sorry to see you
go, but I know it must be done. You will make a living there
and find your way. It's all for the best. Now drink this and
read the letter.'

"And so I did. A small neat hand, and I wondered
reading it whether this Eliza was anything like her sister.
Was she as pious and severe? And what was this Frenchman like? I would be sharing a house with those people.
Suppose the husband looked at me a certain way? Made
secret demands away from the eyes of his wife? Weren't
Frenchmen great fornicators? Yet what was left for me in
Worsley? Whispers and catcalls and life next to a woman
who hated me despite what Jack thought, a woman who
just wanted to be rid of me. She was passing me on to her
sister, and probably without telling her the truth of my circumstances. How she would square that with God I did not
know nor care. As I read Eliza Boyer's words, I could see
in their arrangement something of her sister. Eliza wrote
that I would need to work hard and not expect too much

except my board and a modest wage; they had an infant daughter and some of my duties would lie in looking after the child. She would see in time how I worked out. The wording was cold and precise and sounded very like something your Aunt Sarah might have written.

"Still, I was encouraged. For the first time in months, I could see something beyond the terrible visions in my dreams, and now I was to go and live in London, a place I had never imagined even seeing. Yet hadn't Goody Figgs read my hand and predicted a journey within a year? After reading the letter I felt as though I wanted to get out of bed and walk through the wet fields and woods to her hut to tell her so. But I knew I wasn't strong enough yet and there would be time to say goodbye to the old woman, for when I asked Jack when I might go, he said, 'In a few weeks. As soon as the roads are dry and I can arrange a place for you with a carrier. Davey Jessup, perhaps. He goes into London and sometimes will take a traveller. There is time enough to think on it, Lizzie. But just imagine now. London. You will be living in a great city.' Before he left the room he looked down at me and smiled. 'I think you might say a word of thanks to your sister-in-law about this. I know she can be difficult, but she is not a bad woman and she has your best interests at heart.'

"Or, as I've said, she just wanted to get rid of me, Aerlene. You could take one or the other reason. Jack's sweet temperament chose one and I the other—but what did it matter anyway? I was going to London to start my life again and I vowed to myself I would be careful about men, and if this Boyer was forward with me I would defy him. I would lead a chaste life and a solemn one. At night before sleep in those weeks of waiting, I imagined the streets and churches and shops, the palaces, the great river that was said to run through the city. Why, people from all over the world went to London! The Queen herself lived there, and perhaps I might see her one day in some procession or another.

"When my health was restored and I had thanked my sister-in-law for getting me employment in London, my thanks acknowledged with only a nod, I visited Goody Figgs. Goody's expression never changed, whatever you told her, and so she greeted my news as if it were nothing. Had she not predicted a journey? She never said as much, but I could tell she had great faith in her own powers. I drank a cup of her horrible tea and felt again light-headed, as if I'd swallowed a liquor, while she told me to beware of the French pox in London. I didn't tell her about Philip Boyer, for I had no intention of ever again lying with a man. I smiled as the old woman stirred the fire and told me to watch myself in that city. 'I have heard it is filled with the French pox, so mind your honey-pot, girl. Scour it well and apply this ointment before you lie with a man.' She handed me a small bottle of something that smelled horrible, and that I later threw away, for I didn't alto-gether trust Goody's nostrums, remembering the story of a girl who had nearly died from something prescribed by the old blister. 'And stay away from gentlemen,' she added, her back to me as she bent across the fire. 'They lie with too many and are all pox-ridden, so I'm told. Settle for less. You're better off with an honest joiner or a green grocer's boy. But always remember to scour well, for neg-lect will hasten woe. Those who carry the pox have a sorry end.' And then, as if the idea of my lying with joiners or gentlemen or greengrocer's boys was amusing, she began to cackle, and perhaps it was her awful tea, which had prop-erties for lifting the spirit, because I too laughed. I judge we both might have been a little off in our heads from the tea. Oh, I shouldn't be telling you such things, Aerlene. You'll think ill of your poor mother."

I told her that I would never think ill of her, for I loved her too much. But I wanted her to go on with her story. How did she get to London? What awaited her there? How did she meet my father? She smiled, but I could see she was weary enough.

"Tomorrow, child," she said. "I'm all out now. Get me up to my bed."

I sometimes used to share Mam's bed, but her sick-ness had induced a restlessness in sleep and often she would talk or cry aloud or thrust an arm about as if tormented in her dreams. Once I lay down beside her in hopes of offering comfort and was almost myself asleep when her arm lashed out like a whip and struck me across the face. I feared my nose was broken, and though it wasn't, it was yet sore for days. Thus it was best to leave her by herself, and I slept in the truckle bed nearby. I missed lying beside Mam; I remembered the bolster of her big, soft breasts as I lay listening to her breathe and sometimes murmur words or softly laugh in her sleep. But all that would soon be gone from my life.

THIS HAS BEEN A cold, wet spring with the weather so foul that Maypole Day was cancelled. Under Cromwell, the day itself is no longer the frolic it was in olden times, but it is still celebrated after a fashion, and so the young of the village are disappointed this year. Mr. Walter is also out of humour, and with good cause, since many fields have not yet been seeded because of the dampness. We all seem vexed by one thing or another. I myself have been hampered all week by gravel in the kidney; for three nights now I have paced about my room drinking ale in hopes of moving the stone along, in time staggering off to sleep, only to awaken an hour later to piss. Still I must try not to complain, as many throughout the land are suffering from plague. This morning Charlotte told me that Mr. Thwaites was in Oxford Wednesday and saw posted the Bills of Mortality for London. Nearly six hundred for the week just past. Bristol too is sorely afflicted and Southampton and other coastal towns. We must be thankful that it has not touched us here, so when Charlotte asked me to pray with her for deliverance from the sickness, I said I would, though I told her it was too arduous to get down on my knees and back up again—I would make do with a bowed head from my chair. The truth is I haven't prayed much since childhood; yet I wanted to please Charlotte because she has been diligent these past weeks and even says she is enjoying the labour of taking down my words. She is a good girl and I am often too hard on her. So I closed my eyes in the chair, thinking myself not unlike the King in *Hamlet,* who prays with empty words while the Prince looks on, postponing his revenge. And did the King too not recognize the futility of his gesture?

> *My words fly up, my thoughts remain below:*
> *Words without thoughts never to heaven go.*

When Charlotte arose, I said, "On Monday, my dear girl, we shall get my mother to London, you and I."

She smiled. "I look forward to that, Linny."

Despite the weather and the plague, Charlotte alone among us is happy, for, I now believe, she is in love.

WHEN MAM WENT TO London over seventy years ago by horse, the journey took two full days with an overnight stop at Wycombe. For the poorest traveller, the walk was four days, three if your pace was firm and you weren't accosted along the way. Mam told me that she could not exactly recall the month she left Worsley, but reckoned it was late May or early June in the year 1587; everything, she said, was fresh and green and the weather fair. Uncle Jack put her in the company of the carrier Jessup, who did regular trade between Woodstock and London. My uncle paid the carrier, but Mam thought Jessup might be doing it more as a favour. As she told me, "From the beginning, I could tell this Jessup didn't like me. I am certain he had heard of me and thought I was little more than a bawd. I rode behind him on a poor, thin horse, a more miserable-looking beast you couldn't imagine, though it was gentle enough. There were three other men with their packhorses carrying goods, mostly lambskins and linen. Your aunt Sarah went so far as to wish me God-speed, reminding me to pass on greetings to her younger sister. We left at first light and your uncle Jack rode with us as far as Oxford. When we parted he was in tears, as I'm sure he thought he would never lay eyes upon me again. He had provided money for my lodgings along the way and a piece of paper with directions to Boyer's shop on Thread-needle Street, warning me to set the words to memory in case I lost the paper, as he knew how careless I could be about such things. 'And mind your money,' he said. 'London, I'm told, is thick with thieves.' But I knew that much at least and had made little pockets in my petticoat to secure the coins."

"How did you feel, Mam?" I asked. "Were you fright-ened going off to London like that by yourself?"

Mam said, "Yes, I was frightened. Of course I was, but a part of me was happy too. I told myself that I was having an adventure. I had a little money and prospects and a place to stay when I got to London, so matters were not so bad. It was cheering too that I would no longer have to endure the gossip and looks of people in Worsley. No longer have to put up with tavern louts calling me names, or children leaving turds on our doorstep. In London, not a soul knew me, or how I had so far lived my life. And even had Sarah told her sister the true account of my habits, the Boyers had accepted me and I was determined to work hard in their service, earn their trust and lead a good life. So in sum, I have to say that I was probably happier than I was sad to be leaving, though I knew I would dearly miss my brother."

I was trying to picture Mam on that ill-fed horse, following the back of the carrier Jessup, who didn't much like her. She told me that on the road she saw all manner of rough folk and she felt sorry for those on foot. Men and their women with children, turned out from who knows where or why, with little more than the rags on their backs, filthy with living in woods and fields.

Looking down at them as she passed, she thought herself fortunate. "There were many far worse off than I," she said, "and there they were in the dust of that road. I saw a blind man led by a young girl—his daughter, I suppose— and half-mad men gibbering to themselves and making faces. Some gave us terrible looks and others offered hands outstretched for alms. From time to time Jessup cracked a whip above his head and so too did the other carriers, yelling to those afoot to stand aside. I remember one woman with terrible sores and blemishes about her face, a child at her breast as she walked on the side of that road in dirty bare feet. I don't believe I had ever seen a more wretched-looking soul on the face of this earth. I wanted to give her a penny, but the carrier behind yelled, 'Give her nothing, Missy. Not a groat or we'll be harnessed to her all the way to London.

Mind my words.' And he cracked that whip again to scatter those about him. At the time I thought him heartless, but he knew his trade and perhaps he was right.

"I recall too there was trouble that morning, and though I didn't think it my fault, Jessup didn't like it. On the edge of a village a drunken man was dancing a jig in the middle of the road, twirling around like a child's top and dressed outlandishly in layers of clothes; though the day was warm, he had on an old canvas doublet and a long coat and a bonnet with brightly coloured feathers. A kind of roadside jester singing and dancing and expecting money for it. A ragged devil of a creature, perhaps a former soldier, for he had but one arm, the other a mere stump at the elbow; the long coat had only the one sleeve and I could see that naked lump of flesh where once a healthy arm had been. He may have been an Abraham man pretending to be mad for pennies, but Jessup was having none of it and nearly knocked him over as we passed. Drunk or not, the fellow was nimble and jumped aside at the last minute, cursing Jessup and all of us. Then as I passed, he looked up at me and grabbed my ankle and called me a filthy name. I could smell his foul breath, and he wouldn't let go of my leg as he tried to run his hand over me. But we had stopped, and Jessup jumped down and applied that whip. Such a hiding he gave that man, I thought he might murder him. The man crawled away into the bushes beyond the verge like an animal to escape the blows, dragging himself along with only one arm for purchase. Worthless creature that he doubtless was, I still pitied him. Before Jessup climbed back on his horse, he gave me the darkest look, as if I had invited that beggar's hand on my leg. I told him I was sorry if my presence had caused trouble, but he said nothing, turning his broad back to me and cracking the whip, and on we went.

"In the late afternoon, we stopped at a respectable inn in Wycombe, where I ate supper and shared a room with a farm woman who had walked from a village ten miles away. Jessup ate with the other carriers and drovers at a long table, and they soon grew loud with drink as men in taverns do at the end of the day. This woman—and it's odd, but I still remember her name, a Mrs. Earle—was a widow who had lost her husband within the month. She told me he had received a hurt with scythe or axe. A bad wound in his leg which had broken the shinbone and the wound became infected. Within a fortnight his leg below the knee had turned black as charcoal and smelled of rot.

"She fetched the doctor, who had the man drink as much ale as he could hold, and then they laid him on the kitchen floor with two others holding him down while the doctor began to saw at his leg above the knee. 'I couldn't bear to look,' she said, 'and he wasn't drunk enough, poor fellow, and so awakened screaming. In all my days, I never heard such shrieks,' said Mrs. Earle. 'I covered my ears and fled from the house. The children came too. We stood in a field and listened to the howling, and then finally it was quiet and when we went back into the house, he was dead. The doctor told us that the hurt from the cutting must have stopped his heart.'

"Mrs. Earle told me all this as we lay abed in our room. Her husband, she said, had been young and vigorous and then within a fortnight he was gone. It was hard to fathom. I felt sorry for her and so decided to tell her about Wilkes. I felt no great loss over him, and it had been a long time before, but I thought it would make this woman feel better to hear of another who had lost a husband. I told her Wilkes's death had happened only last winter and I changed its causes; it was, I said, a sweating sickness that overtook him. But she wasn't listening to a word, and soon interrupted to tell me that she was on her way to Uxbridge to visit her sister-in-law. It had to do with money owed to her late husband and she foresaw a dispute. That woman kept me awake half the night with her story about the sister-in-law and the money owed. I was grateful when at last she fell asleep and I could lie there with my own thoughts, looking out the window at the stars, listening to the laughter and songs from the tavern hall below, wondering what might become of me in the years ahead. When the tavern closed, the silence of the night settled in, and before I fell asleep I heard the watch-man on the street below calling out his round:

Give ear to the clock
Beware of your lock
Your fire and your light
God give you
Good night
One o'clock.

"I slept little, however, for I was fearful of not being ready and angering Jessup further, and so I was dressed by three o'clock, when the boy knocked at the door. I left the widow snoring. The morning was wet, and Jessup's head, I gathered, heavy from the night's drinking. I had a miserable time of it on that horse with only a shawl to keep the rain off my head. Wagons were stuck in ruts, as the road was muddy, and men were cursing. Terrible mouths on some of them. But as we approached the city the rain let up, stopping finally as we came along by Shepherd's Bush, passing the gibbet at Tyburn. It was something to see the great houses farther on in Tyburn Road. We had to walk the horses up Snow Hill, and so through Newgate, where Jessup stopped at the market by Christ's Hospital. This, he told me, was where I got off, for he was going elsewhere. He got a boy to take me to Threadneedle Street; it wasn't far, he said, and the boy could be trusted because he'd used him with travellers before. The streets were filled with such urchins who loitered about the hitching posts of inns and taverns.

"The boy was small and ragged, but cheerful enough when he took my penny. He wanted to carry my bag, but I said I could manage; he didn't seem to like that and turned away, beckoning me to follow. I remember how frightened I was once I left Jessup and the other carriers, because the streets were crowded and the noise was something I could never before have imagined: the church bells alone would deafen you, but there was the grinding of cartwheels on paving stones and the cries of hawkers with their wares and beggars plucking at you with pleas for money. 'A groat, Miss, only a groat,' they would yell with outstretched hands. And there I was, following this boy through the crowds at New-gate market, trying to keep pace with him. Why, I thought, he could lead me anywhere or nowhere, since all the streets and laneways looked the same to me. And the infernal racket of it all. I couldn't think as I hurried after him, trying to avoid the beggars and barking dogs and stepping around the kites squabbling for scraps. I'll never last a month in this place, I said to myself. Over the roofs of the shops and houses I could see a great building and imagined it was the cathedral Jack had told me about. But I feared I would lose sight of that boy, who was taking me through laneways and side streets where a rougher sort hung about. This was to be my first encounter with the sharp practice of London-ers, because the boy stopped and demanded another penny before he would take me a step farther.

"I told him I wouldn't give it to him. We had agreed on a penny, I said, thankful that I'd had the good sense to hold on to my bag. The boy only laughed, while others, watching from the tavern doors, idlers and bawds from the look of them, laughed too because they could see a newcomer being worked over, and such people enjoy laughing at a stranger's misfortune. So the two of us, the boy and I, were at odds and I wasn't going to weep, though I felt like it. Then a happy surprise when two gentlemen happened by and took pity on me. They were both in good humour, a little affected by drink, I imagined, and one asked me what the matter was about, and I told him I was newly arrived in London and had paid the boy fairly for directions to Threadneedle Street. Now he was demanding another penny. The other gentleman then took hold of the boy and might have given him a thrashing then and there had the tavern idlers not begun to grumble. A crowd soon gathered and so there I was, in London not twenty minutes and already in the midst of a street broil. Then one of the gentlemen said, 'Come along now, Miss, we'll show you the way to Threadneedle Street. It's not far. This young rogue is not for you.'

"The crowd, however, was with the boy, and some began to mutter about gentlemen minding their own affairs and leaving the common folk to their own. One of the gentlemen reached into his doublet and withdrew a handful of coins, flinging them into the air. As they fell, the people were soon on hands and knees, quarrelling among themselves in search of the money, quite forgetting me and the boy, who freed himself from the gentleman's grasp and ran off cursing us all. The gentlemen merely laughed and together walked along with me to a broad street with many fine shops. This was Cheapside, and as we walked, the gentlemen hardly took notice of me, engaged as they were in remembering bits from a comedy they had seen that afternoon at a playhouse. By the church, which I came later to recognize as St. Mary-le-Bow, they stopped and, pointing ahead, one said, 'You go that way, Miss. You are walking eastward and soon this street will part into three, so keep to your left and that is Threadneedle Street.'

"I thanked them with all my heart, but they had already turned their backs on me and were still talking about the play. So I walked on as directed and no one took any notice of me, and I soon found the street and the shop with its sign of a yellow hat. The shutters were still open because the day's business was not yet done and well-dressed people were going in and out. It was not rough and busy on Threadneedle Street, and I was glad, and felt more at ease. The shop itself looked prosperous and this was cheering too, and I prayed that Sarah's sister would take kindly to me and give me a chance to show how I would amend my life and make them proud of me.

"When I stepped inside, I was overwhelmed by the bustle of it all; I was used to business in your uncle's shop in Woodstock, but here were more gentry and they were buying finer goods, all manner of fancy apparel and wares, not only hats and bonnets, but ruffs and ribbons and gloves, fans and even cutlery—items of all sorts favoured by those with means. As I was to learn, Philip Boyer was not only an expert hatter, but a great importer of goods from Antwerp and Milan, where he had lived for several years learning his trade. I was to learn also that he had customers at court, both ladies and gentlemen, and a contract for boys' caps at the Merchant Taylors' School. In his warehouse at the back of the premises were two apprentices and two maids busy at lacework and hat making. But on that first afternoon, I stood alone just inside the entrance with my bag, watching the servers at the counter and the customers, who were fingering gloves and fans or trying on hats and laughing with their husbands or paramours. Such beautifully dressed women! And the men handsome too, unafraid to show their legs in hose of violet or crimson. I can only imagine what a penny I looked standing there in my plain country clothes with my hair not as it might have been because of the weather earlier that day.

"A woman behind the counter was frowning at me, and I knew at once that this was Sarah's sister, Eliza, as she had similar features, though she was younger by several years; I judged her not much older than myself. She had once been pretty and still was to a degree, but her beauty was marred somewhat by her scornful expression. So, I thought, another Sarah with a temperament soured by piety, for Jack had told me that the Boyers were devout in their own way. Eliza was serving a lady but looking over at me from time to time, her head, I imagined, filling quickly with judgments, and none of them in my favour. I am certain that with those unfriendly eyes she saw only a bedraggled creature with damp clothes and hair and a simple bag. But I vowed yet again that I would do whatever was asked of me, because this shop and this woman and her French husband were all that stood between me and the street beyond the unshuttered windows, where all who passed were strangers.

"When she had finished with the customer, Eliza came over and said, 'You must be John Ward's sister, the widow. Come along with me now—you look a proper sight, I have to say.' And with that, she turned and I followed her through the shop to the back, where I could see the long room with the apprentices at work and the lace maids and beyond them piles of trade stuff. We went up the stairs to the third floor and a small room, where I was at once informed of my duties. I had assumed that with my years in Jack's shop, I would be serving customers, but Eliza Boyer told me that I would be looking after her child, who was then nearly a year in age and only recently weaned. I was replacing a girl who had got herself with child and was turned out, and in Eliza's telling me this, I caught a hint of warning. So I was to be a nursemaid then, and I must have looked disappointed, for Eliza gave me her bitter smile. 'Unhappy, are you? Thinking you are above such work?'

"I was quick to say that I thought no such thing, adding, 'It was just that with all my years in Jack's shop I thought perhaps— '

"But she interrupted me. 'You are not in Woodstock now, girl. Your duties lie with our child. That and nothing more. And you will take your meals with the other servants.' So that was that, and fairly put, I suppose. I had been told my place in the household and I need expect nothing more. Whatever Sarah had said in her letter, she had poisoned her sister's opinion of me, and I had to live with that.

"As I would soon discover, the child, Marion, was a cranky, obstinate little creature who could not be pleased or made to smile by anyone but her father, to whom I was introduced later that day, since he had been occupied earlier with a visit to the wharfs, where he was expecting the arrival of goods from abroad. Philip Boyer was small in stature, but not unhandsome with his fine dark eyes, delicate features and a small beard. He was a precise man who I sensed immediately admired female beauty. I could see his appraising look of me in those eyes and I have to confess I felt a wavering pleasure in it, though I wondered if all this might prove troublesome. Would I awaken one night to find him standing by my bed, and what then? But I soon learned that Boyer was not interested in amorous adventuring; the only female for him at that time was his infant daughter, upon whom he doted and who returned his intense affection with smiles. Not even her mother could contain the child's rage when a distemper was upon her. Yet once in her father's arms, she lay quiet and serene. The rest of Boyer's time was spent in the warehouse instructing and admonishing his apprentices and overseeing the work of the lace maids. Now and again, he made an appearance in the shop to deal with an important customer, a servant from the court, perhaps, requesting samples for display to his lord or lady. Boyer would then arrange for a showing on a day assigned and take his satchel of bonnets to court or to one of the great houses along Holborn.

"As for his child, Marion, she liked me no better than she did anyone else except her father: most nights I walked with her in my arms to encourage sleep, taking the blows from those tiny fists as she struggled in my arms. Her wailing sometimes brought her mother to the doorway of my room in her nightdress, demanding to know what I was doing to her daughter. But no sweet or syrup could soothe the child and I was often beside myself with worry that the Boyers would discharge me for incompetence."

Apart from looking after the child in those early

days, Mam's only recreation was going with the Boyers to St. Anthony's, the church most favoured by those of French descent. After a few weeks, Mam was allowed Sunday afternoons to herself and so began to explore her surroundings, venturing beyond Threadneedle Street, growing each time more accustomed to the muddle and scurry of life in London, just as I myself would some years later. As Mam talked about those early days, I imagined her walking in some bewilderment on Sunday afternoons among so many strangers, holding close within the fear of losing her way in the narrow streets and lanes, for even now, many years later, I can remember such apprehensions: recall how it felt to be among rough people, men and women alike who would cut a purse or pinch your backside, run a hand across your bubs or even grab your quim in a throng. You had to be watchful around the brawling apprentices and idlers who seemed ever bent on making trouble for honest folk. To Mam it must have appeared as it did to me fifteen years later—that the entire world was on sale in the streets of London, and that nobody cared for anything but taking advantage for profit. During my first weeks there I often wondered how my father ever wrote a line of poetry amid the city's clamour. I could only imagine that he worked on his plays in the dead of night. Oddly enough, it was a question I forgot to ask him when we met.

Mam told me how in those first weeks she accustomed herself to the signs of taverns and shops, recognized the churches and conduits as signposts to familiar streets, sharpening her wits and elbows in the crowds, giving back as good as she got, growing bolder with custom and pushing aside those who got too familiar, for Mam then was still a strong young woman. Before long, as she told me, she came, if not to love, at least to wonder at and by times enjoy the variety of life in the crowded, dirty old city.

THIS AFTERNOON THE SOUND of something heavy falling below stairs, and then Emily shouting, a dreadful racket which I surmised came from the kitchen. Making my careful way down the stairs I hoped that Mrs. Sproule had not dropped dead on the flagstones. When I reached the kitchen, she was indeed on the flagstones, though very much alive on hands and knees, mopping and muttering about clumsiness amid the broken crockery and pickled cucumbers that littered the floor. With arms folded across her chest, Emily looked on with an expression suggesting that old women make too much fuss over a broken crock of pickles. The air was pungent with the smell of spices and vinegar.

"The last of the lot," Mrs. Sproule kept repeating as she squeezed the rag into a dish of soiled pickle juice. "Mr. Walter will not be happy. You know, Miss Ward, how he likes his pickled cucumbers with his bacon. There was enough in that crock to last until the summer garden. What will he say now?"

Nothing much, I thought. Mr. Walter may like his cucumbers and bacon, and may even mildly wonder at the absence of the pickles, but such is his unassailable incuriosity about household matters that likely it will never be mentioned. At the moment he is more concerned with getting his fields in order with the weather warm and fair at last. Still I had to appear concerned, and after a fashion, I was. Emily, it seems, in reaching for something on a shelf, had contrived to knock over the jar. I wondered how the girl had managed to tip such a heavy vessel: it must not have been securely placed on the shelf, and that would have been Mrs. Sproule's responsibility. I foresaw a squabble and had no stomach for overseeing it. Emily is clumsy and Mrs. Sproule forgetful, as am I. However, Mrs. Sproule was clattering on about Emily's mind being forever elsewhere when going about her duties and feeling little or no contrition when things went awry. For her part, Emily claimed that the pickle jar had been in her way, and the jar ill placed on the shelf to begin with. When she reached for something behind it, she said, the jar toppled. She very nearly received a hurt on her foot. Right there on her ankle. See that. And of course Emily pointed it out to us. Nothing is ever her fault, and so it followed that we need expect no apologies. I told her to get on with other things and said to Mrs. Sproule that I would make her some tea. Mrs. Sproule was in tears because the girl had been saucy to her. "I shouldn't have to put up with that after all my years of service in this house, Miss Ward." And so on. And she was quite right, and I assured her on that score and then made the tea.

Later I spoke to Emily in the hallway, where she was sulking as she polished the large mirror near the front door, reminding her yet again to watch her manners, to remember her station in the household and to concentrate on the work at hand. Charlotte had gone walking with Mr. Thwaites, so thankfully she wasn't there to hear me, for she hates the slightest hint of disorder in the household. While I was talking, Emily wore an air of grievance, as though she longed for someone to knock on the door and rescue her from this tiresome business. At one point, the damnable girl actually shrugged as I spoke. Perhaps she senses that my heart is no longer in all this.

To calm myself, I went upstairs and sat in the nursery, which is just as it always was, for Charlotte, who loves this room more than any other, wants it to remain as it was in her childhood. I am glad enough that she has insisted on this, because the nursery settles me when my mind is astir. In one corner is the old rocking horse, which was ridden by all the children in their turns, but mostly by Nicky, who would almost tip it over in his exuberance. It saddens me yet to think of a musket ball striking him dead as he sat astride a real horse, his beloved chestnut stallion, at Naseby. The storybooks once read to the children are still here by the window seat, where they listened on rainy afternoons. At other times, I dressed them in cast-off clothes and they performed plays I had composed from stories.

Sometimes we enacted shortened versions of my father's plays, for by then I had bought what was available of his works in print at a stationer's in Oxford. I never, of course, revealed the author's relationship to me; such an admission would have been far too outlandish for the children to believe, and would have occasioned some awkward conversations with their parents. I was content enough to introduce them to my father's work. Nicky enjoyed the histories and especially *Henry V*; the older girls liked the comedies. As for Mr. Walter, his nature inclined him to regard the everyday world as more important than the realm of the imagination. Yet stolid and dutiful child that he was, he could be persuaded to play a minor part in our entertainments, a Sir Walter Blunt or a Salisbury. Just to please me. His sisters enjoyed indulging their younger brother in his fondness for heroic roles, so Catherine might play Mowbray to Nicky's Bolingbroke, or Mary as Edmund suffer the insulting remarks of Nicky's Edgar:

And from the extremest upward of thy head
To the descent and dust below thy foot,
A most toad-spotted traitor. Say thou "No,"
This sword, this arm, and my best spirits are bent
To prove upon thy heart, whereto I speak,
Thou liest.

He was not yet twelve years, his clear, treble voice declaiming my father's words in this nursery.

That year on Christmas Eve, the children and I performed a pageant in the hall before their parents and servants and neighbours with brief scenes from various plays. The last piece of all was Nicky's delivery of King Henry's Saint Crispin's Day speech to his troops before the Battle of Agincourt. Even the old squire, a man not given much to fancy, had tears in his eyes as he listened.

When the girls left for America, Nicky was fifteen and out of sorts with play-acting. This nursery fell silent until Charlotte entered our lives and grew old enough to ask for stories and other enchantments.

One day not long ago, she asked if I remembered frightening her with a scene from one of the plays about the kings of England. That day she had been reading yet again a letter from one of her sisters in America, in which either Catherine or Mary was recalling her childhood in Easton House and the plays and stories I had told them. Charlotte said how she wished she had known her sisters, how she regretted growing up without them, how pleasant it might have been to have older sisters in the house. It saddened her to think how alone she often felt. I told her that she had at least been spared the bullying of older sisters, and anyway, I said, I myself grew up alone and didn't mind much. "You had Mr. Walter," I said, "and still have, for that matter. And you had Nicky too for a dozen years or so."

"Yes," she agreed, "Nicky was a wonderful brother to me. As a little girl, I do remember him so well. Still, it would have been agreeable to have sisters in the house. Even had they bullied me."

She brightened. "But I had you, dear Linny. The stories you told and the scenes you enacted of all those kings. You once had me stuff a pillow under your shawl and then you drew the curtains by the window and had me sit in the darkened room while you left. You told me to hide because the King, who was a wicked man, was coming to get me. Then a moment later you returned. Was that Henry the Fourth or Richard the Fourth? You clomped about the darkened room with that pillow strapped to your back beneath the shawl and said you were going to kill the children."

"Charlotte," I said, "there was never a Richard the Fourth on the throne of England. That particular dramatization was of Richard the Third. Old Crookback, so-called for his deformation."

She'd scarcely heard me, so caught up was she in her reminiscence. "You came into that room and began to search everywhere. Behind the rocking horse. By the bookshelf. Clomping around like a mad thing. You were looking for the two children . . ."

"Yes, Charlotte. Rightful heirs to the kingdom. The hunchback was going to kill them and claim the throne."

"You terrified me. When you opened the cupboard door next to where I was peeking out from behind the curtain, I shrieked." Charlotte laughed at the memory. "I think I must have wet myself."

"Indeed you did," I said, "through and through. I had to change your underthings."

"Oh, Linny," she said, "that was such a long time ago."

"For you, perhaps," I said, "though not for me. Twenty years."

"Yes, I must have been only three or four."

I told her I had invented that scene, as Richard didn't kill the children himself but hired assassins.

I lightened the darkness of some of the plays because, like my mother, Charlotte could not abide sorrowful endings: so in the old King's tale of woe, the hangman's knot is imperfect and Cordelia survives. "Look, look," cries Lear, "she lives." And so she did, at least in the nursery of Easton House before the eyes of a ten-year-old girl. The same happy fate awaits the voluptuous Cleopatra, when

Charmian plucks the asp from the Queen's breast with news that Antony is still alive, and the famous lovers are reunited. Desdemona awakens to embrace and forgive Othello. I could not bring myself to tamper with Hamlet's story, even for a child's amusement, and so I kept it to myself. Perhaps even to this day, Charlotte believes these great tragedies ended happily.

I was still in the nursery with these memories when I heard voices below stairs in the hallway. Charlotte and Mr. Thwaites had returned from their walk, and standing at the top of the stairs out of sight, I heard Charlotte tell Mrs. Sproule that the rector would be staying for supper. I retreated at once to my room to allow the cook time, as I expected her to be flustered by this news. Old people grow accustomed to routine and dislike unexpected requests, and so I would soon get an earful. I allowed a few minutes and then went down. Passing the closed door to the library, I could hear Mr. Thwaites saying something to make Charlotte laugh. In the kitchen, Mrs. Sproule was busying herself but grumbling too.

"Such a day, Miss Ward. First, that girl's clumsiness and impertinence, and now the rector for supper on scarcely any notice. What next, I ask you?"

I told her I had little idea what was next—death perhaps at one fell stroke—but we must cope as best we can. Charlotte then came into the kitchen, her colour high, for she was happy and excited to have Simon Thwaites in the house. And this I thought was a herald of things to come, and good for her and all of us. Charlotte apologized again for the late notice, but she and the rector had walked farther than they had expected and the poor man had talked of an appetite. Mrs. Sproule, however, was not to fuss. Bread and butter and cold meat would do. Charlotte had asked Emily to light a fire in the hall—and would I fetch a glass of wine for Mr. Thwaites? I would indeed, I said, and one for her as well, I hoped.

In the hall, Emily had laid a good fire in the hearth and smiled pleasantly at me. I have to say on the girl's behalf that she quickly gets over hard feelings. Mr. Thwaites, who had been standing by the window with his hands behind his back, turned to accept the wine and thanked me. When Charlotte came in, I could not help noticing, even with my poor eyes, how Simon Thwaites regarded her. Yes, I thought, affection is flourishing between them and clearly on display.

Though not overly handsome, the rector is well formed and has a clear, intelligent look about him. If they marry, he will instruct her in the ways of the world with patience and doubtless he will do a better job than I have done. To his credit, he is no firebrand like his predecessors; Charlotte has said that he is moderate in his views, an even-tempered soul—and with a sense of humour, as I soon found out. When he asked me why I didn't attend

Sunday service, I told him out of nothing more than mischief that I was a Quaker, but with no Society of Friends hereabouts, I made do with quaking by myself.

"Upon my soul, Miss Ward," he laughed. "A solitary Quaker in our midst."

But I could see he didn't believe a word of it and no more was said about attending Sunday service.

From the open doorway, we could hear Mr. Walter talking to Mrs. Sproule in the kitchen, and when he came into the hall, I could smell the not-unpleasant reek of horses and leather. The rector arose to greet him and Mr. Walter could only wag his large head in cheerful dismay at this Thursday evening surprise. I hurried off at once to get his ale.

When I returned, he said, "The cup that cheers, eh, Linny?" and drank deeply.

"Indeed, sir," I said, refilling Mr. Thwaites's glass and stirring the fire. With warmth and drink, awkwardness receded and Mr. Thwaites was soon asking about the fields and the weather. When I left, the conversation had turned to the sickness, still common in the larger towns and cities, but mercifully still absent from us.

In the end, the evening was successful. Mrs. Sproule put together a simple meal of cold beef and mustard with bread and early greens. There was also raisin pie. Afterwards she and I tidied up and had our boiled eggs in the kitchen. Later I listened to Charlotte saying goodbye to the rector, who had decided to walk back to the village despite Mr. Walter's offer of the light carriage.

I lay awake then for the longest time thinking about my next day's words for Charlotte.

I COULD PICTURE MAM IN the Boyers' house on her first night all those years ago, lying in bed, listening to the great city settle around her. That summer, she told me, the pestilence was in abeyance and people were unafraid to walk abroad. She could hear them passing in the laneway below her window, just as I would years later. Her work as nursemaid, however, was not agreeable. "I did my best," she laughed. "But either I was unsuited for it, or the child simply would not take to me."

"Or," I said, "she was just a brat, as you once told me."

"Perhaps so," said Mam. "Yet nothing I did could please her."

For many weeks she had to make do with restive nights and pinched cheeks as the squirming child clutched at Mam's face while she walked the floor with her. Then her luck changed. One of the shop assistants left abruptly and did not return. No one knew why, but Mam guessed the girl had run off with someone. "She was very pretty and a flirt and one of the gallants caught her, I expect," said Mam. "I don't imagine it ended happily, for such encounters seldom do."

To her surprise, she was asked by Philip Boyer to replace the girl and was given some of Eliza's old skirts and bodices, for they were much the same size. She took to her new duties and proved so adroit and personable that Boyer was soon praising her at some length. He could see how gentlemen especially enjoyed Mam's presence as they bought shawls for their wives or mistresses, or hats for themselves; moreover, with each passing day she grew more confident and more useful. Her modest demeanour and friendliness impressed the patrons. She was making money for Boyer, and this was pleasing to his thrifty, Protestant soul. Even Eliza could see this and it helped to temper her hostility.

One evening Mam heard them discussing her below stairs, Boyer putting forth the argument that Mam was more valuable behind the counter than upstairs with the child; they could hire a girl for that because "Elizabeth's gifts," as he put it, lay elsewhere. His wife reluctantly had to agree.

"How they both loved money," said Mam, "but like so many that way, they were close with it. Tight as a nun's crack, both of them," she said, then laughed at the simile, and I did too, though I wasn't sure why. "They decided to keep me in the shop but paid me hardly anything," said Mam. "Boyer was a good man and I knew he liked me, but not as I had feared at first. Not as a man likes a woman whom he may one day charm and seduce. No, Philip simply liked me as a person who knew how to work without complaint, because he told me once that he got nothing but gripes from the apprentices and often was provoked to box their ears for it. But I never complained of anything; I was so grateful to be free of that child.

"Boyer even told his wife that they must be fairer to me. 'Elizabeth should have more time for herself,' I heard him say. And so I was granted Sunday and Wednesday afternoons off plus an hour after closing in the evening, with a warning to be home before dark. I felt I was being treated like a school-girl, yet I was happy to get away by myself."

Mam then went even farther on her walks, and her favourite was by the river. On Sunday afternoons, she liked to watch the boatmen ferrying people across to Bankside, hearing, sometimes, the shouting and applause from the bullring and bear pit. At St. Magnus Corner at the north end of the great bridge, she watched the throngs of play-goers on their way across to the Rose playhouse. But especially she enjoyed the river itself, the swirling, dangerous water surrounding the abutments of the bridge and the smell of fish and mud. Sometimes she missed the country-side in summer: the quiet woods at dusk, the cattle and sheep in the fields, with darkness seeping into the fading light between the trees. But as she said, those were but passing moments of a loneliness, intense and urgent, then quickly gone, replaced by the noise and vigour of the life around her.

One afternoon she gave a penny to an old woman who was sitting with her bundle near St. Magnus and calling out to passersby who wished to know their fortunes. "She might have been Goody Figgs's sister," said Mam. "She read my hand, traced its lines and told me the strangest tale I'd ever heard."

I laughed because I put no store by the notion that your future lay in signs on the palms of your hands, but I was always amused by Mam's touching belief in such things. "What was the tale, Mam?" I asked.

"Why, I couldn't fathom it," she said. "The old woman told me I would meet a shepherd. A shepherd, mind you, in the middle of London! I supposed there were shepherds on some days, bringing their masters' sheep to market, but I had never seen one. Furthermore, she told me this shepherd came from a far-off land, and he would slaughter many folk and rule the world."

"And you believed this nonsense, Mam?" I said with a smile.

"Don't be impudent, Aerlene," she said crossly. "I believed what I believed. You shouldn't ridicule others' dreams and fancies. It comes easy to you, all this scoffing, but it's an unkindness, a failing in your character."

True enough, I thought, though I could no more change my nature than I could the size of my head. Such things had been placed upon me, whether by God or by the devil, I had no idea, but there they were. Still, I was sorry I had hurt her feelings and said so. She told me then that the next Sunday on her walk she had met someone.

Before I could stop myself, I asked, "And was he a shepherd, then, Mam?"

This time she laughed.

"No, *she* was not a shepherd but a woman, though large enough to be a good-sized man with broad shoulders—and the hands on her, the size of a drayman's. For all that, her face was amiable and like many large folk she had a hearty manner. I was leaning on a railing looking at the river and the sunlight on the water. There were long shadows beneath the bridge. And this big woman, well dressed, chose to stop by me and also lean against the railing. I seldom spoke to a soul on my walks, for I was wary. But when she offered an admiring comment on the fine afternoon, I could only agree, and hearing me she said I must be from the country.

"'Oxfordshire,' I said, 'near Woodstock.' And she nodded.

"'Not all that far from where I was born, a village called Coxton in Gloucestershire. Most people in this city are from somewhere else,' she added. 'We all have come to make our fortunes or our misfortunes.'

"Her name, she said, was Mary Pinder and she had been in London five years. I was grateful for someone to talk to, someone who knew the countryside, and so I told her my name and circumstances—a widow and working in a milliner's shop for my brother-in-law. She nodded and listened, friendly enough, though she had an air of menace about her. I imagine it was her size, as she didn't look like anyone you'd want to meddle with.

"She told me she rented a room near Bishopsgate. 'Beyond the wall,' she laughed. 'Shoreditch. A free-and-easy neighbourhood and a lively place, especially on Saturday and Sunday evenings when the players have done with their work and are refreshing themselves. They're a merry lot when they're not quarrelling. Have you been to a playhouse yet?'

"'No,' I said, because I could not imagine ever telling Philip or Eliza that I was bound for a playhouse. I had heard them remark on what foul places they were and how they should be scourged from the earth even though many of their customers, especially the young men from the Inns of Court, often talked with approval of a performance they had seen.

"Pointing across the river, Mary said, 'The new one over there, the Rose, is offering a colourful spectacle. It's full of blood and death, but there's poetry in it too. Called

Tamburlaine the Great and half of London is flocking to
see it. I've gone myself and plan to go again. Composed by
a young Cambridge wit called Marley. He's got London by
the short hairs, I can tell you that for a fact.'

"I told her that I would love to see a play performed,
but the Boyers did not approve of such entertainments.

"'Puritans, are they?' asked Mary. 'Well, they hate the
playhouses, and with some cause, perhaps. The plays can
draw a rowdy bunch and sometimes the apprentices with
too much drink can fight among themselves. It's nothing
to fret about, though the city aldermen do, fearing a general uprising of the people with every little brawl. For my
part, I find plays diverting. They take you out of your life
for an hour or two, and where's the harm in that?'

"'None, so far as I can tell,' I said.

"'Well put and true, Elizabeth,' said Mary Pinder, and
turned to me with a broad smile. 'Why don't we talk more
on this and other subjects? Do you have free time from that
milliner on Saturdays?'

"I told her I was finished at six o'clock and then given
an hour or two in the evenings, though with the darkness
closing in sooner now, I had to be careful.

"'They have you on a curfew? And you a grown woman?'
She shook her head in astonishment. 'Can you find your
way to the Dolphin after six o'clock next Saturday? It's a
worthy inn up Bishopsgate, a little beyond the wall, with

proper food and drink. Some of the players can get a little rough, but you are not to worry. I can handle that. We'll talk about getting you to the playhouse. Tell your Puritan relatives that you've had a change of heart about your spiritual health and are going to Evensong.'

"I said I would go, though I wasn't at all sure at the time. Why, I had only just spoken to this big woman for half an hour and I knew little more than that she came from a village in Gloucestershire. But I never asked what she was doing in London, for I hadn't the nerve. I certainly couldn't tell the Boyers I was going to Evensong, as they would never believe me. In the end, I decided to tell them that I was going out for an hour or two of air, and so I did, though Eliza thought my best dress a little proper for just a walk. I told her that presenting a well-dressed appearance discouraged idlers, and her husband nodded in agreement.

"It was only twenty minutes to the Dolphin, and Mary was waiting for me under the sign of the fish just as she had promised. It was September by then, but a lovely mild evening. From within came voices and laughter spilling out onto the street, and when we entered, I could see that the place was crowded with both men and women, some seated at long tables, but others in private rooms at the back; a blue haze was in the air, which I asked about as we took our seats at a small table. Mary told me that many people of fashion now used a herb brought lately from the Indies called tobacco. Even some of the women were burning this herb in long clay pipes, drawing in the smoke and then expelling it with an air of great satisfaction, although I watched one young woman with a group of gentlemen coughing as though ready to expire. Some of the gentlemen were laughing at her, another clapping her on the back.

"'It's her first time,' said Mary. 'They are teaching her how to smoke this tobacco. It's all the taste now with the young.'

"The young woman recovered with the help of some wine and the merriment resumed. I thought it the oddest thing, this pipe smoking, and by women too. Yet in the Dolphin there were many women finely apparelled, and no one had taken any notice of Mary and me as we entered. When Wilkes was courting me, if you could call it by that name, we sometimes frequented the alehouses and taverns along the Woodstock road and there were always a few women in those places, but they were mostly bawds. In the Dolphin the women all seemed to come of good estate, very like those I served in the shop. The men too were fitted out with velvet doublets and feathered hats, buckled shoes, some of them telling stories in an extravagant manner, striking poses, reciting lines into the air and causing great laughter to those listening. Mary told me they were players who had finished their performances for the day and were now enjoying themselves with drink and banter and bragging.

"'It's in the nature of their profession,' she said. 'Some of them never leave the stage. Life itself is a performance to them. They are very pleased with themselves, these fellows, but excellent company if they are not too much taken in drink, whereupon they are apt to turn quarrelsome.' She smiled. 'They are like children, forever performing, always wanting to be noticed. If you praise them, their chests puff out like guinea cocks at mating time. But just mention a play you liked in which they had no part and they'll soon heap scorn upon your poor judgment. Then you are no more than an object of ridicule. Catch them in good humour, though, and there is no better company.'

"Mary had money enough that night and wouldn't let me pay my share of the reckoning, though I had a little in my purse. We drank sack possets, which were sweet and sticky in the gullet and left me light-headed after only one. I vowed to drink no more than two, as I was fearful of getting back to the shop along streets that were already growing dark. As for Mary, her face was flushed and I wondered if she had been drinking before we met. She was in fine humour, and when I asked how she came to be in London, she was happy enough to tell me, for as she said, 'There is many a rogue in this world, Elizabeth, and we poor country women must stick together. You will soon find that in this city, a good friend is better than gold.'

"I said I didn't doubt it, and Mary smiled—she had a warm, pretty smile, that big woman.

"'Five years ago,' she said, 'I came to London with a friend, or one I took as such, for we'd known each other all our lives. Sally was small and fair, a little beauty for certain. We both wanted out of that village in Gloucestershire. I saw nothing there for me but more trouble from my father, a drunk and a brute, who interfered with me until I came to eighteen years or so, when I broke his nose one night, and after that he left me alone. But that's another story that I won't tell now. As for Sally, with her good looks she was pestered by half the louts in Coxton. I'll not lie to you, Elizabeth, I loved her myself. She was frightened of men but drew them to her as a flower draws bees. When she was seventeen, two of them got hold of her one night and had their way, God curse their miserable souls. She worried that she might have a child from all that but told no one but me. Mercifully her courses came on, and so we began to make our plans to escape down here to London. I had some money saved from my job as a dairymaid at the manor farm, and so we left together before daylight one morning, walking, sleeping by the roadside or in the woods at night, careful with our money and wary of strangers. It took us a week to get here.'

"'There is always work serving others and across the river in Deptford we found service in the house of a brewer, a vile man with terrible children and a worse wife. I could have brained them all with few regrets, though I had little enough to do with the family, since I worked in the laundry, washing their filthy bedclothes and other things. Sally worked upstairs as a maidservant and couldn't help but be noticed by one of the sons, a boy about her age with his eye on her from the first day. Beauty brings its price, does it not?' said Mary, who then finished her drink and ordered another. I said I'd had my last and she only shrugged. 'So you're wise as well as pretty, Elizabeth Ward? Well, good for you, though I dare say you've had your troubles with men.'

"I said nothing to that, for she was telling me about Deptford and how unhappy she and her friend were. But she liked some things about it too. 'I liked the afternoons, when the joiners and caulkers were coming back from the shipbuilding yards and I was taking in clothes off the grass from drying. Those fellows were in good humour after their day's work with a glass at the tavern ahead. "Come and work with us," they used to say. "You look big enough for it." I didn't mind their jesting. But the whole place stank to heaven from the breweries and the tanneries. And the Queen's slaughterhouse was nearby and sometimes you could hear her hounds baying in the kennels from the smell of the blood. That and the constant hammering from the shipyards and the gulls squawking over the river—it was a racket, I can tell you, and I sometimes thought of the ships setting out for the Indies and what it would be like to be on one. Could I carry it off if I dressed like a man? But it was all only daydreams. Besides, I had Sally to look after and I worried about her.

"'She was so unhappy in that brewer's house. She wanted to go back to Coxton because she was finding it hard to keep that boy's hands off her and she feared he would try to board her one day while she was cleaning his room. She was in mortal terror of having a child by him and being put out on the street, and she'd tell me all this as we lay abed. And one night I took her in my arms and kissed her so that we lay together, and she enjoyed that and afterwards I vowed to her that if that boy laid a hand on her, I would break him in two, and she just cried like a child in my arms until she slept. And that night is the sweetest memory of my life and I'll say no more about it.'

"Mary sounded angry, as if warning me or anyone to deny the truth of her statement, and again I could see this strange mix of tenderness and threat in her nature. But her story had caught me up and I asked her where Sally was now. Were they still together?

"You know, Aerlene, how I enjoy a tale that ends well, though I know in my heart that most true ones don't. And so it was with Mary's. She told me that one night Sally left. 'Just like that,' said Mary, snapping a thumb and finger. 'And not a word to me about it, and that was hurtful. Before leaving, she took some silverware. She might have settled for something lighter, linen or jewels, but I suppose she was fearful and in a hurry to be away. So she was going to walk back to Coxton with a bundle of stolen silverware on her back, poor little mutt.

"'Needless to say, she was soon caught and taken to Bridewell. I visited her there. Brought her food and what little money I could spare, but she was never sturdy and already looked little else but skin and bones, her eyes so large and dark. They'd flogged her too, with all the fishwives jeering, and that took the heart out of her. I don't think she was interested in living after that, and she wasn't nearly strong enough for a place like Bridewell. I should have stolen something myself and gone in there to look after her, but I didn't, and I never saw her again. When I went back, they told me she had taken a fever and left in a winding sheet. Already in the ground and no one could tell me where. London has plenty of stories like that, Elizabeth. This city can break you easily enough if you have no money or friends.'

"I didn't need to be reminded, for by then I was worried about overstaying in that tavern. I was sure the streets were dark by now and the Boyers would be waiting for me.

"As if reading my mind, Mary said, 'You'd better be on your way soon. Your Puritan keepers will be wondering where you are.'

"Just then, a man stopped at our table. He wore a fine doublet and white silk stockings. Bending down, he kissed

Mary's cheek. 'As my life is my own, it's Mary the Great. I haven't seen you in weeks. How are you faring, my dear?'

"'Well enough, Tom,' she said, and praised the man for a recent performance. 'Best I've ever seen you do.'

"He preened. 'Kind of you to say so, but it was a trifle only. A mere few minutes in a man's lifetime.'

"'Even so,' said Mary, 'you were good, Tom. Praise paid where praise is owing.'

"'Bless you, Mary.' He bent again to kiss her. 'I intend a visit soon. Perhaps next week.'

"'Send a boy ahead with your time.'

"'You may depend on it.'

"After he left us, Mary said, 'That fellow is in Marley's *Tamburlaine* and he was good. I told no lie. They are all good and especially Ned Alleyn. Would you like to see it, Elizabeth?'

"'I would,' I said. 'I have Wednesday and Sunday afternoons to myself.'

"Mary startled me and others around by smacking the table with one big fist. 'Done, then. We'll go this Wednesday. Meet me at St. Magnus Church at noon. Now listen,' she added, leaning forward. 'At first you may not recognize me but don't alarm yourself, because I will speak my name.' When I asked her why I wouldn't recognize her, she only shrugged. 'Let's get you back to your quarters. I have an engagement, but I've arranged for a boy to see you home.'

"When I told her about my first experience with street urchins, she said, 'Well, you were just off the pack train, so what did you expect? But that carrier should have known better. This boy will do what I tell him and he's been paid, so give him nothing. He's strong too and will see that you come to no harm.'"

Mam told me then she was worried walking back with the boy. "I knew I had overstayed my time allowed, and I feared Eliza's tongue. But after the boy delivered me to the shop and I knocked, Philip himself came to the door in his shirtsleeves. He let me in and nothing was said, and that was that. I can't tell you how relieved I felt."

The following Wednesday Mam walked to St. Magnus Corner, wondering, so she told me, if Mary Pinder earned her living in a house of sale. All week she had thought about the man who had stopped at their table in the Dolphin on Saturday night, and then about Mary telling her later that she had an appointment. Mam asked, did I know what she was talking about? I said I thought I did. I knew a girl in the village a year or two older than me, dull-witted but comely enough, who, it was said, allowed boys to put their things into her down by the riverbank for a groat or an apple core. Was it not something like that? I asked, and she said it was, though in London men paid more than a groat or an apple core. I told her I couldn't imagine having boys or men poking their things into me, and she said I was well advised to hold to that opinion.

As Mam told me about this part of her life, I imagined her walking along the London streets on that September afternoon. She must have felt buoyant with hope for a little happiness in her life; she was going to a playhouse with a new friend, and what did it matter if the friend did sell her favours? Mary Pinder, at least, was no street bawd. As Mam said, "I saw any number of those forsaken souls hanging about street corners, poorly dressed and looking ill used."

As the noon bell tolled, Mam was watching out for Mary, while being jostled by others and trying to affect a knowing air, as if she did this every afternoon. "Then," she said, "I was surprised by a gloved hand on my arm, and there in front of me was this large gentleman with a small moustache in a broad face beneath a hat.

"'Well now, Miss,' he said. 'On time, I see.' A snort then of familiar laughter. 'Yes, Elizabeth, my dear, it's Mary,' and I had to laugh.

"'So help me God, Mary,' I said. 'You gave me a fright. I thought I was being taken for a pickup.'

"'Well now,' said Mary, leaning closer, 'were I really a man I would ask you, and since I am playing the part today, I shall. Will you along to the playhouse with me, Miss?'

"'I will,' I said, and Mary took my arm.

"'And how do you fancy me, by the way?' she asked. 'Am I not handsome?'

"Looking at her in the velvet doublet and breeches, the stout legs in silk hose with buckled shoes, the broad feathered hat, I had to smile.

"'Am I not in the fashion, girl? Have you ever seen better in that hat shop of yours?'

"'I don't believe I have,' I laughed.

"'There you are, then,' she said as we made our way through the crowd, Mary parting others before us with no apology.

"'But why those clothes?' I asked, though Mary pressed a thick finger across my lips as we walked. To those nearby it could have been taken for nothing more than a flirting gesture.

"'Here we are,' said Mary, 'crossing London Bridge on a fine afternoon. Off to see Mr. Marley's play, a gent with his lady.'

"Mary then bent towards me as if in intimate talk, because as she said, going to the playhouse was a great occasion for courting. Gentlemen took their mistresses to the plays to better acquaint themselves.

"'And look around, Elizabeth,' she said. 'It's not only gentlemen about with their lady friends. It's the rabble too you're in company with, so you're better off with a man. A woman by herself is fair game and two are not much better off unless one of them has my proportions. Look at all these unruly fellows half-filled with ale. You're a pretty sight, girl, and I've watched some of them eyeing you. In no time they'd be asking about your tariff. How much for a two-minute stand-up against an alleyway wall on the other side? If you were on your own and in the pit, they'd think nothing of standing behind you and rubbing their pricks against your backside. Having it off while your eyes are on the players. Oh yes, I have seen them at such things. But they'll not lay a hand on you today, or they'll get a cuff from me and it will smart where it lands. Besides,' she added, 'I enjoy the disguise. And men sometimes like this too, this dressing-up business. It's part of the game, Elizabeth. Part of London.'

"And on we went as Mary parted others before us, passing apprentices in their blue jackets and cloth caps, and older, scruffier types, masterless men who had scrounged a penny for an afternoon's escape at the playhouse or bull-ring. When we reached the playhouse, the pit was already filled and people were quarrelling for space. The fruit and ale vendors had scarcely room to peddle their wares, holding their baskets aloft as they made their way. 'You couldn't make room for an eel down there,' said Mary, paying two pennies more for gallery seats.

"'We're better off up here,' she said as she settled herself on the bench beside a gentleman whispering to his lady friend.

"Below us the groundlings were jostling one another and laughing, drinking bottled ale and cracking hazelnuts, spitting out the shells and shouting as they stretched their necks for a better view of the stage. But even in the galleries there was much roistering and the exchange of coarse jests among the lawyers and merchants' sons and courtiers. Mary nudged me with her elbow so I would glance at the man with his hand beneath the woman's skirts.

"'They like to bring their lady friends,' Mary whispered, 'or whoever to the playhouses. Watching the plays is supposed to influence their appetites, if you take my meaning, Elizabeth.'

"It was like being in another world sitting there with Mary Pinder. Only three months before, I had been in Worsley avoiding the eyes of neighbours and the taunts of tavern oafs inviting me out to the woods and meadows, putting up with your tedious aunt and the pitying looks of your uncle. Now I was surrounded by people who knew neither me nor what I had done; for all that, they might well have done worse. Soon I was transfixed by the blare of the trumpets announcing the beginning of the play.

"When Tamburlaine, in his crimson hose and doublet, strode on stage, leading his beautiful captive, the daughter of the Egyptian King, the crowd gasped at his magnificence, and Mary whispered in my ear, 'That's Ned Alleyn. Is he not a fine specimen of manhood? And listen to the tongue on him, Elizabeth!'"

Mam told me the play was noisy and colourful, with

flags flying and cannons roaring and blood-soaked men groaning as they died on battlefields, and everything governed by Tamburlaine's ruthless will. "But," she said, "I had trouble keeping track of all the names and the people and where they came from."

"But was there poetry in it?" I asked. "Were there words to recall?"

She shrugged. "I suppose there were. This Tamburlaine was forever bragging about himself being once a lowly shepherd who was now conquering the world.

"And that," said Mam, smiling, "reminded me of the old woman by the river and I began to laugh, and when Mary asked me what was so funny, I told her about the fortune teller who said I would meet a shepherd who would become a king. And there he was in front of me, a player pretending it was all true.

"Mary derided me, just as you might have done, Aerlene. 'Of course, she told you that,' said Mary. 'She probably told a hundred others too for a penny a turn. She saw the play herself, or more likely heard the story, and so she knew most people wanted to see it. She took your penny for telling what many already knew. You are green as lettuce, Elizabeth, and the old fraud could see it. There's enough like you in London to make a thousand beggars' livelihoods.'

"She was right," said Mam. "But I didn't care. That

afternoon was happiness to me and I loved it all. The gentlemen and ladies in their finery, the apprentices in the pit throwing their caps in the air at the end of the play, the excitement of it all. It wasn't the play itself so much. All that killing and blood was not to my liking. But it was everything around it that I enjoyed. This, I thought, was living."

I remember Mam stopped and looked at me. "And since you're wondering—and I can see from that pinched, quizzical face of yours that you *are* wondering—it was on that afternoon, on our walk back across London Bridge, that Mary Pinder first mentioned your father."

"And what did she say about him, Mam?" I asked.

"Well, Mary told me that a week before, she had met a pleasant young man apprenticed to the Queen's Players. 'Now usually, Elizabeth,' she said, 'I wouldn't commend an apprentice player, as they're mostly rapscallions, but this fellow seems different and I fancy myself no bad judge of men. He's newly arrived in London, not above six weeks or more, for they were touring this summer past down in the south, Canterbury and Rye and other towns. But they were in the Dolphin last Monday celebrating someone's birth date, and this young man was sitting at a table next to mine, looking on and not saying much. I knew many of the players and we had our usual jests one with the other and soon they fell to playing cards, and while they were at it, this young fellow asked me what part of Gloucestershire I came from, as he recognized my speech right off—and me in London now five years!

"'When I said Coxton, he told me he knew it, for years ago when he was just a boy he'd gone there with his father who dealt in wool at the time. They'd visited the very manor farm I'd worked at as a dairymaid. His father, he said, was a brogger. That is to say, he didn't have a licence to deal in wool, but there was good money in it then, and some of the farmers, like our squire, looked the other way and got their price. Will said he was only eleven or twelve at the time, but he remembered the farm and the visit. He told me they had a meal at the manor house, he and his father, before they set off for home. He was so glad to meet someone from that part of the country. Oh, we must have talked above an hour on country ways, for he is from Stratford in Warwickshire. Well spoken too, and not one for carousing. He made his only tankard last the night. I asked him how he came by London, and he told me he'd joined the troupe in Stratford and they had been travelling all summer and were only now settled in London these past six weeks or so. He is working at the theatre and we talked a good deal about plays, including the very one we've seen this afternoon. But I could see he wanted to talk more about the countryside, which I believe he misses, for he spoke so feelingly of the woods and meadows of Warwickshire. These past few days I have been thinking, Now here is a young man well suited for Elizabeth, who also misses her columbines and daisies. And truthfully, I don't believe there's any harm in this Will Shakespeare, so why shouldn't you share some time together and see what happens? The rest lies in your own judgment. I told him about you, Elizabeth, a pretty young widow from Oxfordshire, I said, and he told me he would like to meet you. He will be at the Dolphin next Saturday about six in the evening. Now what do you say to all this?'

"We had crossed the bridge by then and I was unsure. I had got myself into trouble with men over the years, and I wanted no more. At the same time, I needed someone, if only to talk to, so when Mary said, 'If you're interested in meeting this Will from Warwickshire, I'll make him known to you on Saturday.' I told her I would think on it."

THIS MORNING CHARLOTTE RAISED some questions about the composition of my work. Beyond the library window was another dark, wet day. The middle of May is usually fair, but this year the rain has been relentless. Poor Mr. Walter is not a happy man, for already the swales in some fields are under water. I myself have been feeling gloomy too, whether from the rain or from this damnable stone, I do not know. Our conversation went as follows, more or less:

"Did all these things really happen, Linny?"

"Yes, they did. More or less."

"What do you mean by 'more or less'?"

"Exactly what the phrase suggests."

"Are you saying, then, that some things have been invented?"

"Things are always invented in the telling of a story, Charlotte."

"Then this is more like a novel we are writing?"

I took note of her pronoun in the first person plural.

"By which I mean," she continued, "that your mother and this Mary Pinder are having a conversation at a playhouse in London. But I must wonder how your mother could recall that conversation in such detail and so convey it to you, and you to me after more than seventy years. How can we account it as true?"

"Charlotte," I said, "that is an uncommonly literal reading of events and, if I may say so, does a disservice to your intelligence. In relating anything we only *approach* the truth; we are never exactly there. Moreover, does not another truth besides the factual lurk in any account of events? A truth perhaps far more important? Given what my mother told me when I was a girl, I have imagined her in London. She told me she went one day to the Rose playhouse with Mary Pinder. They must have talked about something as Mary, disguised as a gentleman, cracked hazelnuts while they awaited the performance. Am I then to write, 'That day they went to the playhouse,' and leave it so? Is the reader not entitled to a little more, even if it is not *exactly* what happened? And is it not also possible that out of that imagined conversation, a truth beyond the factual might emerge? Something, for example, that casts light on what my mother and Mary Pinder were like at that time?"

I wondered if she was listening to all this, for she had the faraway gaze of the child in a classroom who is alone in a world of her own devising. But yes, Charlotte was listening, indeed she was, for at once she said, "How odd, because the other day Simon told me something very like what you say. He enjoys poetry and novels, and he was commenting on some character in a book, remarking on the soundness of this person's views. And I said, 'But he is only a character in a book, Simon. He doesn't really exist, does he?' And he said something about the character existing within the words on the page." Charlotte laughed. "Am I not getting a little too philosophical, Linny?"

I said I hoped not, adding, "But is your Mr. Thwaites not an estimable man? Should I not therefore fetch something from the decanter and ale cask so that before dinner we might both drink to his good health?"

So we did, both of us greatly heartened and with no more questions raised.

On that Saturday evening in late September 1587, Mam went to the Dolphin as arranged and found Mary Pinder at a table by herself looking ill-tempered. The tavern was filled with song and laughter, and there was this great solemn presence by herself at a corner table. As Mam sat down, Mary was already ordering another glass of sack and said, "And how are things in the haberdashery with those Puritan relatives of yours? Still turning a profitable trade, I trust."

Mary was in a dangerous humour that evening, Mam told me, glaring around the crowded, smoky room as though seeking out someone to quarrel with. "I didn't know what to say to her. And where was this young man from Warwickshire who wanted to meet me?"

"Mary then turned and said, 'I'm talking to a green girl, am I not? A simple soul from,—what is it?—Worsley?'

"'Yes,' I said, 'Worsley under Woodstock. You know that now, Mary.'

"The barmaid brought her wine and I said I would have nothing, for to tell the truth I thought of leaving.

"Mary said, 'I don't imagine, however, that you're not so simple as to know what I'm about. Sometimes I fancy you look at me with the face of a churchwarden.'

"'I do no such thing,' I said, and I must have shown some colour, for Mary shrugged.

"'Well, perhaps not. But I'm sure by now you've guessed that I don't sell bonnets for a living.' She laughed. 'Look at you now. Your face is a beetroot, girl.'

"'It doesn't matter, Mary,' I said, and she gave me another glare. Mocked my voice.

"'*It doesn't matter, Mary.* My, aren't you the generous little gospeller! Do you pray every Sunday morning for my salvation, Elizabeth?'

"'You're too quarrelsome tonight,' I said. 'We'll meet another time, when you are better humoured.' I was so confused and disappointed. I was dressed as smartly as I could be to meet this fellow she had so praised. And where was he? I was angry and said to her, 'It's nothing to me what you do. I haven't the right to call anyone to account, because I have done things myself that merit little praise. I am in London on sufferance, and you are the only person who has troubled herself to befriend me. If you have changed your mind, so be it. I'll take my leave.'

"But Mary had grasped my wrist by then and was close to tears. 'As God is my witness, Elizabeth, I'm sorry. I've had too much wine and it's soured me. You take what you get in this trade, but I had a nasty one this afternoon. Some like it rough, and I'm all for that if they pay well. But this one. A devil out of nature and I didn't at all take to his inclinations. Then didn't he quibble over payment and laugh about it? Slumming in Shoreditch, he said. Out for an afternoon with his friends and he'd heard I was good sport.' She looked away. 'I promised him a clout if he didn't pay as we agreed and he said I could swing for my threat. I had to shake the coins from his breeches and his friends were laughing at him while he cursed me. I may not have seen the last of that arsewipe.'

"Our faces were close while she confided this to me and therefore we didn't notice the figure above us until he said, 'I fear I am late and I offer apologies to you both.'

"We looked up and there was your father standing above us looking grave and polite.

"I wondered if he'd overheard Mary's last sentence, but if so he didn't let on.

"Mary brightened at the sight of him. 'Ah, Will from Warwickshire. I'd almost forgotten about you, but your arrival is timely, as I am to leave. But first let me introduce you to our young widow from Oxfordshire, Elizabeth Ward. And this young man, Elizabeth, is Will Shakespeare, late of Stratford, now resident in Shoreditch and a player with the Queen's company.'

"'Apprentice player,' he corrected.

"'Gainfully employed, at any rate,' said Mary, standing and towering over him. 'I will pay my reckoning and be off now. And you two can become acquainted. I wish you both well.' Then she was gone, shouldering her way through others near the door."

As I listened, I was trying to summon up the scene in my mind's eye: Mam as a young woman sitting in that crowded inn with the man who would be my father amid the tobacco smoke and laughter and loud talk. I remember asking Mam endless questions: How did he seem at first? Was he handsome? What height and form? How did he talk? He must have had a good wit, for look at all the plays he composed. Did she see that gift in him then?

Poor Mam. Putting up with all my chattering as she grew more haggard each day from the sickness that was consuming her. My uncle had called in a doctor, a churlish fellow from Woodstock who examined her and said the sickness was caused from an impostume in her parts. Mam laughed when she told me this. "I may tell you, Aerlene, that he had his hand in there long enough." Mam was duly bled, much good that did her, for already she was grey as wood ash. Only my reading from the *Dream* each night could soothe her into sleep.

But in the afternoons for an hour or two, she was yet strong enough to tell me what happened to her in London. As for her first meeting with my father, she could only laugh at all my sifting.

"Goodness, Aerlene," she said, "I can no longer remember what we talked about that first meeting. Very likely where we came from, as we both loved the countryside. And since you asked about his looks, I can say he was of moderate height. I wouldn't have called him handsome, but he had a pleasing aspect, was of good proportion, his brow impressive."

"Like my own," I said.

She smiled. "Yes, yes, very like your own, I suppose. He had good legs, your father. I had noticed them before he sat down. And later, when we knew each other, I was bold enough to compliment him, and he was pleased because there was vanity in him. Not huge conceit like many others, but he liked to think well of himself. He told me he had done a great deal of dancing as part of his trade, and he was well practised in the galliard and the pavan. He *was* graceful on his feet, and once danced for me in his room to prove his worth."

She thought further on it and said, "We must have talked that first time about how we came to London, because that's what you did if you were newcomers to the city. I told him about Worsley, and he talked about his childhood in Stratford and how he liked to get out into the countryside. He said he had been with the company since early summer, when they had passed through his town and he heard they were short a man, killed, he said, in a brawl. The troupe then spent the summer touring in the south. Will had seen Canterbury Cathedral and Hythe and Rochester, and the cliffs of Dover, which had amazed him. He told me about the samphire gatherers perched on the cliffside high above the sea, and wondered at the time how a man or woman could work at such a dreadful trade. So he had been in London only since July's ending. He liked the city well enough, though he found it noisome and clamorous and often longed for the quiet of the country. We soon learned that we both loved walking in the woods and meadows, and I remember how he spoke knowingly of herbs and flowers and all manner of plant life: of wild thyme and cowslips and musk roses and woodbine. He knew such things and I thought it strange knowledge in a young man who was not a farmer's son, for he'd told me that his father was a glover. But his feelings for nature were delicate and I found that attractive in him. Aerlene, you remember Oberon's speech about the riverbank in the *Dream*, the one that begins, *I know a bank whereon the wild thyme blows, | Where oxslips and the nodding violet grows?* "

"Of course I know it," I said. "Haven't I read it to you enough times?"

Mam was scarcely listening, so rapt was she now in her memories. "I love that speech," she said. "And it's true, I have seen the woodland violets nodding their little heads in an April breeze. And sometimes when I am trying to find sleep in the middle of the night, I tell myself that I once knew the man who wrote those words and I had his child. It is still a great wonder to me by times."

"And to me as well, Mam," I said.

"I may say that I remember your father's hands from that first meeting," she continued. "He had fine hands, not large but shapely, though it surprised me to see that the palms were as callused as a wagoner's. Some weeks later I asked if I might read his hand, which made him laugh and he asked me did I really believe in such things and called me his pretty witch. I asked him then how he came by such hard hands, and he said it was from practice with the foils. 'All players must master fencing,' he said.

"That first night he saw me back to Threadneedle Street. I remember that. We walked along the dark streets and he told me about his father and mother. He expressed a great affection for his mother and called her an excellent, quiet woman of deep faith. And his father, he said, was a good man who had suffered some misfortunes in business, but I can't recall him saying much more about him at that time.

Your father seemed a bit lonely and homesick, and I believe he could see that I was not like most women who hung by the players in those taverns in Shoreditch. Your father, Aerlene, was not one for trugging-houses and debauchery. He was a quiet and thoughtful young man who wanted to better himself. I noticed how favourably he looked upon the address and shop of the Boyers."

"So," I said, "he liked you well enough at your first meeting, Mam?"

"Oh, he liked me well enough," she laughed. "He may have talked of country fairs and nodding violets, but he could scarcely take his eyes off my bosom. We agreed to meet the next morning after service, for Sundays were the only days free to him. They worked apprentices hard in those playhouses. Sometimes we met on a Saturday evening at a tavern, where he would sit a full two hours over a tankard of ale, for he can't have had much money then. I understood that and I always paid for my own wine and he didn't resist.

"In the autumn there was great demand for Boyer's wares with masques at court and dances in guildhalls and the lawyers' inns. Philip and Eliza were often so occupied at week's end with their money counting and ledgers that my free time was not as severely governed.

"A walk costs nothing but shoe leather and soon your father and I were discovering the city together on Sunday mornings with all those bells ringing around us. Sometimes we almost had to shout at each other and then we'd laugh. What curiosity he had! I see that in you too, Aerlene. Always asking questions about this and that, puzzling over how things came to be. Casting looks at passersby and imagining how their lives were lived. He took so much into himself, your father, but he was good company for all that, even if he sometimes wore me thin with his questions and observations. We might be walking eastward by the Tower with him surmising who might lie within and what privations and what tortures awaited him, what thoughts might course through a man's restless mind the night before the scaffold or the block. Or we might walk westward to gape at the great houses near Whitehall. And then he might be wondering what they were eating for dinner that day. Or how many servants it took to dress the lady of the house.

"One day he asked about my husband and how he died. Oh, your father was a great one for talking about death. A favourite subject, and no mistaking that. So I told him some things about Wilkes, but not others, dwelt at length on his brutish nature, and said he died of a fever, so ashamed was I of his brawling end. Another day I could not help myself and mentioned Henry Chapman and how kind and gentle a man he was, though he had no words to speak. This affected your father greatly and he stopped there on the street.

"'Tell me about him,' he said. 'No words at all, this fellow, and yet right enough in his mind?' He seemed astonished.

"'Yes,' I said.

"'But he could hear? He could hear words?'

"'Yes,' I said. 'It was strange. A defect at birth, perhaps.'

"He couldn't get over such an affliction. 'Not to be able to use words,' he kept saying. 'To hear them and not be able to shape a response with words. How horrible!'

"Another time we were in Finsbury Fields near the archery butts, and some gallants and their lady friends had gathered nearby. They looked to have been carousing all night, and they were still drinking wine and singing bawdy songs. One young man was standing behind a girl showing her how to hold a bow and draw the string to guide the arrow to the target. Both could barely stand with their drunkenness, and your father said something about fools and wine being poor bedfellows, and we took care to walk to one side of them, advancing perhaps fifty paces. Then, didn't an arrow pass not ten feet in front of us, followed by a great roar of laughter? When we looked, we saw that the drunkards had fallen forward and were on the grass laughing. The arrow had gone astray with their falling, and they found it amusement itself. And not a word of apology from any of them.

"We walked on, but your father was brooding on the event. He was very good at brooding, your father, and it could get on your nerves, all those dark thoughts of his. When finally we sat upon the grass near the windmills, he said, 'Just think on it, Elizabeth. Had our pace been swifter by a step or two, or had we set out a few moments earlier, that arrow might have struck one of us. And all because those rich young fools were playing drunken games.' That set him off. 'It's all a matter of chance, is it not?' he said. 'Imagine you pass down a street where a madman awaits, his head filled with voices. Or there is a horse alarmed suddenly by the sting of a bee and it rears above you as you pass, those hoofs coming down upon your eyes. Or an arrow carelessly released flies through the air and into your throat. A welling of blood in your mouth and in an instant all is gone, the morning's bright air, the grass, the blue sky above these milling blades. All gone forever. Are we then not simply at the mercy of fortune's wheel?'

"I told him I could not see life that way: walking about as if forever on the brink of untimely events. Besides, I said, there were charms enough to ward off misadventure—old sayings and rituals that kept you from peril by reminding the spirit world of your innocence. 'Perhaps God in his wisdom is behind it all.'

' "'But,' he said, 'what of those innocent souls who are still waylaid by chance?'

"'Well,' I said, 'there must be a reason behind all things—and there's an end to it, as I don't care to dwell on talk like this on such a fine day.'

"He could tell I was angry and said nothing more about it on that autumn morning. But it was like your father to hold such forebodings. The more I got to know him the more I saw..."

She paused as though trying to fasten her memory of him firmly in her mind so that she might encompass him by a single feature of his character. In her illness, Mam seemed determined to tell me of my father's essence as she saw it, and this was not like her, for usually she preferred to skim across the surface of things like a water fly; anything too deep was troublesome to her nature. But perhaps, nearing her end, she wanted to discover for herself a stronger impression of the man who had fathered her child.

"Aerlene, your father was a cautious young man, watchful not only of misplaced arrows or lanes where madmen lurked with knives and voices in their heads; he apprehended danger everywhere. I have seen him push away a plate of oysters that another might eat heartily, and he was careful in boisterous company. Now and then we dined with fellow players on a Saturday night and your father was merry enough; he could trade a jest with anyone, but always I sensed his discomfort when others got drunk and quarrelsome. He used to say that our wits weaken in drunkenness and a misplaced word can lead to blows and blows to swordplay or cudgels and thence to severed hands or broken heads. Do not misunderstand me. Your father was no coward, but he was careful at all times, measuring the consequences of an action."

"Prudence is a virtue, is it not?" I said.

"It is."

"But my father was good company, Mam?"

"Excellent company, as I have already told you," she said. "Pay attention, Aerlene, please."

Mam's pain often put her out of patience with me and my questions, and I felt bad for upsetting her, but I couldn't seem to help myself, so eager was I to learn more about my father.

"I have already told you how curious he was about everything," Mam said. "How filled with strange facts and stories. Your father read a great deal, and he was delighted when he discovered that I too could read. He hadn't expected it of me."

"And how did he discover that?" I asked.

"You are old enough now to know that we must have lain together to have you, so it was on one occasion at his room in Holywell Lane, which he shared with two others. And this was not long after that Sunday morning in Finsbury Fields. Indeed, a part of me thinks it might have been that very day. The other fellows were at the playhouse working on the properties for the next day's performance.

"The room he shared was poor and barely furnished. Only a pair of truckle beds and an old dresser and chair. A chest and a small shelf of books. I had picked up a book from this little shelf—there were only five or six—and I said, 'Who is Ovid and what is the meaning of the title?'

"And your father said, 'Why, you can read, Elizabeth!'

"'Of course I can,' I said, 'and write my name too, though I can't pretend knowledge of any subject, as I haven't read much. Parts of the Bible,' I said. 'My brother and his wife are Puritans, and the few books in the house make dry reading.'

"'Still, you can read,' he said, putting his arms around me and hugging me from behind. I remember his breath on my neck. 'A beginning, at any rate. I'll read some of Ovid to you. He was a Roman who lived about the time of Christ, but he got into trouble with the authorities in Rome and was banished.'

"Ovid was your father's favourite writer and he told me the title of the book, but I have forgotten, though I do recall the stories. All had to do with changing forms: they were about a spirit world in ancient Greece or Rome where humans lived with gods and sometimes mated with them or were changed by them into plants or trees or other creatures. I liked them, because this Ovid was very good at describing nature. But to your father, this book was like a Bible. He could not get enough of these wondrous tales and told me he had been reading them since he was a schoolboy, when he studied them in the Latin tongue. However," she added with a little smile, "I must tell you, Aerlene, that your father was full of earthly passion and I too had sorely missed the touch of a man, and so the reading of Ovid was soon put aside."

"Yes, yes, Mam," I said, for like many girls on the edge of such feelings, I was nervous and impatient about matters anatomical. I had seen a stallion mount a mare in the fields of the Easton estate, and stray dogs in the village were always about it; I had heard too the coarse words of schoolboys, so I didn't want to picture my parents doing such things in any detail whatsoever.

That autumn, Mam and my father found what time they could to be together, sometimes lying in Finsbury Fields; cold and damp as it was, Mam said, it scarcely mattered, so compelling was their passion. But they also talked about many things during those weeks. Not only of their childhoods, but also of their lives in London. Will Shakespeare, Mam said, was interested in everything about millinery; already he knew a great deal about hides and skins and the various apparelling trades from helping in his father's shop.

Such was his mind that he often drew her into topics she had never thought about. Once, passing Bethlem Hospital, they heard a shriek, a prolonged wail of distress from some poor mad soul, and my father wondered aloud what it must be like to be so afflicted: to lose your wits and inhabit another world. He also talked about his trade and the men he worked with, delighted when Mam told him that she had been to a playhouse across the river with her friend Mary, who had dressed as a man. He loved the story.

"It's like the stage," he said, "where the woman is played by a man, while in the audience, a man is played by a woman and all is topsy-turvy." He wondered then if Mary Pinder dressed as a man at her work.

Mam affected surprise at this remark. "Why would she do that?"

"The reason?" he said. "Why, there are plenty about who enjoy such games. Undressing a man and finding a woman. There are many playful themes in the arts of love, Elizabeth."

"And all of them in London, I expect," said Mam, "as I never heard of such things in Worsley."

"Nor I in Stratford," he laughed.

He asked her then what play she had seen at the Rose and she told him.

"Ah yes, *Tamburlaine*. Marlowe's made a name for himself with it. And he has written a second part that is now playing."

Mam told him she thought *Tamburlaine* was good but long-winded. "And this Tamburlaine," she said, "is so puffed up with himself. And a tyrant too. Putting that King in a cage and driving him mad. I couldn't bear to look at the man braining himself."

"But your father appeared not to be listening and said nothing for the longest time. I thought he had forgotten about it or was in his own world, as he often seemed far away from me.

"Then he said, 'Yes, *Tamburlaine* is good in its own way. It is a spectacle with some fine verses. Marlowe has a talent, there is no doubt of that.'"

They had stopped at the door to the shop and he kissed Mam and said, "I too enjoy writing verses, Elizabeth, and one day I will write something better than *Tamburlaine*. On my life I will," he said, laughing. "There you see, Will proclaims his will." He told her he could already find scenes in plays they were rehearsing that he could do much better. "I am hoping that in time I will join others in fixing them and one day I will write my own *Tamburlaine* and others like it and beyond. That is my hope. I am mostly an indifferent player, Elizabeth, and I fear I never shall be anything more. My heart lies in writing. I have felt so for some time. And now, I truly believe it."

"He told me this outside the shop," Mam said, "and I took him at his word, Aerlene, because your father was not a man to make idle boasts. I discovered that about him in our weeks together. I could tell he was envious of Marlowe's success. They were the same age, and there was Marlowe already with a great following. I could see that it bothered your father."

Mam told me that one night they were in a tavern in Bishopsgate Street. "The Four Swans, it may have been," she said, "for that was a favourite of the playhouse crowd. In one of the backrooms was much shouting and laughter, and Will said, 'Greene is with us tonight. You can hear him in there braying like a donkey.'

"I still knew little of poets and players and asked about the man with the loud laugh.

"'Robert Greene,' he said. 'A poet. He had something of his performed earlier this year called *Alphonsus, King of Aragon*. Another imitation of *Tamburlaine* and mostly laughed off the stage, I heard. But Greene is thought well of by some. Like Marlowe, he attended the university at Cambridge and so thinks well of himself. Our paths have crossed a few times, and one day not long ago in St. Paul's churchyard, I was looking at a new edition of Ovid in Latin. It made me think about my schooldays. I could not afford it, but it was a handsome book with very pretty woodcuts. Greene happened by in the company of friends and was amused to see me there with Ovid in my hands and made some slighting jest about an apprentice player enjoying such rich fare. "Bad for my digestion if I weren't used to it," he said. Or something like that. He clapped me on the back and all had a good laugh, and I suppose I smiled too, for I didn't want them to think I was that affected by his damnable forwardness. He can be difficult. Contentious as a tavern lawyer who lives for disputation. It's said he'd rather score points in an argument than win at cards. He delights in parading his wit. He is a man upon whom courtesies are apparently wasted, and overfond of wine, though he's only pennies from the street. But enough of him. I don't suppose you have heard about what happened this week at the Rose during a performance of the second part of *Tamburlaine*. Everyone is talking about it.'

"I said I had overheard something in the shop from customers about a mishap, but I didn't catch it all.

"'A fearful mishap,' Will said. 'A cannon shot in a battle scene went astray and killed a woman and a child. The owner, Henslowe, I'm told now fears the authorities will close the place, though Southwark is beyond their province. The woman's husband is bringing a suit against him.' I asked if he had seen the second part and he nodded. 'Yes, I saw it Monday last. The day before the accident. It's not half as good as the first part. I'll wager Marlowe wrote it in a week and never blotted a line. Too many devices, too little poetry. But no matter. The spectacle packs them in and they cry for more.'

"Just then the roisterers from the backroom emerged led by a red-haired man whose face was inflamed by drink. His doublet was soiled and though he swaggered, he was unsteady on his feet, gripping the shoulders of those he passed among the tables. The others were laughing at something Greene said. But the red-haired man had seen us and, coming over, swayed above our table grinning. 'Well now,' he said, 'it's young Will from Warwickshire. And with a pretty one too. Is she also from the country, Will?'

"'Yes, Miss Ward is from Oxfordshire.'

"'From Oxfordshire? Well now. Not so far from your own little town. You must be talking of country matters.' This made others laugh and I didn't know why, though Will explained later that in the city the term meant love-making. 'So,' continued Greene, 'you are no longer sleeping just with Ovid.' More laughter."

Whatever Will's thoughts that night, Mam said, he took it all in good heart, expecting such raillery from so-called wits like Greene, though she hated the man on sight. A brute and a bully and already wasted in dissipation, though he couldn't have been much older than she was at the time, she said.

Listening to Mam, I hated Robert Greene as well, and was much satisfied years later to learn that he died of debauchery and in debt some five years after the events described by Mam that night in the Four Swans. He was then thirty-five and, as I also discovered, had written something called *Greene's Groats-Worth of Wit*, in which, out of spite and envy, he delivered an ugly rebuke to my father's talent. Had I known his burial site when I went to London, I would have spit upon his grave. Many years later while reading *Twelfth Night,* I wondered as I read about the drunken blunderings of Sir Toby Belch if my father had Greene in mind when he fashioned Belch's character, though I dare say he met many like him in his lifetime.

"Before he left the tavern that night, Greene said, 'And are you well pleased with this woman, Will?' And your father said, 'I am, Robert,' and Greene affected an air of being insulted, splaying his fingers across his chest. 'Oh, if you please, Will, it's Master Greene to you. Should a 'prentice player not know his place among poets?' And then the fool placed a finger alongside his nose and farted. 'And what a pretty and pleasing procession of the letter *p* the foregoing line provides. And the letter *p* stands too for piss, which I must needs take, and so adieu, all gentles. I'm for the laneway.' Amid this mirth he staggered out, followed by the others, except for one, a man whose name Will told me later was Peele; he placed a hand on your father's shoulder and told him to pay no mind, 'for you know Greene's humour when he's in drink.'

"Afterwards your father said, 'He's well named, isn't he, for he's green with envy over Marlowe's triumph.' After finishing his ale, he muttered, 'But then, alas, so am I. So are many in this city.' He was staring across that noisy, smoky room as though he were looking for things that weren't there, and then he said, 'How the devil did he do it? And only weeks older than I?'"

"And what did you say to that, Mam?" I asked. "Did you give my father heart?"

She laughed. "Why, of course I did, Aerlene. But then, what would any woman say to a man she likes who has ambitions? I took his hand and told him the lines foretold a future in which lay triumphs in the playhouses. I knew he put no store by palm reading, but it does no harm to hear such things when you feel beset by life. Yet I must confess that I did not believe it myself. I think I lacked the imagination to foresee your father's success. To me he was then just a young man who loved words, and who wanted to write plays one day. But I could not see him writing anything to equal Marlowe's play. Perhaps it was that I could not imagine myself being that close to a man who could ever accomplish such things. And so I valued your father's gift too lightly—until last summer when I saw his name on that playbook in Oxford."

THIS MONTH HAS BEEN fair and fruitful and the estate occupied with haymaking. All the rain that so dismayed us weeks ago has proved a benefit, with an abundance of good hay now mostly gathered; and only one mishap this year, a boy of eleven years who broke an arm in a fall from one of the wagons. This morning we set out the trestle tables in the orchard for the haymakers' supper, and by four in the afternoon, the benches were filled with the workers and their families enjoying Mrs. Sproule's cold mutton and capons with peas. There was bread and later fruit pies, and plenty of ale.

It is now nearly ten o'clock, and I can still hear shouting from the bonfire, where the young men are leaping across the flames to win the hearts of girls with their daring. Most of the older folk will have left by now. No doubt Emily will still be at the fire, for she has been a fetching sight today in a new smock which nicely shows her bosom, much to the consternation of Mrs. Sproule, who thought the girl too brave in dress. But I said it was only sensible to take your fruit to market when ripe.

"Where is the harm, Mrs. Sproule?" I said. "It's the middle of June and love is in the air."

She didn't argue. Mrs. Sproule was pleased with herself. She worked hard all week roasting her mutton and shelling her peas and the supper was a great success, and I told her so. Charlotte and Mr. Thwaites walked among the tables greeting the workers and their families. The rector will have a full church tomorrow morning.

When Charlotte is with Simon Thwaites, you can see the colour rising from her throat into her face, a veritable glowing in his presence. Before the meal, Mr. Walter thanked the men and women, the boys and girls, for their labour, and Mr. Thwaites said grace, offering a prayer of thanksgiving for the bountiful hay. Then, amid great cheering, the two men raised their tankards of ale and drained them at once. Watching Charlotte as she looked up at Simon Thwaites, I wondered if I had ill prepared her for married life. She has been thinking lately of men and women and what transpires between them.

Yesterday, after we finished our work, she said, "Your mother was certainly attracted to men, was she not, Linny?"

"She was, Charlotte," I said. "Without question, she was."

Charlotte had got up to walk about the library and was flexing the fingers of her writing hand, a small frown appearing as she paced. What did she know of mating? I wondered. You can't live on a large farm for twenty-four years without observing some copulation.

Charlotte said, "This Mary Pinder—what a life she must have led! All those men having their way with her. Last year, when Annabelle and I went to London for a week—do you remember?"

"I do, yes."

"We went for a walk one evening in Drury Lane with her brother and his wife, and Annabelle whispered to me that many of the women on the arms of gentlemen were very likely prostitutes, and that we should not admonish them but pray for their redemption. They were only poor lost souls at the mercy of men. I didn't know what to make of her remarks at the time, and so said nothing, but really I thought those women with their gaudy dresses and painted mouths looked rather hard. Why could they not get honest work as servants? I could not summon much pity for them. Selling themselves like that. Inviting vile diseases into their bodies."

I decided to tease her. "Did Christ himself not counsel forgiveness for the fallen?" I asked. "What of Mary Magdalene, for instance?"

"What of her?"

"Why, it's generally acknowledged that she was a prostitute, Charlotte. Yet Christ forgave her after she washed His feet with her tears and dried between his toes with her hair." Now this wasn't so. It was Mary of Bethany who dried Christ's feet with her hair. But I couldn't help myself.

"Mary Magdalene was a prostitute?"

"Yes, she was," I said. And as far as I know, that at least was true.

Her pretty little face was perplexity itself. "I didn't know that, Linny." And then, since Charlotte never worries a thought for long, she said, "What shall I wear tomorrow, do you think? For the haymakers' supper? Simon will be coming."

In the presence of Simon Thwaites, Charlotte is radiant, even today on the thirteenth anniversary of Nicky's death. For the first time, she has forgotten to mark the day. But I remember a rider bringing us the news two days after the battle, and then Nicky's body returned the week following in a farm wagon, his passage home safely warranted by the Roundheads, for which I credit them. We buried him that evening in St. Cuthbert's churchyard behind the iron railings of the Easton plot.

Yet I cannot blame Charlotte for allowing this day to pass unnoticed. Love promotes happiness, banishing old sorrows, and that is as it should be. Leave sorrowful memories to the old.

LIKE JULIET I WAS born on Lammas Eve. That was in the year of the Great Armada, so by my reckoning I was conceived on or about All Saints' Day in 1587, perhaps in that small room in Holywell Lane or perhaps on the grass of Finsbury Fields near the windmills. Within the month, Mam would have noticed her courses not running and other peculiarities that I remember Mrs. Easton relating to me with the onset of each of her four pregnancies: the flushing and tingling and peculiar cravings. She once whispered to me with a small, gay laugh that at such times she often craved her husband more. Listening to Mam, I wanted to know how my father took the news. Did he clasp her hand and cover it with kisses?

As always I overwhelmed the poor, sick woman with my questions, and by then it was winter and she was nearing the end and lacked the strength to protest in words.

She merely waved a languid hand, saving her breath for her story.

"I first told Mary," she said. "It was perhaps the second or third week of December, and by then I was certain. I used to weep at my foolishness for believing that Wilkes's stillborn child had rendered me barren. I had been fooled, you see, by all those times with Henry Chapman. When I was told years later that Henry had married a widow with children and was living near Chipping Norton, it occurred to me that the children must all have come from the first husband, for the woman who told me said she didn't believe the widow had any from Henry. So perhaps it was his seed that was worthless. And all that time I thought I couldn't bear a child.

"One Saturday afternoon in December, Mary and I were by St. Magnus Church and I went in and prayed, which surprised her. Afterwards, as we walked along Thames Street, I told her. She shook her head and squeezed my arm. I was filled with the wildest thoughts of Bridewell or the streets.

"And bless her, Mary said, 'That won't happen, Elizabeth. You'll not go to Bridewell and you'll certainly not be on the streets. So put such thoughts aside.'

"On we walked to St. Andrews Hill, and my mind was everywhere, Aerlene. A terrible day, as it was all coming true. It was going to happen, and I felt entirely undone."

It is something to listen to your mother explain how the advent of your birth created such unhappiness for her, but it was my own fault for asking and I had to bear the unpleasant truth that I had not been wanted. Yet given the circumstances, I could understand that, so I felt no rancour towards Mam. Mary Pinder, she said, was a comfort.

"We will manage this if you like, Elizabeth," said Mary. "I'll look after you, but you must tell young Shakespeare of your state. I doubt he has much money, but he must have a little to spare. You will need attention and we'll need money."

Mam brightened and said, "Will has often expressed great affection and in the sweetest terms. You don't suppose he might agree to marry? I could still work for a while and we could save. It could turn out well."

Mam said they were then on Carter Lane near St. Paul's. She could remember it like yesterday, a cold afternoon with people hurrying past muffled up against the weather. She recalled the chestnut vendors calling out for trade and Mary stopping to face her, taking her by the shoulders with her big hands.

"Elizabeth. Has he not told you? But then, why would he? How would telling you advantage him?"

"Tell me what, Mary?" asked Mam.

"Why, Will Shakespeare is already married, Elizabeth. He has a wife and three children back in Warwickshire. It's known well enough among the playhouse people."

"But how can that be?" asked Mam. "He's so young. Only three and twenty, he told me."

"Old enough to sire three and more than three," said Mary. "But one thing's certain. He won't marry you because he *can't* marry you. A man can't have two wives in this country, Elizabeth."

To which Mam said, "Can there possibly be another woman in London as simple-minded as me?"

"Yes," said Mary, "and more than one, and they arrive each day by every gate. But there's no dwelling on that. What's done is done, and now what do we do about it? How far along are you?"

Mam guessed about four or five weeks.

"Well," said Mary as they walked along Watling Street, "if you want to rid yourself of it, I know people. But there's always peril in it, and I can't bring myself to tell you of things that have happened to others I've known."

Mam said she wouldn't do it anyway, as she was too fearful. She could think only of the young woman who had visited Goody Figgs and later sickened and died. Could she expect any better in London from people Mary knew?

"What about your in-laws?" Mary asked. "Did you not tell me that the husband has treated you kindly? Is he not a decent man?"

"Decent enough," Mam said, "but his wife won't have me in her house when she finds out. Bad for business, and I can't be sure he wouldn't agree with her. She'll make a good case against me."

"What about your brother, then? Surely he will take you back?"

"I have already injured him enough in name and reputation. This news will grey the hairs on his head."

"Well, you will never lack a place to keep your child, Elizabeth. As I've said, you can stay with me."

They turned northward to Cheapside, and Mam told me she was then walking the very route she had taken on her first afternoon in London months before, when the gentlemen had rescued her from that urchin. What had she learned in all that time? she asked herself. Here she was in trouble again. And why? Because it seemed she couldn't keep her legs closed. And now if she had the child, she would be raising it in a room with a prostitute. Good-hearted or not, that's what Mary Pinder was. And yet was she, Elizabeth Ward of Worsley, any better? It was hard to see how. What self-loathing Mam must have felt as she listened to Mary going on about not behaving rashly and how matters often look desperate at first but in time settle into something manageable. Words. Just idle words in the smoky, cold air of nightfall on Cheapside. Mary told her again that she should press the young man for money.

"Few rides are free in this life," she said, "and Will Shakespeare better than any should know that, for it's said his bride was quick with child when the wedding vows were spoken."

To which Mam could only remember muttering, "Dear God in Heaven, will I never learn anything in this life? I am a foolish woman and no argument."

"And how did my father take your news, Mam?" I asked. "Where did you meet and what did he say?"

But she had already reached out to press a finger against my lips. "Hush, Aerlene, for the love of God. Your questions are irksome. Just listen, please."

She drank some water, for her sickness provoked a great thirst. I was careful to keep the cup filled, as she no longer had strength enough to hold the pitcher.

"As I've told you," she said, "it was our habit to go out on a Saturday evening, and we went to the Cross Keys Inn on Gracechurch Street. I liked the Cross Keys, for the patrons there were not a rough sort. I imagine I was nervous that night. Who wouldn't be? But at first your father didn't seem to notice, for he had something to tell *me*, and he could scarcely hold it inside. At one point he took both my hands and, leaning forward, whispered, 'Do you want to hear something wonderful, Elizabeth?' I had no time to answer before he said, 'Our troupe has been invited to court to present a comedy before the Queen, and I am to be one of the dancers at the play's end. Now what do you think of that?'

"How difficult it is to tell someone filled with glad tidings that you have contrary news! I couldn't bring myself on that night in the Cross Keys to tell him. He was so . . ." Mam looked away for a moment. "He was so very young and happy. Perhaps he was a little drunk, but just with excitement. We went back to his room. And then he saw me to Threadneedle Street, where I wept until morning."

"But when *did* you tell him?" I asked.

"I didn't tell him. I couldn't bring myself to do it. It was Mary who saw him in the Dolphin a week or so before Christmas, when he was with friends. I had not seen him for a fortnight because the shop was busy, and it kept my mind off things. Only at night in bed did I worry. But Mary said that in the Dolphin she took your father aside and told him, and he said to her, 'Knapped again, then."

"What did he mean by that, Mam?" I asked.

"I don't know. But what does it matter anyway now? That night Mary told your father that he couldn't be expected to leave his wife and family, but he should do the right thing by me and provide some money, because it was likely that I would be turned out by my relatives when the truth became known. Yet apparently, all your father said to this was 'I have no money. I live at Mr. Burbage's pleasure.'"

I had never heard of that verb *knapped,* but years later when I saw a performance of *King Lear* at an Oxford Inn yard [one of only two plays by my father that I ever saw enacted, the other being *Hamlet*], I heard it used by the Fool when he mocks the old King for ranting over his treatment at the hands of Cornwall and Regan:

Cry to it, nuncle, as the cockney did to the eels
when she put 'em i'; the paste alive; she knapped
'em o' the coxcombs with a stick and cried, "Down,
wantons, down!"

The word suggests that at the time my father felt "knocked about" by Fortune in the guise of another woman wanting either marriage or money.

When I asked Mam on her deathbed whether she ever spoke to him again, she said, "Aerlene, that season your father was occupied, so I can't believe he made himself scarce on purpose. As for me, I felt so apart from everything around me that I was sick unto myself. It may have been the morning illness coming on, but I was sick at heart too, distraught by all my foolish longings. I still worked in the shop because I was needed, but on Christmas Day I took to my bed and wept. I think Eliza suspected the cause, though she didn't approach me in my room. I remember Philip Boyer himself bringing something up to me, but I couldn't touch food. If his wife had confided her suspicions to him, he didn't let on. The next day was the Feast of St. Stephen, and I lay in bed thinking of your father dancing a jig at the end of a comedy before the Queen.

"A few days later came a letter from your uncle Jack telling me how satisfied he was that I had settled and was finding my way in London. And there I was trying to imagine writing a reply asking if I might return! Those weeks of grey frost in January and I seemed to be passing through them like a shadow of myself, not knowing what to do, hoping that I might miscarry as I had after Wilkes's death."

Mam was not one to spare my feelings even when it came to relating how she wished I'd never been born, but I was used to her ways. I don't think she meant harm by it; she just wasn't aware of how it sounded to me.

"One day," she said, "Mary came into the shop dressed as usual like a gentleman and she was frowning as she looked at me."

"'You're not caring for yourself,' she whispered. 'Get out of this place and live with me. Come to the Dolphin on Saturday at six o'clock and we'll talk.'

"I could see Eliza watching us," said Mam, "and I wondered if she was thinking that Mary was the father of the child I was carrying. The absurdity of it made me smile.

"On Saturday night when I told Mary about Eliza, we both laughed so hard you might have thought the two of us were the happiest doxies in London. I told her too about your father dancing a jig at court, but she only said, 'And well enough he should dance. I'd have him upturned with his pockets emptied for whatever they held. And look at you—thin as a pikestaff. Are those Puritans starving you?'

"'Not at all,' I said, 'but I have little appetite these days.'

"Mary again talked about my living with her, but I had been thinking long about that. In her own way Mary was a good friend to me, but when all was said and done she earned her living as a prostitute, and I couldn't see myself bringing a child into such a life where one day perhaps I too might find myself beneath a man to pay the rent. And Mary's temper was so inconstant. I could never get the measure of it; she could change on the instant from mirth to rage, a harmless remark igniting her. In Worsley, I could at least manage Sarah's disdain without the fear of blows.

"In January I wrote to your uncle, and in three weeks or so came his reply. I kept that letter for the longest time by my side, as I wanted to give it to you and it is still somewhere about. It might have fallen into some crack or cranny of this house and you may one day come upon it. It is a fine letter in which your uncle told me that I could return, but that I must amend my ways and this would be my last chance, as Sarah was already hard-pressed to forgive me, anticipating the laughter of the village. He told me not to expect an easy life, but said with the grace of God, I might still find salvation, and he would pray for me daily.

"A few days later I told the Boyers. I had been waiting

to catch them in good humour, and one evening at supper Philip said that he had spent the day with the accounts and it was pleasing to see their profit over the past month. The baby was below stairs with the maid and quiet for a change. I judged it a good time to thin the syrup with vinegar, and so I told them I was with child.

"At once Eliza made a face, reminding me of her sister when she had caught me out in some wrongdoing. 'I knew it,' Eliza said. 'I've known it since Christmastide. This is the thanks we get for taking you into our home.'

"Her husband had placed his elbows upon the table and pressed fingers against his brow while his wife rattled on about my wantonness. I was quick to add that I would be no burden, as my brother would take me back.

"'And the sooner the better,' Eliza said, getting up from the table and leaving the room.

"Philip Boyer looked at me and said, 'I'll see what I can do about getting you back. If this frost lasts, the roads should be passable. I'll talk to some people tomorrow.'

"He too left the room, while I thought of how much easier it is to deal with those who hate you than with those who are merely disappointed in you.

"Yet within the week he had arranged for me to travel with a family that was moving to Oxford, where the father had been appointed rector of a parish. They were leaving in two days, because the carriers feared a thaw that would muddy the roads.

"The next day I sought out Mary to thank her for her friendship and wish her well. I didn't know where she lived, but one of the ostlers at the Dolphin knew and gave me directions to her lodgings. He said he hadn't seen her about lately and was told she'd received a hurt. I found the house in Shoreditch, a warren of rooms where a young woman, looking tired and out of sorts, as though I'd just awakened her, showed me the way to Mary's room. It was early afternoon and Mary was still in bed, but little wonder, as she was bruised about the eyes and mouth, with a great welt along one arm, as though it had been wrung by strong hands. She was as surprised to see me as I was by her state, but she soon told me how she came by her trouble.

"A week before, in darkness near Hog Lane, she was set upon by two men while a third looked on; even in darkness she recognized this third man as the gallant she had upended weeks ago for disputing the tariff. The other two were brutes—rivermen, Mary thought, for she could smell the mud and fish on them while they held and struck her. They gave her a proper hiding and she feared some ribs were broken because any cough was now distressful. She lay there looking up at me.

"'It will all come right in time,' said Mary, 'and anyway, I had the last laugh on that trotter. At the end of my thrashing, he stood over me and made his water. Can you fathom it? Laughing as he pissed all over me. When he was shaking himself dry, I said, "I'm glad that miller's thumb of yours is good for something, for it was no use to me and I doubt not but that your poor wife thinks the same." That set him off and he began to kick me. It hurt like the devil with these ribs, but then one of the rivermen stepped in front of him and said, "Now she's had enough, sir. She's had enough. We're not homicides." And they led him away.' She smiled up at me. 'I should have been more wary. I knew he'd come back, for I'd shamed him that day in front of his friends and his kind don't soon forget things. My own fault. I'm growing careless in my late years, Elizabeth.'

"I asked her if she was well enough looked after and she waved a hand. 'The other girls tend to me now and then. I'll make do.'

"I told her that I was leaving next day, returning to my brother's house in Worsley.

"'That's good,' she said, 'but I want a kiss before you go. Only don't hold me too close, for these old bones will complain.'

"I was happy enough to kiss her, but as I left, I wondered what would become of Mary, and I still do, yes, even to this day, though it would not surprise me to learn that she is now in her grave. But walking down Bishopsgate Street that afternoon I felt happy, and this was a source of great wonder to me, for there I was, unmarried and carrying a child, with a life ahead in the same house as your aunt Sarah.

Yet still I felt this lift in spirit. I passed the lunatic hospital where your father had wondered aloud one day what it was like to be mad. Was I mad then to feel as I did? But I judge it had more to do with escape. I was getting out of the city with its squalor and noise and confusion. I had enjoyed my time there; I had met your father and given myself to him with no thought for the next day, and now here it was, the next day upon me. But at least I was getting out and I was set firmly in my mind to be a better person, vowing that I would do well by my brother and the child I would bring into this world. I was being given another chance, and perhaps it is only on the brink of another chance that we find such happiness.

"That very night Philip Boyer took me to the Castle Inn on Wood Street, where I met the clergyman's family. Reverend Tuttle and his wife had six children, from an infant in Mrs. Tuttle's arms to a girl not much older than you now, perhaps fourteen. Her name was Kate and we shared a room that night with three younger children. Boyer had given me money for food and lodgings along the way. Kate took a liking to me and indeed the whole family was agreeable company, cheerful and not much minding the cold, bumpy ride, for the Tuttles were transporting their furniture in two great wains drawn by oxen. The wagoners were sturdy fellows and one had an harquebus in case we met highwaymen.

"Oxen are slow creatures and the journey took us nearly a week. Mr. Tuttle sat next to one drover in the morning and with the other in the afternoon so that each might share his thoughts on theology and the religious life. One day I overheard him offering his views on whether Papists would be allowed into Heaven. The rest of us sat behind amid tables and chairs and dressers and dismembered beds, telling stories to one another, while Mrs. Tuttle nursed her infant son in a rocking chair from which she gazed out at the passing villages and countryside. Nothing, not even a child once falling off and bruising himself, seemed to upset her serenity. We stayed at inns and the weather remained cold and fair until the last day, when it turned mild and the roads softened. Yet those stalwart beasts pulled us through the mire and we arrived in Oxford about two in the afternoon and said our farewells, Mrs. Tuttle drawing me apart and whispering in my ear, 'Are you not quick with child yourself, Elizabeth?' She wished me well. Somehow mothers know such things.

"I had managed the money carefully, and on that afternoon I spent my last penny on a loaf and walked to Woodstock, arriving at my brother's shop as he was closing for the day."

"So," I said, "you left London without ever again speaking to my father?"

"I did."

"Did you not at least feel the need to say goodbye?"

"I may have felt the need, but I couldn't see the benefit. I had no heart to face him again, Aerlene, for I knew by then that we didn't love each other. And what could he do about my situation? Him with his wife and children back in Warwickshire? And that's another thing," she added, struggling to lift herself in bed. "Put the pillow behind me," she said.

I could see I had angered her with my questions.

"Calm yourself, Mam."

"You are asking me why I didn't say goodbye to him? But he hadn't told me he was married and I found that vexing. I not only had committed fornication, but was now also an adulteress. And not for one moment had I ever meant to commit adultery. I was terrified that someone might find out. Can you imagine what your aunt Sarah would say if she knew I had lain with a married man? So I was ashamed of myself and eager to put it all behind me. It was better to get out of London. And to tell you the truth, as the years have passed, I mostly put your father out of mind, until I saw his name upon that book in Oxford. And then I felt you deserved to know."

I told her it was all right. I hadn't meant to upset her.

In those final days, Mam lost track of her senses from time to time, wandering off to other worlds, murmuring old names and often crying aloud from pain. In the hope of easing her mind, I was still reading the *Dream*, but I was weary of it and perhaps she wasn't even listening. Yet I felt I should continue reading. I had the notion it was keeping her alive, and I knew it helped to settle my own wits. One evening, for a change, I took up *Romeo and Juliet*, and was reading the scene in which Mercutio invokes Queen Mab to mock the lovelorn Romeo for believing that dreams mean anything at all:

> *She is the fairies' midwife, and she comes*
> *In shape no bigger than an agate stone*
> *On the fore-finger of an alderman,*
> *Drawn with a team of little atomies*
> *Athwart men's noses as they lie asleep.*"

I thought Mam was asleep, but then I heard her say, "He got all that at his mother's knee. The agate stone on the alderman's finger. I remember that."

"What, Mam?" I asked.

"Your father," she said, opening her eyes to look up at me. "It's 'Queen Mab's Ride' he's talking about, and the words made me think of a day in Finsbury Fields when we talked of our childhoods. We'd only just met, and he said how his mother used to tell him stories of the little people and how they got around at night. I loved it, for I too knew such stories. But your father had a great memory for such things, and he told of how his mother described for him Queen Mab's little carriage made from a nut . . ."

"Her chariot is an empty hazel-nut."

"Yes"—she smiled—"an empty hazel-nut."

Made by the joiner squirrel or old grub, / Time out o' mind the fairies' coachmakers."

"That's it. He used to say how artful in detail it was. As a child he never tired of hearing his mother describe Mab's carriage and how it took her through the night and into lovers' dreams."

"And in this state she gallops night by night / Through lovers' brains, and then they dream of love."

"Yes," said Mam, "that's right."

Not long after, perhaps a day or two, I got up from the truckle bed one morning, and when I saw her lying grey and still, I knew even before I touched her cold face that she had left me in the night.

TODAY AFTER EVENSONG, CHARLOTTE and Mr. Thwaites came back to the house to announce their engagement, the banns to be read on the first three Sundays of September and the wedding to take place on the Saturday following. Amid the congratulations Mr. Walter remarked that seeding time for winter wheat was always considered propitious for marriage, if we would forgive a simple farmer saying so. This made Charlotte colour prettily and we all laughed. Charlotte then displayed the gemstone on her finger and had a little weep in my arms. Mr. Walter had me fetch the brandy, and we raised glasses to the young couple's future happiness.

MY STORY

MAM DIED IN JANUARY of 1601 at the age of forty years and ten months. It was cold and I remember a little snow on higher ground. In our parlour I was asked to put chunks of sea coal on the fire, and I was glad to have something to do; sitting before the grate I willed the coal to burn faster to keep me occupied.

That morning the rector, Obadiah Littlejohn, came by, and he and my aunt talked in the kitchen while Uncle Jack stood by the coffin staring down at his dead sister. Now and then I looked up from the fire to watch him. He appeared more angry than sad, and I wondered if it had to do with the rector and my aunt talking apart from him. My uncle had never taken to Littlejohn, who was new to the parish—only a year or so then at St. Cuthbert's—and a gospeller. Uncle Jack didn't care for his fiery sermons and told me once there was too much hatefulness in them; they worked people up in the wrong way. He even wondered if the burning of Goody Figgs's hut had been provoked by the rector's sermon on witches and demons. I didn't like the man either, but more for his looks than anything else. He was short and thick-set with a great black beard, his bald, egg-shaped head fringed with more black hair; by appearance at least he seemed more in league with the devil than with God. Or so I used to imagine.

When he came into the parlour with my aunt, I listened carefully. No one took any notice of me crouched by the grate; still they conferred in whispers as though my poor mother might overhear and disapprove of their arguing above her corpse. Uncle Jack had quietly maintained that his sister was one of God's children and deserved a Christian's funeral. But Littlejohn was adamant about the service. Mam, he said, had been a fornicator. It was common knowledge in the parish, and the congregation wouldn't tolerate a Christian service for her. He said he would stand at the graveside and offer words from Holy Scripture, but nothing more. Beside him Aunt Sarah was silent, but she wouldn't meet my uncle's eyes. I guessed that she and the rector had agreed about the funeral in the kitchen. Uncle Jack was an even-tempered man, but I could see his face darkening as he listened to Littlejohn. Where was Christian forgiveness in his teaching? he asked. Had Jesus himself not urged forgiveness to those who had sinned? Did he not teach us how to pray for sinners in Matthew, chapter 6, verses 14 and 15?

For, if ye forgive men their trespasses, your heavenly Father will also forgive you. But if ye forgive not men their trespasses, neither will your Father forgive your trespasses.

"Those are the words of our Lord as transcribed by St. Matthew, sir," said Uncle Jack, looking down at the ugly little man. "How do you square them with denying my sister a Christian service in the church?"

I was proud of my uncle for opposing Littlejohn, whose great round face had also reddened, though he stood his ground and said it was indecent to have such a woman's body accorded the full service. Uncle Jack left them then and went upstairs. I should have supported him by leaving the room too instead of poking at the fire and watching my aunt and the rector whispering by the coffin.

Later I went out by myself to the churchyard and watched the sexton and another man digging the grave. They were talking about the snow and cold weather and about how they feared catching an ague. After they left, I stood above the open grave looking down at the hole in the earth. I had seen maggots at work in dead dogs and birds, and I knew that the same happened to all living creatures when they died. Mam's body, which I remembered as being so warm when I lay next to her, would soon be cold as winter earth, and in time, it would be filled with worms, and I wondered how long it would take before all the flesh was gone and only bones remained. Years later at an inn yard in Oxford, while watching a performance of *Hamlet,* I received a start when I heard the Prince ask the gravedigger, *"How long will a man lie i' the earth ere he rot?"*

I have now come to believe that such questions are perhaps not so unusual to those with a particular cast of mind.

On that winter morning in the churchyard, I also recall wondering if what they said in churches about the dead was true: that we all had souls within us, and that at the death of the body the soul was released and either ascended to Heaven or sank through the earth to Hell. Uncle Jack had once told me that Papists believed their souls went first to a place called Purgatory and the entrance was somewhere off the coast of Ireland. He thought the notion fanciful—but if any of it was true, I wondered, what judgment awaited Mam, who had lain with men outside marriage and brought a bastard into the world? That was a sin and even Uncle Jack had said as much. Would Jesus and his Father take into account her kindness, her love for her brother and for me, her tolerance of Aunt Sarah's mean-spiritedness, her unwillingness to utter an unkind word to others, including the louts who called her names beneath our windows or schoolboys who threw stones and ran off laughing? Would all that goodness not count in her favour in God's court? I had read enough of the gospels to know that people like my aunt and the rector paid little heed to the notion of forgiveness. They were scolders and punishers, and to them that was what religion was about. This led me to wonder further if such hard-hearted people went to Heaven, for they certainly expected to; it seemed that it was all they talked about. This life on earth to them was little more than time spent rebuking and punishing those they accounted sinners. Would such as my aunt and the rector then go to Heaven as a reward? If so, would I want to spend eternity with them?

I may have decided on that very day as I stared down at the empty grave in St. Cuthbert's churchyard that I no longer believed such things, if indeed I ever had. They were all made up, like stories for a child at bedtime to comfort her into sleep, or for those who were sick and feeling hopeless about their lives on this earth. Like everyone and every other living creature before her, Mam perhaps was neither in Heaven nor in Hell; perhaps she was just dead. As dead as the cat I had seen a few days before, stiff and frozen on the midden in Market Lane. And being as dead as that cat, Mam no longer cared about anything, including me. These were dark and terrible notions, and perhaps I was wrong for thinking of them. But true or not, I knew I must keep them to myself.

Standing by that open grave a good long while with my thoughts cost me dearly, because that evening I came down with a fever and could not attend Mam's burial next day.

Over the next several weeks a distemper kept me listless and it was thought I had lost my will to live, and perhaps that was true. Aunt Sarah brought me bread and broth and religious books, which she said would see me to Heaven if all else failed. To humour her I looked briefly at *The Path to Rightful Living*, but when she'd left the room I took out my two playbooks and read them aloud as if Mam were still there to listen. In the evenings, Uncle Jack often sat with me, urging me to drink a little more broth, telling me stories about growing up and looking after Mam, his little sister. I wanted to know what Mam was like when she was my age, and he would tell me of how she enjoyed being by herself, wandering the woods and fields, a dreamy girl but pretty. The boys were always after her and he had to keep an eye out, for she liked to be admired, a failing in his estimation. But mostly Uncle Jack sat fussing over me, worrying about how frail I had become, and finally he fetched the doctor, the same fellow who had once attended Mam. He bled me too, and as I watched my blood drain into a dish I thought I might die even then, for it so weakened me. Only bread soaked in milk and apple brandy revived me, and when I awakened Uncle Jack was there holding my hand.

"I've lost your mother," he said. "I can't lose you too, Aerlene."

He begged me to tell him what he might do to revive my spirits, and so I said that I would like something other than Aunt Sarah's tracts to read. I told him that I needed something to take me out of my thoughts, which, dark and unwholesome, were depleting my will. This was guileful, I admit, but I wanted to know—perhaps at that state in my life it was the only thing I wanted to know—whether my father had written any more plays. I knew my uncle would do anything to help me recover health, but I also knew I was asking him to go against his conscience. Still, I took out the copies of my father's plays and showed him.

"Could there be other books by this man Shakespeare?" I told him how Mam had bought these books a year before, and how I had read the *Dream* to her and it lifted her spirits. By then he was leafing through the pages of *A Midsummer-Night's Dream* and frowning.

"But this is a playbook, Aerlene," he said. "With fairies and sprites and magical properties. It's the devil's handiwork, child. Why would your mother have bought such a thing?"

"It was only to entertain herself and me," I said. "In her last months I read the play to her time and time again."

He looked greatly puzzled by this. "But, my dear child," he said, "why were you not reading Holy Scripture to your poor dying mother? This stuff is mere fancy."

"Because," I said, "the poetry was a great comfort to her, else she would not have asked so many times to hear it. We both enjoyed it. It's quite harmless, Uncle. It's not the work of the devil."

"But who is this man Shakespeare?"

I was ready for the question. "Just a writer of plays that

my mother happened to find interesting as she was looking through the books at Gladwell's in Oxford one Saturday when you were with friends."

He looked doubtful, but I sensed I was winning him over. "I just want to know," I said, "if he has written others that might divert me from this illness. When you go into Oxford next could you perhaps bring back one?"

"I don't know, Aerlene," he said. "These stories are presented in playhouses and taverns, and I am told all manner of vulgar people attend such gatherings. I have heard of drunkenness and riots and lewd behaviour. Why, it is said the authorities in London close down these playhouses by times."

"Well," I said, "if it so troubles you, Uncle, don't bother, for now I must go to sleep, as I am tired," and I turned away from him and closed my eyes.

It was my trump card and it won, because as he bent down to kiss me, he whispered, "If I do bring you one of these playbooks, you must be careful with your aunt. This must be our secret. And you must find a secure place where she will not find it or we'll never hear the end of it."

I turned and, opening my eyes, put my arms around his neck and kissed him. "It is our secret, Uncle," I said, "and I shall be careful." And so I was and so was he.

That spring and summer I read *Much Ado About Nothing, Richard II, The Merchant of Venice* and *Henry IV,*

Parts 1 & 2. All these bore my father's name on their title pages, but as the bookseller Gladwell came to know my uncle he told him that he was a great admirer of Shakespeare, and that there were earlier plays and poetry in print that did not bear his name but were surely of his making. And that is how I came also to read *Richard III* and *Henry V*, though the latter was a poor version of the play I would read in the Folio years later.

All this confirmed that my father was still alive and writing and it heartened me; I had a reason now to live and to dream of going to London one day to meet him. In the meantime I had no need of others, for now I lived in the company of new acquaintances: Falstaff and Prince Hal, Beatrice and Benedict, Richard Crookback and Lady Anne. In my room, I performed the plays, taking all the parts, and reading with wonder and pride the words my father put into the mouths of these characters. I knew it went against my uncle's beliefs to bring these books into the house, and sometimes as he handed me another, he would express his dismay, saying something like "I sometimes wonder what will become of you, Aerlene, with your head crammed with such stuff." Yet he was happy enough to see how much improved I was in body and spirit.

By my thirteenth birthday I felt well enough to ask another favour of him. Even such good company as I had been keeping in my imagination cannot over time replace real life, and I was growing tired of my room and Aunt Sarah asking how I occupied myself by being alone so much. I feared her discovery of my pastimes and there were close calls when she would appear suddenly at my bedroom door.

One day I asked Uncle Jack if I could help in his shop. He thought about it and talked to Aunt Sarah, who disapproved of the idea, arguing that a bastard child would not be good for trade. She wanted to place me in service and intended to do so when I came of age at fourteen. Very well, I said, but could I not do something until then in the back of the shop? This was agreed upon and my uncle told me to make myself useful to his only apprentice, Tom Bradley, a quiet boy with a clubfoot who was a year or two older than I. His father was a gamekeeper in the Royal Park where the Queen had once been held prisoner in the palace by her Papist sister, Mary.

Tom's lameness made an outcast of him in the eyes of most; he was seen as a changeling with the devil's footprint in his clumsy gait. He said he'd heard of me; was I not the base-born child of a man who had lived in the woods and had no tongue? Such were the tales that surrounded me in my youth, and so embedded were they in people's minds that there was nothing to be gained by contradicting them.

On that first day, I said to Tom that we were then a

likely pair, a clubfoot and a bastard, best hidden from the eyes of the innocent.

At first he seemed perplexed by this, but then he laughed. "Why, yes," he said, "that's right enough, though it seems odd to hear it put that way."

In no time we were good friends. He showed me how to measure cloth with the yardstick and how to cut a straight line with the shears. I swept up the cuttings for him and put away things in boxes. There was really not that much to do, but I tried to keep busy. Tom was easy to talk to, and we shared our bread and cheese and cup of ale at eleven o'clock; he told me stories of his father chasing poachers in the park. Tom said that he loved living in the park and, but for his leg, would have followed his father into gamekeeping, for he preferred animals to humans and enjoyed the quiet rustle of forest life. I was soon telling him stories about magical creatures who lived in the woods and how the little people travelled by moonlight and lodged in people's ears, where they fashioned dreams. Borrowing shamelessly from my father's playbooks, I took on as my own the stories of Richard Crookback and the young lovers of Verona and the fat knight who once beguiled a future king of England. Tom listened like a child asking endless questions. "Who told you such things?" "Is what you say true or not?" "Where is this forest with the magical creatures?"

I was a terrible chatterbox, but I enjoyed myself, and sometimes Tom would look up from his bench and say, "How can I work with you jabbering on so? Your uncle will scorch me if this stitching isn't done within the hour." But not a minute later, as I watched his long clever fingers at their work, he would mutter, "So what happened next?"

I think I must have loved Tom Bradley a little, for one day I asked him to step behind a rack of wall hangings and there I kissed him full on the mouth. Tom had pock scars from childhood—just a few—and you could never call him handsome, but his smile was so pleasant and he had a pretty mouth. He was shy at first, for he feared my uncle coming upon us, but soon he was enjoying our innocent little games behind those tapestries. Then he said that I was the strangest little creature ever he had known, but that he wouldn't trade me for another.

At the end of the workday, Uncle Jack and I walked down the long hill from Woodstock to Worsley and I would get him talking about all manner of things. Away from his wife and the worries of his trade, he answered my questions about his family and how Mam came into his life. He had been the first-born, a healthy son for his mother and father, but then ill fortune struck their household as child after child died before reaching the second year. He said his parents felt cursed until Mam was born. By then my uncle was ten or eleven and he told me how he marvelled at his baby sister, at the tiny perfection of her hands and feet. Even then he vowed he would protect her as best he could.

"Your mother, Aerlene," he said, "was a little miracle for my parents and me."

On those early evening walks I asked him too how he came to meet Aunt Sarah, and he told me that he was apprenticed to a mercer in Burford, and he saw her one day with her sister at church. They sat across from him and he used to steal glances, as did many other young men, for the sisters were much sought after.

He told me that the greatest pleasure of his week was going to service on Sunday mornings for a glimpse of Sarah. Sometimes he worried that God would punish him for these thoughts, which strayed far from the preacher's text. I wondered about that. How do you keep an impure thought from straying into your mind when you are looking at someone you desire? I myself already had "impure thoughts" of Tom Bradley, imagining him undressing me in a forest glade. But I never asked my uncle such a question because he would have said only that those playbooks were corrupting me.

To hear Uncle Jack speak with such feeling about my aunt was instructive, since youth often has difficulty in imagining passions that might once have burned in their elders. I thought my aunt still a handsome woman, though a lifetime of frowning and reproach had pinched her features into a disagreeable wryness. Yet once she had been desirable enough to capture hearts, and this was worth remembering. These walks home with my uncle were a great pleasure at the end of the day, and they continued through the late summer of that year and into autumn and on to winter, when we had to pull our cloaks about us against the northerly wind that often struck the brow of the hill leading down to our village.

Then one evening towards the end of that winter, the walks abruptly ended. The day itself had been peculiar from the beginning, because when I first arrived Tom Bradley wasn't there, though a few minutes later I heard his voice at the front of the shop. No customers had yet arrived and he was talking to my uncle, and I could also hear a woman's voice. When Tom came into the back, he wouldn't look at me but went straight to his bench and tied on his apron. My "good morning" was greeted only with a murmur as he fell to his sewing. All week he had been talking with exuberance of the Lenten preacher who was giving sermons each night at St. Mary's Church. He told me these sermons were so good that one could not help but rejoice in the Lord. I was not much interested in such things, but always I kept that to myself and listened. Until that morning, when he arrived so silent and morose. Nor did he say anything the whole day, and even my jests, which usually met with laughter, were turned aside with a shake of the head. There was scarcely any point in thinking of kisses.

I thought about him all day and was doubtless still wondering on the walk home with my uncle. He too was so quiet that I was moved finally to ask, "Is there something the matter, Uncle? You seem in an ill humour."

We were nearly to the village and he stopped. "Yes, Aerlene," he said, "something is the matter and I must ask you not to return to the shop from this day forward."

"And why is that, Uncle?" I asked.

"I spoke this morning to Tom Bradley and his mother," he said. "Tom is a good lad and he has been attending the Lenten preacher's services at St. Mary's this week, and so was moved to tell his mother of what's been going on between you and him in the back of the shop."

"But it is nothing, Uncle," I said. "Only kisses."

"Only kisses," he said scornfully. "And where do kisses lead if not to embraces and then to other matters? Your mother's troubles began with kisses."

"What Tom and I were about was innocent enough," I said.

"That's not for you to judge, child. Your lovemaking was on my premises. I could dismiss that boy from his trade for this."

"Don't do that, Uncle, please," I said. "It was all my doing."

"So Tom said, but one cannot act without the other, and as he is older, he should not have taken advantage. It would appear that you are both at fault." He began to walk on, and I hurried after him. "I will keep him on for his mother's sake," said my uncle, "but you must not set foot in the shop again, Aerlene. You must stay at home now and learn household matters from your aunt. You will be fourteen this summer, and she has hopes of placing you in service."

Next day my aunt summoned me to the parlour and we sat by the window from where I could look out at the garden and the stone bench where Mam and I had spent so many afternoons together. It is difficult so many years later to convey the intensity of the dislike that poisoned the very air between Aunt Sarah and me when we found ourselves alone together. When Mam was alive, her more compliant temperament had acted as a buffer. But now I was alone and, it seems, growing more obstinate with each passing day. I admit it freely now; all those years of enduring my aunt's hostility and righteousness had scored my spirit with a rage that I could barely suppress, and this translated into numbing silences in her presence, or brief, sarcastic answers to her questions.

That day in my aunt's parlour, six and fifty years ago—I can see only its dim outline now, but I can imagine how we might have sounded. A late winter morning and I was probably staring out the window, annoyed at no longer being in the shop at that time of day, disappointed by Tom Bradley's disloyalty, pretending perhaps that I was in love and had been betrayed.

"Your uncle has told me about the boy in the shop."

"Yes?"

"What have you to say for yourself?"

"Very little."

"I have been wondering for some time now if your mother ever spoke to you about the changes that take place when you approach a certain age."

"Yes, she did."

"And what did she tell you?"

"That one day about my fourteenth year I should expect cramping in my parts and a flow of blood once a month."

"Yes. Well..."

"Mam told me to keep a supply of cloths on hand to clean myself. I must change them each day."

"I am glad to hear that you were told such things. And do you realize what all this means?"

"It means that if I lie with a man I could bear a child. But I didn't lie with Tom Bradley, and anyway my courses have not yet begun. Mam told me everything about this. You do not have to speak of it."

"And you do not have to be so insolent, Aerlene. Whatever you may think, your mother set a poor example for you in her habits, and everyone in this village and as far as Woodstock can see where those habits got her."

"Yes. They got her me, a bastard in your house, where neither of us was made welcome. Not by you, at least."

"Your uncle and I took you both in out of Christian charity. We have fed and clothed and housed you all these years. We have always had your best interests at heart."

"My gratitude knows no bounds, Aunt."

"You are a sarcastic, impudent and ungrateful girl and deserve far worse than you have had."

"Thank you, Aunt."

My aunt left the room while I remained staring out the window at the stone bench. It must have been something like that.

Upon hearing of this conversation and doubtless others like it over the following weeks, my uncle finally took me aside and told me I was taxing his patience.

"You are too full of scorn and ridicule, Aerlene, and that is unbecoming in anyone but especially so in the young. You need reminding of what Scripture says about obedience."

I expected this, for Puritans always had a ready verse to illustrate their point. In this case a quotation from St. Paul's Epistle to the Ephesians: *Children, obey your parents in the Lord: for this is right.*

And he continued, "In the absence of your poor mother, your aunt and I are *in loco parentis,* which is to say we are in her place and therefore deserving of the respect and obedience you would afford her were she here. It is God's word, Aerlene, and you must subscribe or risk damnation."

To please him I said I was well rebuked and would endeavour to amend my ways. Yet in my heart, I wondered if it were possible to change so.

Still, I tried. At least looking back from this distance I believe I tried.

Within a fortnight, however, this concern for my manners was left behind in the wake of a letter that briefly transformed Aunt Sarah into a state of excitement bordering by times on agreeableness. The letter was from her sister in London asking if she and her daughter might visit us for a few weeks in the summer to refresh themselves in the countryside. Aunt Sarah, who hadn't seen Eliza since her wedding seventeen years before, was only too delighted to have them, and was soon occupied with planning for the visit, reminding me that her sister would expect proper accommodation. She had married well; her husband was a Frenchman, but a God-fearing man nonetheless with a prosperous milliner's shop in Cheapside. I knew Philip Boyer's shop was not in Cheapside but on Threadneedle Street, though I didn't let on. From Mam's story I knew a great deal more about the Boyers than did my aunt, and I liked having this knowledge and not sharing it with anyone, not even Uncle Jack.

There was much to do and my aunt soon learned that I could work well on my own, and so I settled into cleaning the house from bedroom to pantry: washing and airing bedclothes, polishing pewter and glassware, dusting tables and chairs and chests. In those final days before their arrival, I scrubbed the flagstones and spread fresh rushes across the floors so that the house smelled as clean and sweet as ever it had. My aunt favoured me with a muted "Well done, Aerlene," adding that my labour spoke well for itself and a future life in service. She was already looking for a position on my behalf. Service was not an ambition I was eager for, but I supposed I deserved no better and would be living in someone else's house by the end of the summer. Meanwhile I was curious and excited too about having these visitors from London.

On the June morning of their arrival, I was weeding the garden when I heard voices and the neighing of a horse. When I went around to the front, Eliza Boyer had dismounted and the two sisters were weeping into each other's arms. A maidservant stood by a pony and held the reins of a packhorse laden with saddlebags. Where was Uncle Jack all this time? It must have been a weekday and he was at the shop. The visitors had spent the night at an inn in Oxford after two long days on the road and Eliza Boyer was complaining of the coarse language of the carriers, the many beggars underfoot and the heat and dust. All this while my eyes were fixed on her daughter, who was still on her horse. I was disappointed at how pretty she was, with her fair skin protected from the sun by a broad hat, which she had removed to shake out her long reddish blonde hair.

She too was regarding me, for both of us had our stories about the other. This young beauty was once the squalling brat who could be appeased by no one but her father; this girl had once pinched and pulled Mam's cheeks and nose at will. I was the base-born offspring of the woman who had once lived with them.

Small wonder, then, that with these inquiring looks exchanged, we decided on the instant to dislike each other.

MY SEVENTIETH BIRTHDAY, AND this evening a small gathering with gifts: a fine, bone-handled enlarging glass from Mr. Thwaites to increase my ease in reading; from Charlotte, a new book, which she handed to me, whispering, "The first has scarcely a dozen pages left unfilled"; a handsomely engraved pewter mug for my ale from Mr. Walter; from Mrs. Sproule, a woollen shawl knitted by her granddaughter; and from Emily, a brooch that likely will not last a wearing, for it is poorly made, bought no doubt from a peddler at her mother's door. Still, it is the thought that matters, and besides, the girl has little money. I was grateful to them all.

There was cake and wine and ale, and everything might have been well had I not been suffering all day with the stone; a fiendish pain had me pacing my room from first light until late afternoon, when it abated somewhat, allowing me to pass water. I kept this to myself as best I could and mostly listened to the talk at the table, which was on the harvest that will begin this week. Mr. Walter is hopeful of a good return and said with a laugh that this hot, dry weather is a benefit but will greatly deplete his store of ale, because the workers in this heat soon grow a thirst. Listening to him I thought of how the seasons swiftly pass, folding into one another with barely our noticing. Another harvest, and then the planting of winter wheat and the apples and medlars brought into the cellar. Soon Advent will be upon us, and then Christmas and another winter. And surely I am close to having used up my share of seasons. What then? Heaven? Hell? Nothing?

Mr. Thwaites was in Oxford this week and heard talk of how Cromwell is quite ill and Parliament worried with no successor named and Prince Charlie waiting in France with an army. That made me wonder if our Great Protector was also considering his share of seasons here on earth. I have heard that for all the blood on his hands, he is a pious fellow and so must be readying himself for what's next.

This led me to reflect as I have from time to time on how my father faced his end. When he died, I was twenty-seven, and I knew nothing of his passing until five or six years later, when in Oxford at a performance of *King Lear*—at a courtyard inn in Cornmarket Street—I overheard two gentlemen speaking well of my father and lamenting his death years before up in Stratford. In the last years of his life, my father had lived only forty miles away, and travelling from London he must have passed through our village on his way northward. Yet oddly enough, not once had I thought of him doing so; always I pictured him in London.

In the play I saw that Saturday afternoon, the old King laments the final separation from his beloved daughter with the terrible words

> *Why should a dog, a horse, a rat, have life*
> *And thou no breath at all? Thou'lt come no more,*
> *Never, never, never, never, never.*

And what of the Prince, who leaves this world with only four plain words? *The rest is silence.*

Was this what my father believed? Or were these only words spoken by characters—words that did not express at all what he thought of what comes after?

As he was leaving this evening, Mr. Thwaites took my hand and said what a great thing it was to reach the biblical three score years and ten, adding, "And you may reach further yet in years, Miss Ward."

"Perhaps," I said, "but does the psalmist not end that particular verse with the words 'and if by reason of strength they be fourscore years, yet is their strength, labour and sorrow; for it is soon cut off, and we fly away.' But exactly where we fly, the psalmist doesn't say."

The rector laughed. "Why to God, of course, Miss Ward. Fear not, for in good time you shall go to your Heavenly Father who awaits you."

Still, I wonder.

IN MY BEDROOM ON that first day, Marion Boyer pointed to the girl and said, "Her name is Margaret Brown and she is my maidservant." The poor creature was as plain as her name. "If you wish," said Marion, "I can instruct her to do your bidding as well, and if you find her work unsuitable you may beat her, but you must first ask my permission."

"Why would I beat her?" I asked.

"Because," said Marion, "she is a dull, forgetful girl who wants beating a good deal of the time."

I looked at Margaret Brown, who was placing clothes in a chest which I had opened for her, and I told Marion that I didn't think I would need a servant. I was used to looking after myself.

She smiled. "I thought as much. I am going down to see Mother now."

After she left, I asked the girl how long she had been

working for the Boyer family. She looked at me as if she wasn't sure how to answer. "Some time, Miss," she said finally, but I could scarcely hear her. She was as timid as a spring hare and wouldn't meet my eyes.

I asked her how she came to be employed.

"Please, Miss," she said. "My mam brought me to the family when I was fourteen."

I was surprised, for she looked no more than twelve. "And how old are you now?" I asked.

"I am sixteen, Miss," she said.

I was not used to sharing a bed, and for the first week Marion and I said little to each other. Margaret Brown slept in the truckle bed where I used to lie during Mam's illness. Near the end of that first week, however, Marion and her mother had an argument. I heard them in the downstairs hall and that night Marion lay beside me rigid with anger. Margaret Brown had gone to sleep and I could hear her shallow breathing in the summer night.

Suddenly Marion said aloud, "I hate my mother, but I love my father and I wish I were with him in London. He has a mistress there, but I don't care. He never sleeps with my mother now. He is going to take me to Milan one day with him. He has promised. I hate it here and I wish I were home so I could go to dancing school with my friends. Our teacher is from Paris and is a friend of my father's."

All this was announced in the darkness as if she were

reciting the words to an unseen audience. I didn't know what to say and so turned on my side and went to sleep.

The next day Marion asked me who lived in the great house at the edge of the village and whether we might walk by it together. She was afraid to go alone because of the dogs. That afternoon we walked by Easton House and, standing near the gate, looked down the avenue of elms, which then were so much smaller than they are today. Marion asked if anyone her age lived in the big grey house and I said no, only the squire, who was to be married soon. Marion was excited by this and asked if the bride-to-be was pretty, and I said she was, because I had seen her carriage many times passing through the village. This was true, for Mr. Walter's mother was a beautiful young woman.

Marion decided she could tolerate me, though in her peevish humours she could be cruel and was given to outbursts of quarrelsome rage, while I in turn treated her with a cold reserve, which vexed and puzzled her. I would not rise to an argument, though sometimes in conversation I would use words she didn't understand. "Augment," I would say. "It means to make greater, Marion. To increase." I was happy enough to see that this provoked her wonderfully, the colour rising in her pretty throat.

One rainy afternoon I suggested that we read a play together. This was rash, even dangerous, for if she told her mother, Aunt Sarah would soon find out and demand to know about the playbooks. But I had a good hiding place for them in the rafters of the house and no torture yet devised would force me to reveal its whereabouts. Though it might prove troublesome, I could not resist the urge to show how well I read to this pampered girl from London with her maidservant and her dancing lessons. I guessed that reading was unlikely to be one of her strengths and I was right.

I chose *Romeo and Juliet* and, without revealing how the story ended, outlined the plot and assigned the roles, giving myself Romeo, Mercutio, the Nurse and the Friar. I told Marion she could be Juliet, who was the most desirable girl in Verona. Marion liked the idea of being a beautiful girl in Italy, where her father bought his hats. I expected all this to go badly and it did; Marion could scarcely get through a line without fumbling a word or marring its thought.

"If they do see me, they will murder me."

"No, no, Marion. She is thinking of her lover, not herself. She fears that danger will befall Romeo if he is seen at her balcony, and so says, *If they do see thee they will murder thee.*"

"My beauty is as boundless as the sea."

"No, the word is *bounty. My bounty is as boundless as the sea.*"

"Bondage is hoarse, and may not speak aloud, | Else would I tear the cave where Echo lies, | And make her hairy tongue more hoarse than mine."

"*Airy* tongue, Marion. The word is *airy,* for Echo's voice resounds throughout the air as any schoolchild knows. Do not speak of hairy tongues, for it is foolishness itself."

"This," she cried angrily, "is the silliest stuff that ever I've read."

"Hardly read, I should say. *Mis*read is the truer word."

"It's a silly pastime anyway, reading plays. Mother says only fools and whores attend playhouses."

"But gentlemen from the Inns of Court as well," I said. "And courtiers from Whitehall who favour velvet caps for themselves and laces and ribbons for their ladies."

Marion looked at me closely. "How would you know?"

"My mother once told me. She worked in your father's shop. She often heard the customers talking of the playhouses."

Marion could not disguise her smirk. "Your mother told you, did she? I thought she was my nursemaid."

"She was for a time, and said you were insufferable. Mewling and wailing over nothing. But she also worked in your father's shop."

"When she wasn't at the playhouse, I suppose," said Marion.

Flushed with triumph I had overspent my purse, and so between us that afternoon I called it but a draw. Yet I had other matters on my mind that summer: my fourteenth birthday was fast approaching and I knew my aunt was eager to be rid of me.

One July evening, perhaps a fortnight before Lammastide, I was summoned to the parlour, where she and my uncle were waiting. Uncle Jack looked grave and worried and Aunt Sarah was forcing a smile, and I knew I would hear something adverse. My aunt told me she had been speaking to a Mr. Trethwick, who was looking for a servant girl. He lived in a farmhouse some three miles beyond Woodstock on the Hensington Road with his elderly sister, who was feeble-minded. He had spoken to Aunt Sarah after church about me, wondering if I were yet of age for service. When told that I soon would be, Mr. Trethwick said that though I was small, I looked a good strong girl who could help in the household, since his sister was growing difficult to manage with age. I had seen them in church on Sunday mornings, the sister nodding and smiling as she held on to her brother's arm. John Trethwick was in his late middle years, a severe-looking man with a squint.

Uncle Jack was against my going; he said Trethwick, though cheerful enough in company, was a flint-hearted man and still close to every penny he'd made; none of his neighbours liked him, for he'd quarrel over an inch of dirt between boundaries. As for his sister, there was more to her than just nodding and smiling; she inclined, it was said, to fits of rage. Both brother and sister had lived together alone fifty years. And where does that leave the mind? said Uncle Jack. John Trethwick, my aunt argued, was a God-fearing man who never missed church and was always pleasant in conversation. I would be in good hands.

"Sarah," said Uncle Jack, "you see the man only at the church door on Sundays, when he bears a friendly face to all. At home he lives behind all that."

But my aunt was not moved by his argument and said that when I came of age she would take me herself for an interview.

That night I lay awake listening to Marion as she muttered in her sleep, while I imagined life with the Trethwicks in their farmhouse. I saw a winter night with the rain beating against the windows and the old woman by the fire, her brother telling me it was time to take her to her room and undress her for bed, the farmhouse stale with the smell of soiled underclothes and old bodies and dust that had gathered over years.

All this made me want to know more about those who spent their lives serving others. I pitied Margaret Brown and the way she was treated by Marion and her mother. I wanted to like the girl, but I found it difficult. She had little to say on her own behalf and her meekness repelled me. If I found her peeling onions for dinner or mending an apron by the fire while the others were out, I would ask about her life before she entered service. She had but brief answers to any questions. What of her family? I would ask.

"Oh, yes. I have a mother and father, and brothers, one sister."

What of them? I would say, for I wanted images so I could picture her life before service with the Boyers. But she would add nothing.

"What is your father's work?"

"My father, John Brown, is a cob, Miss."

"And what's that?"

"A water carrier, Miss."

"Yes. And what else about him?"

"He is overfond of ale, Miss."

"And what of your brothers and sister?"

"What of them, Miss?"

I would leave her then to her mending, for I could find no spirit in the girl and this filled me with an obscure anger. Was the serving world filled with such people, and how could I be a part of that world?

That Sunday at church, I carefully watched the Trethwicks across the aisle, the old man's heavy-lidded eyes closing now and then, even under the loud hectoring of Littlejohn's war on pleasure. Beside him, his sister's ever-restless eyes were looking this way and that, the nodding, smiling face a study itself in madness. I vowed I would run away before I placed a footstep in their household. I would go to London and find my father. I would have to walk and I imagined it would take at least a week. That meant living rough, avoiding vagrants and thieves. Could I carry enough food for a week? Would I need a weapon, a small dagger perhaps? What would I do when I got to London? How would I start the search for my father? It was a foolish dream, common enough no doubt among unhappy children, but something at least to cling to when compared to life with a miser and a madwoman. Even as a child I was never much for praying, but perhaps that morning I asked God for help.

My fourteenth birthday came and went and was but lightly regarded, and only by my uncle, who gave me a shilling. But his better gift was his news that John Trethwick would not need me until after the harvest. Uncle Jack surmised that the old man wanted to spend his money only on field hands in August, and so I was reprieved; moreover I had a shilling to put with my playbooks in the rafters and time to think further on my plan.

My bedmate, Marion, was growing more irritable under the slow pace of country life and the heat of the sun, which was ripening the corn. She took up her dancing in the afternoons to beguile herself, and I have to say she was both graceful and adept, though I never told her so. When she asked if I wished to learn some steps, I declined, as I knew her game; she wanted to place her skills at dancing beside mine, which were negligible. She was in poor humour most of the month and getting on the nerves of everyone, including her own mother and my aunt, who asked me to amuse her as best I could.

One afternoon I took Marion into the countryside. She insisted that Margaret Brown come with us, as she wanted the girl to pick some flowers that might dress the night table by our bed. I took her first into the woods to what was left of Goody Figgs's cottage, telling her along the way that a witch once lived there. Saying all this, I felt disloyal to both Mam and the old woman, for she had been Mam's friend and was certainly no witch. But I wanted to impress Marion, who was interested in such things as witches and goblins and expected each village in the country to have at least two or three. Yet she was not much affected as we walked around the charred ruins where the smell of an old fire still clung faintly to a half-burned bedpost and a broken joint-stool.

She was peevish that day, Marion, and told me that her courses were on their way, and though she knew I had not yet had this experience, she insisted on asking me whether I too felt out of sorts at their onset. I said it made no difference to me, and she smiled, for she knew I was lying. We went by the river, now shallow in the summer heat, and I showed her where the bream lay in dark pools beneath the willow trees. I said we might catch a fish for amusement. If we lay on our stomachs and slowly moved our hands through the water, the bream would rise and we might tickle their bellies to entice them. But Marion said it would soil her skirt; already her stockings were torn from the brambles, she said. Margaret Brown was sitting apart from us on the edge of the meadow, where she had been gathering cornflowers and hysop. These poor flowers lay beside her in a clump, already wilting. Marion walked towards the girl while I lay by the river's edge to watch the fish. I could hear Marion scolding her.

"This country living is making you more stupid every day. Look at those pitiful weeds you've gathered."

When I looked back, Marion had taken off her broad summer hat and was shaking out her long hair. She said her stockings were soiled and it was hot in the sun and she hated this place with its cowpats and flies. I was enjoying her tantrum as I lay staring into the dark, still water, studying a fish near my hand. I was gently stirring the water above it while Marion ranted about her stockings, blaming Margaret Brown; apparently there were holes in the stockings and this was Margaret's fault. As I listened, I must have stirred the water too quickly, because the fish disappeared, and when I got up I saw Marion standing over the girl with an alder switch in her hand.

"What were you thinking when you laid out these stockings for me?" she demanded.

Margaret Brown said she was sorry.

"Sorry, sorry, sorry," Marion cried. "It's the only word you know. Get on your hands and knees. You want beating."

I walked towards them. Margaret Brown was now on her hands and knees in the long grass, and Marion had pulled up the apron and dress. The girl wore no petticoat and I could see the pale, narrow back, the ridge of her spine. There was so little to her. Marion began to flail at that back, soon raising welts as the blows struck. When she finished she was panting and looked flushed. She handed me the alder switch.

"You may have ten strokes on her. I shall count them."

Startled, I asked why. "She has done nothing to warrant a beating," I said.

Marion was beside herself with rage. "Why, why, why?" she screamed. "Because she is a stupid, lazy girl who wants beating. That is why."

Her outburst sent a flock of meadowlarks soaring into the hot blue sky, to settle finally in another part of the field. Without realizing it, I was holding the alder switch and looking down at Margaret Brown and those reddened welts, a kind of mad handwriting on her pale back. I felt appalled by Marion's cruelty, yet I was also repelled by the terrible resignation in the kneeling girl. Was she born to endure such punishment without complaint? For a moment I had the greatest urge to strike her. I wanted to feel what it was like to hurt someone who could not hurt back. I may even have raised that alder switch—I can't remember now—but I did not strike her and that at least is in my favour, even if my thoughts were shameful.

I told Marion I was going back to the village, and they followed me as we crossed the field and no one said a word. But from that afternoon on, I sensed that the enmity between Marion and me had deepened. Perhaps she was ashamed that I had witnessed her cruel tantrum, or perhaps she was merely tired of me and her long confinement in the country. We didn't speak to each other until the next morning, when I had washed some clothes and was spreading them on the grass to dry.

Marion came out of the house and stood watching me and said, "May I ask you a question, Aerlene? I know you are angry with me, but I want to be your friend as well as cousin. I want to get to know more about you."

I looked up at her and I knew she was lying. She would never claim a bastard as her cousin. Still, I asked, "What is your question?"

"Do you ever think about your father?"

I felt my heart quickening. My father? What was she on about with my father? I stood up, wiping wet hands on my apron.

"The other day," said Marion, "I heard Auntie talking to my mother and she said your father was either a farmhand or some idler your mother met in London. Did she ever tell you who he was?"

I walked past her carrying the clothesbasket and said nothing. I was determined not to be drawn into argument lest I say something I might regret. I knew that a part of me longed to tell her that my father was a writer whose plays were performed in London playhouses, and a greater man by far than Philip Boyer, a seller of bonnets and ribbons. But I could prove nothing and would only look foolish in the telling. So silence and carefully chosen words uttered with foresight would be my weapons in our little war.

Yet she was cunning, Marion. I give her that. Cunning and capable of surprise attacks, sweetly voiced, the innocent inquiry that was meant to unsettle. I might, for instance, be nearly asleep when she would whisper, "Auntie says the farmhand had no tongue. Is that really true? And you such a clever girl with all those words in that head of yours. I think it more likely to have been the London idler, who was perhaps a man of words and passed that on to you. The subject of fathers and who bred us is important, Aerlene. We should talk about it."

I guessed she had rehearsed these little speeches before delivering them to me in bed. When she grew tired of harping on my father, she turned to my name. One night I was certain she was asleep, so even was her breathing, but I was startled anew by her calm clear voice out of the darkness.

"Aerlene is an odd name, is it not?" I feigned sleep, but she continued, "I have never heard it before."

Then nothing more until two or three nights later when I had forgotten all this, didn't she begin again as though she had just left off this conversation.

"What does the name signify? I wonder. Of all the Christian names, why did your mother choose Aerlene?"

Another night she would wait until I was nearly asleep and say aloud, "Let's play I Spy, Aerlene." The minutes would pass and sleep would draw closer and then the damnable girl would say, "I spy with my little eye, something that begins with *e*."

And I might finally say, "Go to sleep, Marion. I am not interested in your games."

"Very well," she'd say. "I'll play alone. I spy with my little eye something that begins with *e*. And it is an *elf*. Auntie has already told me that your name means 'elf' in some heathen tongue. She said that your mother used to go to the woods and talk to ravens and toads, and was friends with the witch whose house was burned down by young men from the village. That was the place where you took me the other day, was it not?"

It is not easy to share a bed with someone you dislike enough to hurt, and I knew I was capable: Marion was older and taller, but at the time I was something of a hoyden, a sturdy, little brown nut of a girl with a temper. If need be, I knew I could thrash Marion, and as I listened to her it became an ordeal not to pinch her arm or strike a blow across her brow. Yet I was rescued by language; words saved me from behaving like an ill-bred wench in her cups. Words, I decided, must be used, and not as battering rams in an argument, but rather as allies in defence of order. I chose the word *forbearance*, a favourite of Uncle Jack's, and he had ready need of it in his wife's company. But also I liked the sound of the word in my mouth, its three-syllable iambic heft, *for bear ance*.

As I listened each night to Marion's prattle about tongueless men and London idlers who might have fathered me, I summoned up forbearance, imagining a bear valorous and stolid; and in my mind's eye I saw myself riding to sleep on the back of that bear in the middle of a word.

A DAY TO TAX AN OLD HEART, and a day in which I overreached myself in behaving badly. This morning, after sprinkling the sand over the last of my words, Charlotte said that she had something to tell me. I expected to hear more about the wedding, now only six weeks off, for each day seems to bring news of alterations to everything from guest list to wedding supper. The other day, Mrs. Sproule told me that she doesn't expect to survive August. So I thought more of the same was on its way. Yet Charlotte had been more than her usual skittish self in our mornings together these several days past, asking me to repeat sentences, querying words, losing track of the sequence of events. It seemed as though she were only half-listening to me. I expected today's work to be a muddle. With the help of Mr. Thwaites's glass, I can now make out words on a page, but it is tedious and I haven't the patience to see if Charlotte has it right. Perhaps when and if I finish all this I will try.

I was standing by the window looking out at the elms, presenting themselves to me now only as two rows of shimmering greenery in the August sunlight, when Charlotte said, "Linny, I want you to promise not to be angry if I tell you something."

So, I thought, it is not about the wedding after all. I told her, however, that I would promise nothing of the sort. "You are tied to the post, Charlotte, and must face matters."

"Very well," she said. "Last evening on our walk, Simon told me a very interesting story."

"Oh yes? And what was this story, Charlotte?"

"Well," she began, as if relating tea-party gossip, "it seems that in certain circles in Oxford, where Simon has many cultivated friends, it is well known that a certain gentleman, Sir William Davenant, a playwright and poet, has long claimed to be the son of William Shakespeare. It seems that Shakespeare knew the Davenants in London, and when they moved to Oxford, he used to visit them. John Davenant bought a wine tavern in Oxford and Shakespeare used to break his journey to Stratford by stopping there. The story goes that he was enamoured of Davenant's wife, Jane, who apparently was very beautiful and witty, and Shakespeare got a child upon her, or so this man claims. Davenant has a considerable reputation in London. His sympathies with the King in the war got him into trouble with Parliament and he spent some time in France. But he is now back in London and writing plays. Is that not remarkable?"

I said it might be no more remarkable than two plus two equals four if you consider that actors or playwrights like my father who achieve success tend to attract female admirers, and may as a consequence spread their seed throughout the land. A glib response, I admit, and I don't really think I believed that of my own father. But really—how little I knew about him. It could have been so with this Davenant woman.

"And how, Charlotte," I continued, "did all this crop up in your conversation with Mr. Thwaites? Could it possibly have appeared because despite your solemn promise to me, you have told Mr. Thwaites the whole story of my mother, my father and my illegitimacy?"

I knew from the way she was looking down at her hands that she was distressed. Why do I take such delight in catching her out? It is a moral failing that I seem unable to conquer. Yet she was quick off the mark, eager to confess.

"Linny, it has been so hard to take down your words and keep all this inside me. Simon has told me much about himself these past few months. His childhood illnesses and pranks. How as a young man he was very nearly expelled from St. John's. How he turned down important livings and chose instead a country parish like Worsley. How he wanted so badly to be a poet in his youth. He still writes poetry, though he says none of it is good enough to show anyone. He wants to know about me too. But what is there to tell? I lead such a dull life. More than once he has asked me how I spend my days. Do I read? And if so, what do I read? Surely I don't just embroider and gossip like so many ladies in the parish? I know you think I am a dunderhead, Linny, but I can't bear the thought of Simon thinking me one too. I so want his good opinion of me and I am trying to improve my mind with reading. So when I told him that I was writing down your memoirs because your eyesight was failing, he told me it was a virtuous act and one to be admired. But I felt I was not doing justice to our mornings together, Linny. I wanted Simon to know how important your story is. That it is not just the account of a lifetime as nursemaid and housekeeper in a country home, filled with tales of children and harvest suppers. You are the daughter of the greatest poet our country has produced. Simon has read all his plays, and when he was a student he even saw two or three performances and was reported to the authorities by Puritan enemies. He said he saw *Hamlet* only weeks before Parliament closed down the theatres. So when he told me about this man Davenant, and of how he boasts of being Shakespeare's son, I could no longer contain myself. I said to him, 'Simon, this man Davenant's story is nothing to what I am taking down each morning. I am recording the words of a woman whose mother was Shakespeare's mistress and had a child by him. And that child is now a woman who has lived in this parish for seventy years and no one has known.'"

Charlotte stopped. Even with my poor eyesight, I could see how flushed she was with the telling of all this. And I felt . . . Well, how did I feel? All my life I have been terrified of ridicule. Who would possibly believe such a tale? I seem to have convinced Charlotte—but others less credulous? She had turned in her chair and was again looking down at her hands like a child who has misbehaved. I felt a fluttering in my chest. Was I unwell, I wondered, or merely confused— angered by her broken promise, yet curiously thrilled that an educated man like Simon Thwaites might know the true condition of my mother's history and mine? And if it came to that, had Charlotte really meant any harm by revealing the truth? I suppose she wanted to impress the man she loves, and what was so terrible about that? It was perfectly understandable. But old termagant that I am, I said nothing except that I had to lie down.

The rest of the day in bed, then, with the curtains drawn. Below me the sounds of others moving about. Voices drifting up from the partly opened windows behind the curtains, the gardener Johnson talking to someone. Then a knocking on the door and Emily peering in with a smile. "Is there anything I can get you, Miss?" What a big, healthy-looking girl she is! "Mrs. Sproule would like to know if there is anything she can prepare for you. Is it your stomach or the other end, Miss Ward? She can put together some rhubarb and tartar."

"No, thank you" came the faint reply from the old child in the bed. And yet I did feel the onset of something. Some mild agitation about the heart, which perhaps foretells a weakening.

After Emily left I thought of how I might have told Charlotte that all was forgiven. Was that so difficult? My damnable pride. What difference did it make if Simon Thwaites knew my story? Perhaps he didn't believe it anyway and was only humouring Charlotte. I ought to have forgiven her.

Then in the late afternoon she came to see me, bearing a tray, which she set upon the table next to my bed. Mrs. Sproule had prepared some chicken broth and cold pork and two tarts made with pippins from the orchard, the first of the season. The old trout is usually frugal with her confections, so two apple tarts was a pleasing surprise. Charlotte still looked worried and took my hand. I was drawn to the strength of her grip on my old veined claw. She was eager to please me. Did I want the doctor? Mr. Walter wanted to send for him. I said I wanted no doctor. Emily too was worried, Charlotte said, and Mrs. Sproule. An air of consternation in the house. I revelled in it all. Told Charlotte I wasn't hungry, though truly I could have eaten the cloth off the tray.

"Linny, I'm sorry I upset you," she said. "After my promise I shouldn't have told Simon."

I then surprised both of us by asking, "But does Mr. Thwaites believe it? Does he not think it passing strange that a servant in Easton House is the daughter of a great poet? I will not be made a laughing-stock, Charlotte. I would rather go out in the rain and die by a hedgerow than be laughed at." That was too melodramatic even for Charlotte and she laughed, and so did I.

"Please don't be silly," she said. "Let's have no talk of lying out by hedgerows in the rain. When I told Simon about your mother and father, he said nothing at first, but he had his thoughtful look about him. It's the look I see on his face when he is thinking of a homily or what he might say on a visit to someone who is ill. Then he said, 'It is remarkable, but why should it not be true? You have told me how Miss Ward's mother met the poet in London all those years ago. It's certainly possible. And why should it not be so? Why do people make up things about themselves? Is it not usually to gain admiration from others? To be noticed? To be seen as more important than they really are? But as you suggested, Miss Ward wants no attention whatsoever—indeed wants none of this known. Imagine, if this were known, how she would be troubled by visitors eager to know more of her father. Many would welcome such attention, but she wants none of it. Take this man Davenant; he bruits it about

London that Shakespeare was his father, not minding in the least the damage to his poor dead mother's reputation. Now she is seen as a woman who had a child by a family friend under the very roof of the house in which her husband slept. And her son is boasting of it. And why? Audacity? To boast of carrying the poet's blood? A kind of fame, I suppose, but at what cost? Yet Miss Ward wants nothing more than that the truth of her story be quietly recorded before she passes beyond all earthly vexations. She doesn't care a pin for fame, and I for one find that admirable.'"

Charlotte's account of Mr. Thwaites's remarks put me into a pleasing fluster. "You're making it up, Charlotte," I said. "You couldn't remember all that word for word."

She laughed. "I have given you the gist of Simon's remarks. Whether exactly word for word doesn't necessarily pertain to the truth. Is that not what you once told me, Linny?"

So I had and I was pleased that Charlotte remembered. "Very well," I said, "but can I have faith in Mr. Thwaites's discretion?"

"Absolutely," said Charlotte. "I have not spent these last few months in his company without realizing how trustworthy he is. And he is so delighted with your story. He can't wait to hear how you get to London to meet your father, and your impressions of him."

"So you have been reading my words to him?"

"Yes. For the past fortnight or so. And he wants to read it himself one day."

"He finds it worthwhile?"

"Yes."

"Believable?"

"Absolutely."

How vanity sweeps away all before it! I now had another reader, an educated man who believed my words. I held out my arms to Charlotte; when all is said and done, she is the only person in the world who truly loves me.

Before leaving she asked whether I wanted the tray removed, but I said I might try a little of Mrs. Sproule's broth. As it happened, I ate everything.

When Emily came in to take the tray, she was carrying a tankard of ale.

"Mrs. Sproule thought a drop might furnish you with cheer, Miss."

"And so it might," I said. "And I thank you for it, Emily."

Then I said her hair looked pretty in the evening light, though really I could make little of her features.

"Thank you, Miss Ward," she said. "And sleep well tonight."

And so I shall, if the stone will grant me peace for a few hours.

THE LAST SUNDAY OF August in the year 1602, a sun-filled day with a light wind, a day in which farmers sniff and scan the clear blue sky in hopes that the fair weather holds. I am fourteen years and twenty-three days old and I am standing under the branches of the two-hundred-year-old beech tree in St. Cuthbert's churchyard, watching Aunt Sarah and John Trethwick stroll among the gravestones as they talk, my aunt in a violet taffeta dress and bonnet, John Trethwick in his Sunday suit and dark hat, his clasped hands behind him, leaning inward to my aunt as he listens. They are talking about me, conducting business over the bones of the dead. *Is that the best you can do on wages? What day shall she have free, Wednesday or Sunday? Will you provide her clothes?*

If this weather lasts, the corn will be gathered by week's end and John Trethwick can pay off his day labour and set aside the pennies for the maidservant, whose primary task will be the care of his older sister, who is now waiting for him to take her home; she is sitting on the grass by the iron railing that encloses the Easton family plots. I am watching her too as she plucks the petals from the Michaelmas daisies she has taken from a new grave.

I have just quarrelled with Uncle Jack, if *quarrel* is the word, for he seldom disputes, and that of course is what angered me. As we left the church, he drew me apart and we walked to this beech tree, where he said there was nothing he could do.

"I am sorry, Aerlene, but your aunt's mind is firm. She will have you in John Trethwick's house by the end of the coming week."

That is when I reminded him that we were only footsteps from my mother's grave, yet he was renouncing his vow to her to be my guardian. I told him he was a weakling and a coward, terrible words to call the man who had protected me all those years, but he now seemed worn down and unable to resist his wife's bidding. He left me and walked home alone while I stared across to the church door where Aunt Eliza and Marion and a few others were still gathered around the rector.

I found it bitterly amusing how over the weeks Obadiah Littlejohn had changed his tune about finery in church; after seeing Eliza and her daughter that first Sunday in June, he had the following week preached a sermon on the vanity of dress. At that time, Eliza and Marion had not noticed that the homily was directed at them, and their London fashion. Over the weeks, however, Aunt Eliza had put Littlejohn into a swoon, and now he fawned over her. And on this August morning, both Aunt Eliza and Marion are at their best because they are nearly done with their long country holiday and are returning to London in a few days. By the churchyard gate Margaret Brown was waiting for them and for the first time she too looked happy.

Watching them all, I was angry and envious. I would soon be living with the mad creature who was plucking at the daisy petals and her skinflint brother with his shifty eyes and manner. My dream of running away was only that, a dream. I had my birthday shilling and nothing besides, and I felt out of touch with everything and everyone. I dreaded the week ahead.

That week began badly too, with a slap to my face delivered by Aunt Sarah. I will try to reconstruct this as best I can. I know we were both in a foul temper that Monday morning, my aunt for reasons of her own and me because the last week had now started and it would end with me in the Trethwick farmhouse. Over that summer my aunt had assigned various household tasks to prepare me for service, and that particular morning I was cleaning pots in the scullery. At one point my aunt came in from the kitchen and made some trivial criticism, a remark that another day I might have received with a shrug and a wry face behind her back. Instead I thrust the pot directly at her stomach.

"Do it yourself, then," I said. "I'll be gone by week's end and you can do them all yourself, every damnable one of them."

Her hands did not reach for the pot. I don't know why—perhaps she was too startled, but I let it fall anyway. Somehow it missed her feet and clattered to the flagstones. With my aunt's perpetual scowl, it was often difficult to detect in her features any increase in the wrath that was so constant to her nature. She was not one for screaming but spoke always in an even manner. I had overstepped myself, she said.

"You will learn obedience where you are going, Aerlene. John Trethwick is not a man who will long tolerate insolence."

"Nor will I his," I said, "and if he lays a hand on me, I'll take the poker to him. Then you can thank yourself for having put me in his house."

Those words brought on the blow, which struck smartly, and when I turned my burning cheek I saw only surprise on the faces of Marion and her mother, who were standing in the kitchen doorway, no doubt drawn there by the noise. Behind them Margaret Brown looked astonished.

I went to my bedroom, and a few minutes later Aunt Eliza came up to tell me that she and Marion were going to

Woodstock to buy a few things for their journey and she had persuaded Aunt Sarah to accompany them.

"It will be good for both of you to be apart a little. She wants you to finish your work in the scullery and keep an eye on Margaret Brown, who has a collar to mend for Marion." She offered a wan smile. "Try to look upward as your life unfolds, Aerlene. Perhaps this man Trethwick will not be a bad master for you."

But I was almost certain she didn't believe a word of it.

After I heard them leave, I went below stairs, as I was restless and eager to be out in the bright, windy morning. I certainly had no intention of staying indoors on such a fine day with Margaret Brown, whom I came upon in the parlour; she was crouching by the hearth while she blew on the embers of the breakfast fire. I saw two buns, one already skewered to a toasting fork, and I knew she had stolen them from the larder, but I didn't care. Let Margaret Brown enjoy her toasted bread. Was it not little enough to ask in this life?

She was surprised to see me, saying, "Oh, Miss, I thought you had left the house too."

"I am going out now, Margaret," I said.

She looked up beseechingly. "I'm sorry you and your auntie had an argument, Miss. You won't tell her about the bread, will you?"

Poor little wheedler, I thought. Aunt Sarah would find out soon enough on her own, for she knew to the last onion what lay in her pantry. And when she found out, it would go hard for Margaret Brown.

Yet all I said was "I won't tell her, Margaret. Toast your bread."

I walked to the end of the village and across a field already gleaned and into the woods by the river. In a nearby glade I lay on my back to watch the tops of the trees thrashing about in the wind and beyond the trees the clouds like great towering galleons coursing along the sky. Later I skirted the Easton estate and watched the harvesters cutting the field in good order, a dozen at least moving steadily forward, the corn falling to their scythes; behind them women and boys were raking the grain into piles for the carters to draw to the barns. The boisterous air was filled with the shouting and laughter of the young gleaners, for the harvest was drawing to an end with the promise of ale and a good supper later in the week in the squire's orchard.

A young girl lost her bonnet in the wind and everyone laughed as it rolled comically across the field. A boy tried to fetch it, yet each time he bent down, the wind snatched it away and off he would run while everyone cheered. I knew the girl; she was no older than I and not handsome, but filled out now and ready for young men. I watched the boy finally capture the bonnet and tie it beneath the girl's chin while others laughed at his red-faced embarrassment, and I wished more than words can say that I was that girl.

Henry Easton came by on his horse and talked to the foreman; from time to time they both looked up at the thickening clouds, pointing this way and that as though gauging the wind's intent. Then he galloped off. I think now of that day and what a fine figure Henry Easton cut on his horse, and his young wife back at this very house and carrying their first child, for Mr. Walter was born the following spring.

That August day, as I continued homeward, I smelled the smoke before ever I saw it, and when I reached the village it was billowing above Market Lane. My first thought was of the dunghill by the blacksmith's, where sparks from his anvil often set manure ablaze, bringing his wife out with her pail of water. But that day there was far too much smoke for a midden fire, and when I turned in to our street, I saw the crowd holding their hands before their faces against the sparks flying in the hot wind and watching our house burn. Smoke gushed from under the roof as the rafters splintered and burned, taking with them my birthday shilling and my father's playbooks. It was too late to do anything about our place, but men and boys were already climbing ladders on nearby houses with pails of water to dampen roofs.

I thought of Margaret Brown in all those flames, but then I saw her at the edge of the crowd sobbing into the apron of the blacksmith's wife, and I was glad at least that I would not have her death on my conscience. The church bell was ringing and I ran towards Margaret, but when she saw me she only turned her head away and clung to the blacksmith's wife. By the grass beneath a casement window, I saw a half-eaten bun.

There came a great rumble of thunder and a woman who lived nearby fell to her knees to pray for her house. And her prayer was answered, as on the instant the rain came down hard, and most bowed their heads to give thanks. Slipping away as fast as I could, I ran to Cattle Lane and hid in an open-ended shed where sheep and cattle were quartered overnight before market day. The shed stank of old hay and cowpats and the roof leaked. But I piled straw in a corner and sat there wondering about all that had happened that day. Within a few minutes, the downpour ended and left a clammy grey stillness in the air. Now and then I saw people passing by in the laneway.

Someone must have seen me near the shed because in time Uncle Jack found me. I could see him in the light of the doorway and he called to me and I told him I was there, and he came and sat down. It was late in the afternoon and beyond the doorway the sky was darkening with more rain. In the shed I could not read my uncle's features; he was just a figure beside me.

Finally he said, "Everyone is in church now for a service of thanksgiving. The rain saved the village, but the farmers' fields are drenched and with the corn not fully gathered.

'The Lord giveth and the Lord taketh away. Blessed be the name of the Lord.'" He laughed mirthlessly as if those familiar lines from Scripture were no more than a bad jest.

But I could be wrong; he may not have thought that at all. Perhaps that was only my thinking.

We said nothing for the longest time and I guessed he was trying to get his mind around the fact that when he left for work that morning, he had had a house and the furnishings of a lifetime. Now everything was gone, and this vast and sudden oddness in his life was difficult to grasp.

As he stared into the darkness at the other end of the shed he asked me how the fire had started and, without waiting for an answer, said, "It was the girl, wasn't it? I have heard she was toasting bread. You should not have allowed that, Aerlene. The girl is slow."

I began to weep and said I was sorry for using those horrible words against him in the churchyard on Sunday. But he only asked me again why I had not watched Margaret Brown more closely.

"There must have been a casement open to that wind," he said. "It carried a spark from the hearth onto something."

I thought of Marion's dress on the settle, where Margaret Brown had put it to mend the collar. That was likely where the spark had landed and Margaret may not at first have noticed; she may have taken her bread to eat by the open casement, where she could enjoy the wind's commotion on her face. It was something I might have done myself. But as she ate, the fire was already leaping across the settle to the wall hangings. When she felt the heat behind her, she turned and, seeing the flames, threw the bread out the window and looked about for something to cover the fire. But what and how could that be done? It was too late and the heat was fierce and she was terrified, her fears multiplying by the moment, racing ahead to consequences.

Sitting on the straw in that shed, I imagined that it must have been something like that. And so she fled from the house and into the arms of the blacksmith's wife.

"I wasn't there, Uncle," I said. "I went out to the Easton fields to watch the harvesters."

He turned his face to me. "Why would you do that? Were you not told to stay with the girl?"

"I am sorry, Uncle."

He looked away again. "That was poor judgment, Aerlene. The girl is slow."

"I never thought her slow, Uncle," I said, "but only shy and uncertain."

For the first time his voice sharpened. "The girl is slow and you shouldn't have left her alone in the house. A spark in the wind and that's how it went. *Everything* went."

I couldn't bear to tell him the truth, that I had encouraged Margaret Brown to toast her bread before I left that morning, and so I asked about Aunt Sarah. He told me she had taken to bed at a neighbour's and the doctor had been sent for; she would stay the night, and Eliza and Marion with her. Uncle Jack said he was sleeping that night on the floor in the back of his shop and I would have to make do there as well. He would lay down some cloth for us near the workbenches. For the rest of the week he had arranged lodgings for us at the White Hart, the best hostelry in Woodstock; he wanted us all in comfort, especially his wife, whose mind, he said, was greatly unsettled. At the end of the week, Marion and her mother would leave for London, and on Saturday afternoon I would go to John Trethwick's house on Hensington Road. He would take me there himself.

He was silent for a few moments before he said, "The girl cannot be found. At first the blacksmith's wife took her in and said she was sitting in a corner of the kitchen with a porringer of soup, and when next she looked, the girl was gone. There were many in the house, she said, all coming and going, all eager to hear the story since she'd been the first to smell the fire. So with everyone coming and going, she didn't notice the girl leaving in all that rain, and now no one can find her. I expect she ran off. God alone knows where."

That night a storm swept over us, and I was glad to lie beside my uncle on the floor of his workshop under old cloth. I lay thinking of Margaret Brown out in that weather, looking for shelter, alone and fearful.

Whenever I have returned to my father's *Lear*, I have been especially moved by the passage in which the old King, thrust out into the storm by his two evil daughters, looks about in his wretchedness and feels at last a sympathy for those in want:

> *Poor naked wretches, wheresoe'er you are,*
> *That bide the pelting of this pitiless storm!*
> *How shall your houseless heads and unfed sides,*
> *Your loop'd and window'd raggedness, defend you*
> *From seasons such as these?*

And always I think of Margaret Brown, cowering in woods or wayside on the night she ran away.

At the White Hart in Woodstock, my two aunts shared one room and Marion and I another; my uncle had his own, for he wanted Aunt Sarah attended to by her sister, and he himself was often awake through the late hours working on plans for a new house. By nature my uncle was a sanguine man, and his disposition soon overcame the bitterness of his loss. By midweek, he was already conferring with masons and carpenters and bricklayers about his plans; and because he was so highly esteemed in the community, all were eager to help. Aunt Sarah, however, fell into a melancholy and stayed in her room all week.

Marion and I unwittingly declared a truce, deciding we could ignore the petty differences that so often soured our time together over the summer. Her intense self-enchantment with her constant primping at the looking-glass, her daily admiration of her dancer's legs, my mordant and grumbling temperament, her muttering in sleep, my prodigious wind—all could be endured for a few days, because each day drew me nearer to the farmhouse on Hensington Road.

As though reading my apprehensive mind, Marion often expressed sympathy, though I soon came to regard her concern as nothing more than spite; she would warn me of things I had already considered and hearing them again only served to deject me. She would tell me, for instance, to be wary of the sister because the mad can be crafty and unpredictable; they can stick a fork in your arm on the merest whim and when you least expect it. How she knew this, I can't say; she had little imagination. Perhaps she had overheard her mother talking about mad folk. As for John Trethwick himself, she didn't like the look of him. Was the door to my bedroom bolted? Masters take liberties with their servants, that's common knowledge. And in a farmhouse far from others? Who would know and who could help? She said that Margaret Brown had told her stories of girls who suffered under men like John

Trethwick. Maidenheads taken with force and many tears. It would do well for me to be watchful in the night; he might climb through a window. I would try to change the subject by asking if she ever wondered what had become of Margaret Brown, but Marion would only say that the girl had been responsible for the fire and was scarcely deserving of thought or sympathy.

When Marion wasn't forecasting the imminent loss of my maidenhead to John Trethwick, her other bedtime narrative contrasted our different fates; by this measuring, she was looking forward to city life with its dancing lessons and parties, its Sunday service at a proper church—her father preferred the French service at St. Anthony's on Threadneedle Street, but her mother now worshipped at St. Mary-le-Bow, where the finery of the ladies could not be surpassed and the admiring looks of merchants' sons were most pleasing to Marion. On Thursday night of that week at the White Hart, she was going on yet again about the various pleasures awaiting her in London when my uncle knocked on the door and told me to get dressed and come to his room at once. I left Marion wide-eyed with curiosity.

Uncle Jack's room was only one floor above the tavern and I could hear faintly the voices and laughter from the patrons. I found my uncle in a curious state, nervously excited, pacing back and forth. It was unlike him, but there he was, walking to and fro, his hands behind his back, pausing now and then to peer out the window at the dark street like a man in search of answers to life's most difficult questions.

Sitting on the bed, I waited for him to speak his mind, and finally he said, "I have news, Aerlene, and it affects your situation."

"Yes, Uncle?"

"I heard not an hour past in the taproom below that John Trethwick is dead."

I said nothing but felt such a welling of relief that it cannot be described; to rejoice in another's death is not laudable in anyone, but there I was—happy enough to hear it.

"How did it happen, Uncle?" I said, only half-listening. John Trethwick was dead. What did I care how it happened? I would not have to live in his house; I could scarcely be expected to look after his lunatic sister alone. Had I been able, I would have danced a jig—yes, a proper jig for this news. But of course I just sat there, quite likely frowning lest I be thought callous.

"The man died in his sleep of an apoplexy," my uncle said. "They say his features were all grimaced as though the devil himself had laid hands upon him. But here is a terrible thing too. It all happened earlier in the week, possibly on the night of the storm. The sister had been going into his room each morning to wake him, and hadn't the wit to see he was gone until today. When he was turning in colour and smell, she ran from the house. It's a dreadful story, is it not?"

"It is, Uncle," I said. "A dreadful story."

"Merciful Heaven, what an end," he said, shaking his head. "Neighbours saw that poor distracted creature wandering and wailing along Hensington Road and took her back to the house, where they found Trethwick in his bed, his face all twisted and dark. I never liked the man, but I couldn't wish such an end on anyone. Three days dead and not attended. They say the storm on Monday may have put him off his head. He was seen in a terrible temper that afternoon, for most of his corn was spoiled and he was cursing the heavens. It may have provoked the apoplexy. Whatever happened we'll never know, but it touches on your situation, Aerlene. The sister will have to be put away. You can't live in that house with her. I won't hear of it and I don't expect your aunt to press the matter, though she knows nothing of this yet and I'll not tell her until her mind settles. I am trying to brighten her with my plans for the new house, but it will take some time.

"I have arranged for rooms at Oswald Thompson's until the new house is at least walled in and roofed. There is no room for you at Thompson's, nor would your aunt be comfortable in the same house. I am sorry to say it, but it's the truth. In the morning I intend to talk to her sister about taking you to London until the new house is ready. You have worked for me and could be useful to Boyer in his shop. Your mother always spoke well of the Frenchman and said he was decent enough and always kind, even in her circumstances. But I have to persuade Eliza. I can't see that she's overly fond of you, and her daughter and you have had your differences too. But I will talk to her in the morning about this, for they are leaving the next day, so time is short. If Eliza agrees to this, I shall have to rent a horse for you and get you some new clothes. It must all be arranged by tomorrow. Now, remember you must be more willing to take instruction and curb this obstinacy of yours. Eliza will not brook insolence, nor should you think of offering it. Meanwhile, do not say a word of this to Marion until I have talked to her mother."

Insolence? I would call upon the bear to stop my mouth before ever I uttered a single word that might offend; I would practise obedience, with an air of humility and gratitude befitting a convent girl in Papist Spain. *Forbearance* would be my watchword. That much I vowed to myself before leaving my uncle's room that night.

After a long talk with my aunt, Uncle Jack told me the next morning that they had come to an agreement; to this day I believe that money changed hands, though I never asked and was never told. Marion took my news with good humour, telling me I would have much to learn about life in the city, a remark that I took to mean she would be only too eager to reprove me for my ignorance. But what did I care? I was free of John Trethwick and his sister and was now going to London, where my father lived and worked. Perhaps one day I would see a play of his enacted? When Mam was in London, he was only three and twenty. That would put him now in his middle years, an established and successful man. How could I meet him? It was an enticing question I would ask myself many times over the next few weeks.

On Friday of that first week in September 1602, Uncle Jack put us up at an inn on Cornmarket Street, and we left Oxford the next day at first light in the company of six carriers whose saddlebags were packed with goods for trade and each man leading another horse packed likewise. Marion and her mother and I rode in the middle of this procession, and so we were fifteen horses in all. The night before, I had lain awake an hour or two imagining myself upon a horse, remembering Marion and how splendid she had looked the day she arrived in Worsley. I soon found out, however, that riding a horse was not so grand as I'd imagined, for I grew tired of the narrow saddle, and the motion itself was upsetting to my stomach. The horse was docile enough, but I found the entire experience a misery and was glad when we reached Wycombe by late afternoon. There we stayed at an inn and I was sick to my stomach in the night.

Next morning it was raining and the horse's motion as we splashed along the muddy road again brought on the queasiness, which improved only when I closed my eyes. Thus I travelled that second day like one half-sleeping with an ague, mildly feverish, my innards unpleasantly astir, wishing only for the moment when I might stand still on my own two legs. No splendour then for me astride a horse. The rain had stopped, but at one point I heard shouting ahead between the carriers and two draymen whose cart had lost a wheel and was blocking the road. I only half-listened, but was still amazed at the range and originality of the curses they exchanged as our horses stepped carefully around the broken wagon. I have yet another memory of that day on the road. As we approached London, I heard from a distance the murmuring of a crowd and then shouting and hurrahs and the carrier behind me saying, "Another gone to hell and good riddance." It was a hanging and probably at Tyburn, but still I kept my eyes closed until I heard the church bells, hammer blows to the brain of the sick, and then we were inside Newgate. When we stopped at the market, I fell from that damnable horse in a swoon, hearing above the sound of the bells a woman crying, "Is it the pestilence? Has she the pestilence?"

One of the carriers told her to shut her mouth. They were rough fellows, those carriers, though kind enough to me, and one said, "We carry no pestilence. The girl is not used to the horse, so leave off, you're waking the neighbourhood." This brought laughter from some, but yet the woman continued to shriek about pestilence.

When I opened my eyes, I saw faces staring down and the hag still yelling until a man fetched her a clout and she was quiet. All this I saw from the paving stones in my first moments in London. One of the carriers then summoned a carter and I was lifted into his wagon with the baggage piled in beside me. As my aunt and Marion moved off through the streets, I followed in the cart, listening to the voices nearby: "Is she dead, then? Was it a fever?"

I remember the creaking axle and the grinding wheels of that cart and a jarring that could loosen the teeth in your head, and on I went, past the cries of hawkers and around me the restless surge of the poor appealing for alms or offering prayers. Opening my eyes, I looked up and for a few precious moments saw between the overhanging roofs a patch of sky and three kites circling, wishing with all my heart that I was such a creature unbound from this earth by flight.

I was trundled then along a busy street—Cheapside, as I would soon discover—and some time on, when the carter stopped, I opened my eyes to the sign of a yellow hat. My aunt beckoned the carter to draw me down the laneway to the rear entrance, and the man carried me up narrow stairs to a room on the third floor, where he placed me on a truckle bed and left. A servant girl undressed me, her hand passing over my brow in search of fever, then reaching under the covers to feel my pubis for swelling. Later she brought me soup, but I had little appetite; I lay there listening to the voices of passersby in the laneway, watching the evening light fade into darkness, and then I slept.

In the night I awoke with a start, fearful that I had wet the bed, and I must have cried aloud, because the servant girl, Jenny by name, came in with a taper and, sniffing the air, muttered, "I know what's wrong with you." Drawing back the blanket, she whispered, "Oh Lord, what a mess you've made."

Not the kindest-hearted creature, she wiped me with a rag, and roughly enough too, and then pulled the soiled sheet from beneath me, grumbling about the nuisance of it all. A big, round-faced buxom girl of sixteen or so, this Jenny, and as bold in aspect and manner as poor Margaret Brown had been meek in both. When Jenny showed me the bedclothes by candlelight, I could see I had neither pox nor pestilence, but only my first courses. As the girl put it with her sour laugh, I was now of breeding age.

For some days thereafter I felt vaguely unwell, as though I were still on that horse counting the milestones to London; I lay in bed vowing that I would return to Oxfordshire on foot before ever I rode a horse again.

On the third or fourth day, however, I was up and approached my aunt in the parlour, told her how sorry I was about the bedclothes.

She was embroidering lacework and, looking up at me, said only, "I hope you realize what all this means now, Aerlene."

"I do, Aunt," I said. "My mother told me of what can now happen."

Returning to her needlepoint, Aunt Eliza said, "Much good the knowledge did her."

Then a man's voice in the room. "That will do, Eliza. There is no need to be unkind."

I hadn't noticed Philip Boyer, who was sitting at a desk in the corner writing something. I was embarrassed to have mentioned my condition in his presence, though it didn't appear to bother him. He was small in stature with a moustache, his dark hair now greying, and he was precise and handsome in his dress.

He got up from the desk and said, "I am your uncle Philip, and you are Elizabeth's daughter."

"I am, sir," I said.

Aunt Eliza said she must speak to the servants and left. Even then I felt a coldness between husband and wife.

Philip Boyer said, "I was fond of your mother. An interesting woman. Not like most English women. I enjoyed talking to her. She had unusual ideas."

I was uncertain what he meant by that and had no wish to pursue the subject; I still felt embarrassed in his presence.

"When you are feeling more yourself," he said, "I will show you some of this city where I have made my living these past thirty years. At first London is a confusion, so you will need guidance. Later we will put you to work in the back of the shop with the apprentices. You must earn your way in this city and it will do you good to occupy yourself. Idle hands make work for the devil. Is that not what you English say?"

I told him I had often heard the expression, but guessed it could apply to the inhabitants of any country who saw value in work and mischief in indolence. He laughed and told me I might be right.

"I can see you are a clever little thing," he added. "I will show you London and then set you to work during your stay with us."

Over the next few weeks Philip Boyer was as good as his word in acquainting me with at least parts of the city, for London has so many neighbourhoods one could hardly know them all in a lifetime. On Sunday afternoons we would set out westward from Threadneedle Street, walking to St. Paul's and along Cheapside to Holborn or the Strand, since Boyer favoured the rich and their mansions; the vast major-ity of Londoners did not interest him and I never saw him give a penny to the poor. As we walked, I was excited to be in the city where my father lived, and I wondered if he was now rich enough to live in one of those grand houses by the river.

Boyer was forever going on about the success of French Protestants in London. "We are good at business," he liked to say, "and we work hard. Harder than Englishmen, if you will forgive a criticism of your countrymen." It had taken him thirty years, but he had succeeded; he had a good trade with the ladies at Court and with gallants from the Inns and with those from the countryside who came into the city to be outfitted for the Christmas season. He had long ago paid his denization fee and was as good as any Englishman alive. He told me that it hadn't always been like this. In his first year in London as a Huguenot refugee, he had found it difficult, "for Londoners have never taken kindly to 'strangers,' as we foreign-born are called." He told me of one night when he was foolish enough to be out after dark and lost his way. When he asked for directions at a tavern door in his bad English, he was set upon by half a dozen bluecoats.

"They gave me a terrible beating, those young apprentices. And when they finished kicking me and I was lying in the street, I wondered how I would ever survive in this city. But I couldn't go back to France. I thought of returning to Italy, but there too thugs resent strangers. So I said to myself, I will work hard and learn their language, and one day I will be rich and it will not matter what accent I speak with, for they will have to listen. Lying on that street I promised myself that I would be careful. I would obey the authorities and one day have my own business. And I have done so."

Philip Boyer was a boaster, but I didn't mind and anyway I felt he was entitled to brag a little, as he had done so well.

One day we walked past Goldsmith's Hall to the liberty of St. Martin le Grand, where he first settled after fleeing the massacre of Protestants in Paris thirty years before. There he had found friendship and safety among other refugees, Italians and Flemish and fellow Frenchmen.

Another day we walked by the river and Boyer pointed to the cranes near Queenhithe. "There now, you see," he said, "that is where the wine barges carrying our good Bordeaux are unloaded. And across the river," he added, pointing again, "are the pits for the bears and bulls that are tormented by the dogs. You hear great shouting from there in the afternoons. It seems barbarous to me, but you English appear to enjoy such things."

"Not all English, Uncle," I said. "I myself, for example, have no wish to see a bear or bull tormented by dogs."

"Yes, yes, perhaps," he said, "but most do. I'm talking of the common people."

I could see that he had no wish to be unanchored from the generality of his observations about England and its people.

"And those big buildings beyond," he said, "are playhouses. I have never been to one myself, but many of my customers enjoy such entertainments. Even some of the ladies, I am told, like the comedies."

So that, I thought, was where my father's plays were performed. In those very buildings across the river. Perhaps one of his plays was being enacted that afternoon. But how could I find out? There was so much to learn about London, but that day Boyer was also remembering my mother, looking at me sideways from time to time.

"You're not as comely as your mother, Aerlene, but you have a ready wit, as you English like to say. Elizabeth was very pretty, but she was also gentle. I used to think that there was about her an air of tender."

"Tender? *Tenderness*, the noun," I said.

"Tenderness, yes. Exactly. A kindness in her. Rare in a pretty woman. They are usually so vain. I see it every day in my business. But vanity after all is my bread and butter. Is that not an English saying?"

"I suppose it is, Uncle," I said.

"Yes," he continued, "your mother was *une femme douce*."

"Well, Uncle," I said, "I will never be as pretty as Mam. When I was younger they called me an elf."

Philip Boyer laughed. "*Une elf*. But that's so unkind. Who would say such a thing?"

"Other children in the village."

"Well, those are unpleasant memories you must put away."

"My head was too big for my body," I said. "Of course, I have grown since those days."

"Of course. And you have a fine head on your shoulders. It's a great storehouse for your wit. Aerlene is a pretty name, too."

"Do you know what it means, Uncle?" I asked.

"I do not," he said.

"It was my mother who named me," I said. "*Aerlene* means 'elf' in some old storybook."

He put his arm around my shoulder. "My little niece, the elf." He laughed, and so did I.

One morning three weeks or so into that September, Boyer showed me the stockroom at the back of the shop, where his two apprentices were at their workbenches. I had seen them coming and going with material to display for customers, but had spoken to neither. The older one, Corbet, was perhaps eighteen, fair and handsome, though his manner was disdainful; the other, Prew, was dark and small, his skin blemished by pox marks that put me in mind of poor Tom Bradley in my uncle's workshop. Prew was shy and kept his head bowed, his eyes on the needle and ribbons he was attaching to bonnets.

Both boys were born in London, but their parents were French and they considered themselves French like their master. Corbet, for instance, soon corrected me on the pronunciation of his name; the ending, he said, rhymed with *say*, not *set*. Prew's name was originally Proulx. When together alone, the boys conversed quietly in French, and if I came upon them they would stop at once. Jenny, who was often coming and going, didn't appear to mind this, but I found it unsettling.

I was put to work unpacking the crates delivered by the draymen to the rear entrance off the laneway. That first day Corbet showed me how to use an iron bar with a claw at one end to open the crates. Uncle Jack had taken me once to see the brilliantly coloured peafowl strutting in the royal park at Woodstock, but never had I seen such glorious plumage as the feathers that lay beneath the straw in those crates: the pink of flamingoes and the blue of egrets, the pure white livery of ostriches and swans from Africa. There were soft grey lambskin gloves from Spain and France and multicoloured ribbons from Milan, cotton fabric to be knitted into nightcaps for elderly men and bolts of wool to make boys' caps, as Boyer had a contract with a nearby chapel school.

Since it is not in my disposition to remain silent long, I asked questions of Corbet and Prew, but neither seemed inclined to talk. I had better fortune with the draymen and was soon trading wits with those hearty fellows in their leather aprons, their ale-and-onion breath. At eleven o'clock Jenny brought in a tray of bread and cheese, and for each of us a tankard of weak beer. Prew always finished his meal quickly and returned to work, but Corbet took his time, eating slowly, even scrupulously, I thought, as I watched him pick the last crumbs of cheese from the trencher.

At the end of the day, I swept the floor of cuttings and began to feel the onset of dread at the long evening awaiting me, for there were no books in the household save two large Bibles, one in English and one in French.

After supper I would go to my room and watch the darkness filling the window, trying to summon up my bedroom in Worsley and the sounds of village life when the air itself seemed to breathe in the darkness; and reading my father's words, I would listen to the cries of a nightjar or the hooting of an owl, or hear my uncle snoring from along the hallway. In my room in London, I heard faintly the voices of people on Threadneedle Street, and now and then I would be drawn to the window to look down at the laneway. In the room next to me Jenny might be moving about, coughing or farting or muttering to herself. She often went to bed early because she had to prepare Boyer's breakfast and he liked his bread and hot chocolate at first light. Other times I heard the murmuring of the two apprentices in the room above me. Lying there I would write to my uncle telling him of my life in the city, but the words remained in my head, for I had no money to post a letter.

One night I was awakened by cries that made me think of village cats, and when I hurried to the window I saw a man and woman coupling against the wall of the building opposite. He was thrusting himself at her as she cried, from happiness or pain I couldn't say, but then above me I heard laughter too. It was hard to imagine Corbet laughing at anything, but there it was, and even more astonishingly there too was Jenny, for her giggling was unmistakable. The man and woman were perhaps too drunk to care, for they soon finished and staggered off arm in arm.

I returned to bed thinking of Jenny with the two boys upstairs and feeling obscurely jealous; but apart from my jealousy, I was more troubled at how wrong I could be in my assumptions. How little I really knew of others. People were far more complicated than I had imagined, and what appeared to be often was not so. I lay thinking that a great writer like my father understood this; he had created Mercutio and Juliet, Beatrice and Benedict, Sir John Falstaff, and Shylock, all of whom are complicated, by turns baffling and surprising us. They were like old friends and I missed them.

A stroke of good fortune, then, because on the following Saturday, Boyer came to my room and gave me a tester. I looked at the silver sixpence in my hand while he told me that Corbet had given good report on my work in the shop, and therefore I deserved a wage and would be paid accordingly each Saturday at noon, when our work was finished for the week. I asked him then if I might venture out by myself to St. Paul's to visit the bookstalls, as I had lost all my books in the fire. It was only minutes away, I said, and by now I was familiar with the streets around the great church. I would be cautious. He looked doubtful.

"I should ask your aunt about this," he said, "but she has gone marketing with the maid."

I promised him I would be back within the hour, and he said he would hold me to the promise.

"I know you love books, Aerlene," he said, "and I see no harm in it, but you must watch your purse and your virtue in this city."

On that Saturday afternoon in October, I was happy, if a little nervous, to be on my own in London with a six-pence in my pocket. At St. Paul's churchyard I marvelled at the variety of books on offer, mostly religious in content: Bibles and prayer books, anthologies of sermons, volumes of inspirational sayings and lessons on Christian living, pamphlets of Puritan zeal on the coming of Armageddon, miscellanies of prayers and devotions. But there were alma-nacs too, and books on travel with accounts of voyages to distant lands, some with engravings of fantastical creatures, enormous serpents, crocodiles and leviathans. Such books were costly and one vendor rebuked me as I turned a page. "No thumbprints on my wares, Miss. That book is beyond your means."

True enough, I thought, taking no offence, for I had already grown accustomed to the rough-and-ready manner of Londoners. But where were the books of plays? They seemed but a small part of the general trade and I was disappointed, for

I had imagined my father's playbooks would be everywhere. Then on a table I saw an old favourite from childhood, *The Hundred Merry Tales*, and beside it a bound copy of *Richard III*. It was like seeing an old if unsavoury friend, and I turned to the opening speech, where the misshapen Gloucester declares his hatred for all those of fair proportion:

> *And therefore, since I cannot prove a lover,*
> *To entertain these fair well-spoken days,*
> *I am determined to prove a villain,*
> *And hate the idle pleasures of these days.*

"Are you reading, Miss, or just looking at the words?"

Scarfe's first words to me, framed, of course, as a sarcastic question. And what a question! Could I read? Looking up I saw watery blue eyes, a foxy grin, the unkempt hair stuffed beneath a cap, this boy of sixteen, as pale and thin as London air. I had seen dozens like him on the streets, apprentices with their insolent tongues and swagger, their caps askew.

"I can read the words," I said.

"Can you, now?" he laughed. "Then read something to me so I know you're not here to filch a book and put us out of business. How old are you, anyway?"

"Sixteen," I said. "Is there an age you have to be to buy a book in London?"

He was still grinning. "Why, you don't look above twelve."

"Shall we divide the difference, then, and get on with our business? How much for this copy of Shakespeare's *Richard III*?" It gave me a shiver of delight to say my father's name to another.

"How do you know it's by Shakespeare? His name is not upon it."

"I know it is his work," I said.

"Could you read a passage for me?" he asked.

I handed him the book. "Select one."

He gave me another of his crooked smiles as he leafed through the book before handing it back. "There," he said. "Begin there."

I can't remember what I read that day; it wasn't an opening scene. Let's say the following, or something like it:

> *Look, what is done cannot be now amended:*
> *Men shall deal unadvisedly sometimes,*
> *Which after-hours give leisure to repent.*

Holding up a hand, he said, "Enough." And taking off his cap he bowed. An absurd gesture and I had to laugh. "Scarfe at your service, Miss," he said. "In the employ of my master, Henry Sharples, London's finest bookseller."

Everything about him suggested a careless mockery, and he reminded me at once of Mercutio. He pointed at another table, where an awkward-looking boy with reddish hair beneath his cap was stacking books.

"That is my fellow slave, Gideon Parrot, and the white-haired gentleman you see within is the master himself. I can see now that you are not just another light-fingered soul, but a small person of some learning. You read that passage well, Miss." Again he took off his cap and bowed. "I am humbled in your presence and offer my apologies."

I could see that he wasn't really sorry and that this politeness was but acting. Those pale, restless eyes were full of mischief. And the underfed look of him, the prominent Adam's apple—he was like so many other boys in that city. Raised in houses whose overhanging roofs shut out the sky. Did they ever see sunlight?

"Where do you hail from, Miss?"

"What business is that of yours?"

"Well, none if it comes to that, but I am interested in the various tongues of my fellow countrymen, since our city appears to be filled with such folk these days." He paused. "I would say somewhere in the Midlands. Gloucestershire?"

"Wrong," I said. "I come from Oxfordshire."

"Ah well," he said, "I've never been to those parts. I'd be frightened to death in those extremes with your wild animals and such. Now, what do you lack, Miss?"

"I can't imagine you pleasing many in this trade with your manners," I said.

He shrugged. "I do hope you can find it in your heart to forgive me."

"I shall take this book by Shakespeare," I said.

"Very well, but we have a third printing of that play freshly out and bearing his name."

I couldn't help myself. "I have read many plays by Shakespeare. He is my favourite poet. I have read *Richard II* and *III*, and *Romeo and Juliet, A Midsummer-Night's Dream, Much Ado About Nothing, Henry IV, Parts I & II, Henry V* and *The Merchant of Venice*."

Scarfe's eyes widened. "Really?"

"Yes, really. How much are you asking for this? It's well used, I see."

"That particular item," he said, "will cost you nine pence."

"I bought one new in Oxford two years ago for six pence. How can you charge nine pence for this? I'll give you four."

"I know where you're from now. You're from Warwickshire. People from Warwickshire are known for their bargaining skills. And you admire the work of the Warwickshire man Mr. Shakespeare. He's a fine fellow. He's been in our shop."

That stopped me. Had my father actually been in this shop? Was Scarfe just lying to me? But why wouldn't my father have been in this shop and others like it? Presumably he bought books, so why not here? I resolved to be careful about what I said.

"I'm not from Warwickshire," I said. "I'm from Worsley under Woodstock in Oxfordshire, but I love Shakespeare's plays."

"So you have said, and with spirit. Did you see his latest, Miss?"

"I did not."

"I saw it last April," he said. "Or was it May? In the spring at any rate. I am a Marlowe man myself, but I have to say this latest work by Shakespeare was excellent with some rare speeches. All about a Prince whose father is murdered and when the Prince finds out that it was his father's brother who did the deed and stole the crown, this Prince decides to seek his revenge. It played well. Pity we don't have it yet in the stalls. Probably next year. I have to say it's much better than what you've got in your hand. Old Richard is thin stuff compared to Hamlet."

I knew I should have been on my way back to Threadneedle Street. "Does he come here often, then?"

"Who?" he asked. "Shakespeare, you mean?"

"Yes," I said. "Does he come here often?"

"You might see him hereabouts on a Saturday morning, or an afternoon if he hasn't a performance, for he's a player as well. He played the ghost in *Hamlet*. Can I ask you a question, Miss?"

"Yes, of course."

"If you've read all those plays by Shakespeare, why would you want to buy them again?"

"Our house in Worsley burned down," I said, "and all my books were lost in the fire. That was my reason for coming to London: to live with my aunt and uncle while a new house is being built. I so miss my books because there is nothing to read in my uncle's house except the Bible." I hated the self-pity in my voice. "I want to own all of Mr. Shakespeare's playbooks and I'll start with this copy of *Richard III*. I'm pressed for time, so I'll give you six pence for it, though I'm being gulled and you should be ashamed of yourself. But I must get back or my uncle will be angry. If you have *Romeo and Juliet* or *A Midsummer-Night's Dream*, I'll take it instead of *Richard III*. You are right. It's early work. I'll save it for another time."

People were now crowding about the bookstall and a red-faced man who had been waiting was growing impatient. Parrot and the owner were in the shop with another customer, but Scarfe seemed unconcerned. "Calm yourself, now," he said. "I'll see what we have in the shop."

As he left, I watched that narrow back with the shoulder blades showing through the smock. What did he live on? Air? Words? Soon he returned with a copy of *Romeo and Juliet*.

"We haven't the other in stock," he said, "but I can get one for you by next Saturday." He grinned. "Tell you what.

Since you've shown such spirit, I'll give you both Crookback and the lovers' sad tale for your tester."

I was astonished. "Can you do that? Did you ask your master?"

"It's entirely within my discretion," he said, handing over the two books.

"Then I must thank you sincerely. Have you a first name?"

"Scarfe will do," he said.

"My name is Aerlene Ward."

"Yes. From Worsley under Woodstock in Oxfordshire. I'll have the other play for you next Saturday without fail." He turned at once to the red-faced man. "And how, sir, may I help you?"

That night I read *Romeo and Juliet,* looking up from time to time at the guttering candle, but when I finished reading, I couldn't sleep. I was thinking of my father somewhere in that city; with luck I would find him. Listening to the rain splashing off the roofs into the alleyway, I thought of Scarfe. He knew what my father looked like. Perhaps I could ask him to help me. I would have to concoct a story to provide a reason for my search.

Lying there, I tried to picture my father at that very moment; perhaps he too was awake, thinking of words, a wavering thought lurking in his mind, waiting to be put down on paper before it was lost in sleep. Up then in his nightshirt to light a candle from the fire in the grate. Sitting down at his desk to sharpen a quill with his penknife, glancing out his window at the dark, wet city. Then looking down to the half-written page and the uncompleted scene. Unstopping the inkhorn and dipping the quill and so he begins, the words arriving swiftly, a scrawl across the page and then on to another and yet another, sprinkling each with sand as it fills with words. Getting down at least the pith of the matter before it vanishes. Amend it in the morning when the brain has been refreshed by sleep. Might he not be doing something just like that as I lay wondering?

FELL THIS MORNING. MISSED that damnable last step on the staircase. Emily was soon by my side, as was Mrs. Sproule. Only moments before I had heard them arguing in the kitchen, but differences were put aside as they helped me into a chair in the library. Emily bathed my foot in salted water and bandaged my ankle, scolding me as she worked.

"These feet of yours want tending," she said as she knelt beside the chair. "What a sight they are!"

How forward and familiar our Emily has become in the household. She was not born to serve because her temperament resists authority. Emily should find a young and sturdy yeoman and emigrate to America, where, I have been told, no one is in service except blackamoors. I wonder if that is really true? Yet I like the girl. I am used to her ways now and couldn't manage without her. So I said that yes, my feet were doubtless an affliction to the eyes of the young, but one day she too would be old with ugly feet. She wasn't impressed with my observation.

"No grumbling about age, Miss Ward," she said. "Count your blessings for all your years. And don't neglect your feet. We're only given two in a lifetime to get us around. Look here at these corns. They want paring. And this nail on your great toe! Why, it's all gone inward with a life of its own."

I dimly saw the top of her head, the dark hair pulled back and knotted; she's often messy, but her apron was still clean. "I wish you wouldn't dispute so much with the cook, Emily."

"It's only habit, Miss Ward," she said. "We don't mind it much. But you should hold on to the balustrade when you come down the stairs. With your eyesight so poor, it's only proper sense."

"That will do now, Emily," I said. "I've had enough rebuke today."

"Miss Charlotte will have a fit when she sees you laid up like this."

"Will you do me the kindness of asking Mrs. Sproule for a tankard of ale, Emily?"

"I will," she said, getting up. "And then I'll fetch a knife and work on those feet of yours."

When Charlotte came in with Mr. Thwaites, there I was, my corns and wayward toenail repaired, my foot raised on a stool like Mr. Walter's when the gout is upon him. Charlotte fussed over me until Mr. Thwaites took hold of her hand and said I looked quite comfortable in the chair with my ale. He then told me that Cromwell died yesterday at three o'clock in the afternoon. The news reached Oxford by late last night and Mr. Thwaites had been told by a friend this morning. No one yet knows who will succeed him, but the wagering is on his eldest son, Richard, who is chancellor at the university, though not highly regarded enough to lead Parliament. I said I didn't much care because our great Lord Protector had never been a favourite of mine.

"Well," he said, "let us talk, then, of greater men. Last evening Charlotte read to me your account of arriving in London and meeting this young man Scarfe. Am I correct in surmising that he will lead you to your father?"

"Is patience not one of the cardinal virtues, Mr. Thwaites?" I asked, and then sipped my ale.

"It is indeed, Miss Ward."

"Then pray be patient, Mr. Thwaites, for my old brain tires easily these days. I am trying to recall details of my time with Robert Scarfe, but such details have lain dormant in my memory for a good long while. I have hopes that some may yet return. And if not?" I added looking at Charlotte.

"Why, then you'll have to invent them, Linny." She smiled.

"Just so," I said.

I think I will give them my books as a wedding gift. The playbooks are mostly now in tatters, but the 1623 Folio is in good condition, save for the marring of *Antony and Cleopatra* where a liquor was spilt, discolouring several pages. Over the years, I have often wondered how that came about. Too many glasses of wine inside the reader? The decanter of port upended by a clumsy elbow? At least those brown-stained pages remind me that someone in that house once looked at the book.

I bought it twenty-five years ago this summer, the year Squire Henry married his second wife, Miss Pentworth. Nicky was eighteen that year and drove me to Harrington Hall near Great Tew. A woman who had once served in the household told me the family possessed a great many books, and so I went in hope, for I had visited other places without success. But there it was and no one taking any notice of it. The farmers in their sober dark clothes had no time for literature. As for the family, they were emigrating to America and had no room for any books in their sea-chests, save the family Bible. I bought the Folio for eight shillings.

Yes, I shall give them my father's words in a fine and durable edition as a wedding gift.

SIX LONG DAYS TO fill before I would see Scarfe again, and the routine of the stockroom was not enough; I could do what was required of me in an hour and so time lay heavy upon me. Corbet ruled the roost and he did not like me. To please him, I imagine, Jenny too treated me with disdain and little Prew kept his head down on his sewing. Nobody noticed or cared if I wasn't there, and after the carters' deliveries in the morning, I took to walking up the alleyway to the street to watch the passersby. At other times, I lingered by the curtain separating the stockroom from the shop, parting it a little so I could see Boyer and his clerks serving customers, or overhear the gossip of the day as gentlemen were sized for hats or ladies were trying on gloves: Lady Somebody was apparently with child and the father a mere household groom but handsome as the devil and half her age ... Lord Such's masque that week was not to be missed ... Have you not yet received your invitation? . . . They say the Queen is unwell and has taken to her bed . . .

The Boyer family life seemed to me embittered and acrimonious, with each going his own way; Boyer had his eye only on the business. I had heard talk that he might be looking for new premises in the Royal Exchange, so he was often away for a good part of the afternoon. But even when he was home for a meal he said little to his wife; they seemed estranged and I wondered if what Marion had said about his having a mistress was true. We no longer took our Sunday walks; he regretted that he could not spend the time with me. Aunt Eliza had many lady friends and often visited them, each, I imagined, commiserating over her husband's various failings. As for Marion, she was either at her dancing class or preparing for parties, and there were several admirers, or so I was led to believe. She seldom took me into her confidence or even bothered to speak to me; I do remember she once told me that if I was reading at night as Jenny had reported, her mother expected me to pay a penny a fortnight for candles. Nothing came of that, however, and I put it down as only mischief on Marion's part.

On the Saturday following my first meeting with Scarfe, I returned to St. Paul's. It was early and he was nowhere in sight, and I went into the great church to await his arrival, as it was raining that day, a light, persistent drizzle. In all our walks around London, Boyer had never offered to show me the cathedral. He dismissed it as nothing compared to Notre-Dame in Paris. But I was both fascinated and repelled by St. Paul's. It didn't seem like a church at all in those days, but more like some vast marketplace, with vendors selling everything from prayer books to trinkets. The nave was filled with shouting and commerce and the everyday life of the street: I saw two men conferring in a corner and money changing hands, a dog wandering by to raise his leg against a column. Apparently a service was taking place, for the preacher was hectoring a few scattered souls, but his voice could scarcely be heard above the din. It was the most curious church I had ever seen, and I thought of a passage that I had read as a child in the gospel of John, in which Christ drove the moneychangers from the temple in Jerusalem. I found it amusing to see holy ground still giving way to the imperatives of commerce.

When I returned to the bookshop, Scarfe was nowhere to be seen. The rain had stopped and left behind a dank, grey day in which the smoke from chimneys seemed to hang above the city, going nowhere. I waited until the red-haired boy had finished with a customer and then asked him if he expected to see Scarfe that day. I think he remembered me from the previous week, for he wore the sneer you expect on the faces of people eager to see others dismayed.

"Oh, he likely won't be in today," he said. "Or maybe he will. You never can tell with Robin."

"But I was here last Saturday," I said, "and bought two books from him and he promised to have another for me today. My name is Ward. Did he by any chance leave a copy of Shakespeare's *Midsummer-Night's Dream?*"

Parrot was straightening a pile of books. "Not to my knowledge. You would be better off looking elsewhere."

"He promised me he would be here. Might he be ill?"

"That's unlikely," he said, carrying some books to a nearby table. "He was fine when I saw him earlier. Sleeping like an infant when I left. Mind you, he had come in only an hour before."

I left feeling puzzled and irritated by my degree of disappointment. I could have bought the book at any of a score of shops in the churchyard, but I didn't. Now why was that? I wondered.

The Saturday following, however, Scarfe was there, head bent and hair falling into his eyes as he carried books from inside the shop to the tables, and I thought as I watched him that those who write love rhymes may not be far wrong. My heart did seem to give a leap at the sight of him, and when he looked up and saw me, I was happy enough that he remembered me.

"Why, it's the girl from Warwickshire."

"Oxfordshire," I said.

He bowed his head. "Oxfordshire, to be sure."

"I came here last Saturday for Shakespeare's *Midsummer-Night's Dream*. You said you would get one for me."

"Ah, last week. Well, unfortunately I was ill."

"Nothing serious, I hope."

"A passing fever. I am now restored."

A liar too, I thought, but let it be for now. "Do you have the book?"

A shrug of those narrow shoulders with the easily placed smile entreating forgiveness. "I'm afraid not."

I was only fourteen and had never met anyone like Robert Scarfe. I knew at once that he could not be relied upon for anything; his swagger and brash knowingness were irksome and he was far from the handsomest about, yet for all that, I was beguiled by the boy.

"I tell you what, Miss. I'll get a copy for you today."

"And am I to come back for it a second time, then?"

He seemed lost in thought for a moment. "Why, it has come to me just now that I saw *A Midsummer-Night's Dream* enacted six or seven years ago. I was only a boy. My father took me one afternoon to the old theatre in Shoreditch. I thought the play was all fairies and foolishness. Why do you want it so? I have others of Mr. Shakespeare's comedies. *Much Ado About Nothing* is better stuff."

"I want *A Midsummer-Night's Dream*, Scarfe," I said. "It was my mother's favourite play."

"Your mother?"

"Yes, I read it to her the year she died. It comforted her."

No grin then, but he fixed his gaze upon me. Those light blue eyes. "Do you live hereabouts, Miss? Parrot said you were here last week. Have you work?"

"I am staying with my aunt and uncle," I said. "My uncle is a milliner with a shop in Threadneedle Street."

"And how long have you been in London?"

"Two months now."

"Have you seen much of it, then?"

"At first my uncle took me on walks, but he's too busy now. He showed me where the houses of the rich lay along the river."

Scarfe nodded. "Listen to me now and tell me your opinion. I've done you a wrong making you come back for your book when you could as easily have bought it elsewhere, and so I appreciate your trade. Let me propose by the way of apology to show you a little of our city. I was thinking that perhaps tomorrow being Sunday, you might go walking with me. What would you most like to see in London? The Tower, where the wealthy villains go?"

I have said that I was beguiled by Robert Scarfe, and I believe I was. But I also had the notion that somehow he could lead me to my father. Would I walk out without knowing him on a Sunday morning? Indeed, I would and said so. I told him that the two places I most wished to see were Finsbury Fields and the theatres across the Thames.

"Well, that's easily done and I'm your guide, Miss."

"Aerlene," I said. "Aerlene Ward."

"Aerlene Ward, to be sure," Scarfe said. "And I'll bring along a copy of Mr. Shakespeare's play."

"*A Midsummer-Night's Dream*?"

"The very one. Do you know Bishopsgate Street? It's not far from your uncle's premises."

"I know of it," I said, "but I've not been on it. Uncle Philip doesn't like that part of the city."

"Your uncle favours the better parts, does he? Well, he has shown you the city's forefront. Allow me to show you its backside. No offence, Miss Ward."

"No offence taken," I said. "And so you will show me Finsbury Fields?"

"Yes, tomorrow morning, and may we hope for a better day. Why, I haven't been to the Fields in years. I shall meet you at the corner of Threadneedle and Bishopsgate at ten o'clock tomorrow. You'll see a great stone and timber house nearby. Crosby Hall. They say Richard, Duke of Gloucester, once lodged in that house before he became King of the realm."

"Old Crookback?"

"The same."

It seemed a favourable omen: a character from one of my father's plays had lived in a house near where I would meet Scarfe.

"Please do not forget the book," I said. "I'll give you sixpence tomorrow."

He shrugged. "Oh, by the way, your Mr. Shakespeare was in the neighbourhood Wednesday last, though he didn't come by us. I saw him browsing the stalls. A well-dressed gentleman too."

It had started to drizzle and Parrot was busy covering the books with canvas, looking flustered. "Give a hand here, Robin, or you'll find yourself on the street. The old man is having a fit in there watching you gossip with this girl and no money yet exchanged." He was glaring at me as he spoke.

"Not so," I said loudly. "There's money exchanged here," I added, handing over my sixpence to Scarfe.

He looked sheepish. "Thank you," he whispered, "but Giddy is right. I'd better lend a hand."

Other vendors too were now covering their wares as the rain thickened, and I began to run, darting among older, slower people who were seeking shelter. As I ran I wondered if I was tempting fortune by feeling so happy. Perhaps Scarfe was lying about seeing my father that week. Perhaps too he had no intention of meeting me the next day. And I had given him my sixpence. I don't think I slept much that night.

But meet me he did the next day, though I waited at least twenty minutes past the hour and was about to call myself the greatest gull ever seen on the streets of London. Then he appeared, looking as if he had just awakened, hair crammed into his cap, but grinning, carrying a woven bag over his shoulder as if intent on a walk to Norfolk.

"Here you are, then, and a good morning to you, Miss Ward."

It *was* a good morning too. The rain had passed in the night leaving behind fair weather, the sky a pale blue and the air mild for the middle of November.

Scarfe was in high spirits and I felt shame for having doubted him. We passed Crosby Hall and walked northward on Bishopsgate Street, already busy with people and wagons. Scarfe shifted the bag to his other shoulder and I wondered what he was carrying in it. I had to walk fast to keep up with his long-legged gait; nor did he mind jostling others on his way, giving an elbow to this one, receiving a glare from that one. It was all one to Scarfe. A Londoner born and bred, I thought, with no time for courtesies, and why bother anyway? All on the street were alike and the few on horseback would as leave trample you as not. Scarfe never stopped talking, pointing out a large stone building beyond the wall on our left.

"That's the Bethlem madhouse, where some bay at the moonrise. I've heard them myself."

Looking at the grim building and its courtyard, I thought

of Mam and my father walking by here fifteen years ago with my father wondering aloud what it must feel like to be mad. I also saw the Dolphin Inn, where they met for the first time.

At Norton Fallgate, Scarfe stopped and set down the sack, and snatching off his cap, he bowed his head. "A brief moment of respect, Miss Ward, for Marlowe, a great wit, who once lived on this street and wrote some of his verses here." Scarfe struck a pose, pressing the cap to his chest, proclaiming,

Ah, Faustus,
Now hast thou but one bare hour to live,
And then thou must be damn'd perpetually!
Stand still, you ever-moving spheres of Heaven,
That time may cease, and midnight never come.

As he stood there in the middle of the street with people stepping past him, some with smiles and others with muttered curses, it came to me that Scarfe was drunk. But I can still remember the clarity of his voice and I loved the sound of the words.

Shouldering his sack again, he took my hand and said, "The sun will have dried the grass now and I have a bite to eat for us and, as it happens, a swiggle or two as well."

"Those lines you spoke just now," I asked, "where did they come from?"

"Why from *The Tragical History of Dr. Faustus* by Marlowe," he said. "Pa claims he would have been the equal to or better of your Mr. Shakespeare had he lived."

"What happened to him?" I asked.

"Some say death by treachery, but death nonetheless. He was killed in a brawl in a Deptford tavern. Nine or ten years ago now, it must be. He was only in his thirtieth year. Pa says *Dr. Faustus* is the greatest play ever written by an Englishman. I wish it were printed."

"No book of it yet?"

"No," he said, adding, "How soon we forget greatness!"

"How can you remember the words, then?" I asked.

"I heard them often enough from Pa, who could recount that play word for word. He said he saw it perhaps a dozen times before he lost his eyesight entirely."

We were tramping across the fields, and I saw the windmills where Mam and my father had rested after that stray arrow from the bow of the drunken archers.

I asked Scarfe how his father came by his blindness. He seemed not to hear me as he bent to feel the grass for dampness. Satisfied, he laid down his sack and began to root about, bringing forth bread and cheese and a bottle of wine.

"No drinking vessels, I'm afraid," he said as I sat down beside him. "We'll take our turns with the bottle." He grinned at me. "Or are you too young for wine, Miss Ward?"

"I can take a little," I said, though I'd had it only once or twice, a tiny cupful from Uncle Jack at Christmas.

The red wine was sweet and strong and Scarfe drank deeply, that Adam's apple bobbing in his throat as he guzzled, then wiped his mouth.

"Pa went blind working for the lawyers at Lincoln's Inn," he said. "He was a scrivener for thirty years and one of the best in London. Gave over his life to writing out deeds and indentures, conveyances. All those words on all those pages over all those years. Took away his sight and palsied his right hand." He took another long draught of wine. "The poor old darling sits at home in the dark now with a useless hand, remembering Marlowe's lines. Everything gone in service to the laws of the land and the bastards who administer them."

He broke off pieces of bread and cheese and we ate for a while in silence, watching housewives across the fields laying out laundry for drying in the pallid sunlight.

"My father," Scarfe said, "has a gift for memory and I suppose I have it too. He can still recall whole speeches from *Tamburlaine, The Jew of Malta, The Massacre at Paris, Faustus,* of course, even one or two of Shakespeare's plays that he liked. Those *Henry* plays were favourites, especially the ones with the fat rogue."

"Sir John Falstaff."

"Sir John, my royal English arse. No more a knight than I am, but yes, that's the man."

"Does your mother like the poets too?"

"My mother's dead. Jumped off London Bridge one night when I was three years old. I've only the vaguest memories of the woman. She was never much at home, it seemed."

"And you live with your father, then?"

"I do," he said, "and Mr. Parrot. But you were asking about my remembering lines. Pa has such a prodigious memory that he used to win money from the lawyers. He told me how in his younger days he would wager that he could recite word for word a two-page deed or will. And he always won. He was famous around Scriveners' Hall for his memory. And I myself have inherited the gift. But only with words. Faces and figures defeat me. I am useless near the counter. But words—well, is that not why I am apprenticed to a bookseller? It is the only trade for me. And kindly old Sharples, whom I am ashamed to say I sometimes take advantage of, is a good master. He's an old friend of Pa's. But I do filch the odd item. It's a failing and I admit it."

"You steal from your master?"

"One has to eat," said Scarfe, holding up the empty bottle, "and drink, of course. The wages of an apprentice scarcely keep body and soul together. And I chose not to live under his roof. Strictly speaking, that's forbidden under Guild law, but old Sharples doesn't mind. I don't think he wants me in his house. He doesn't even much like me. He took me on only as a favour to Pa. He gives me a little extra for lodgings, but it seldom goes far enough and I'm bad with money anyway. Parrot is worse—no more than a child is our young Giddy. We're always in need, it seems. So a book here, a book there. Why, they're hardly missed."

"But if your master finds out?"

Scarfe shrugged. "I wrote a play myself once. For my friend Parrot, who sang in the choir at St. Paul's until his voice changed and they turned him out. No family to speak of, so Pa and I took him in. As you can see, he's a poor figure with all that bright hair. I often think that in a certain light, his head is on fire. He can't play a woman's part, and with that sunken chest and no leg to speak of, he'd cut a poor figure as either hero or villain. So Pa got him a position with Sharples and I wrote this play for him thinking it might get him in the playhouses. I thought he could enact a fool, and so I wrote a comedy about a red-headed fellow who is swindled out of his inheritance by lawyers. Took it to Mr. Henslowe and then to Mr. Burbage, but they threw me out in quick order."

He was at the sack again and cried out, "Now look here what I've found. Another bottle of this horrible stuff. I'd quite forgotten I'd packed it."

He was soon working the cork out with his teeth while staring across the field at the women setting their laundry on the grass. Scarfe's jacket was far too small for him, and his skinny wrists protruded from the sleeves; he had taken off his cap now and the hair was falling into his eyes. Looking at him, I decided that if he wanted to kiss me, I would let him. But his mood suddenly darkened. Now and then he passed the bottle to me and I took only sips, as I already felt light-headed.

Then Scarfe said, "You told me you read to your mother when she was dying. Is that true?"

All this time I had forgotten to ask for my book, and I was afraid now that he didn't have it, yet I didn't wish to make a fuss. I just wanted to sit there on the grass with him and stay as happy as I was. I told him that it was all true, that I wouldn't lie about such things.

"It took her half a year to die," I said, "and I read to her most days. We had to be careful because my aunt was against plays or entertainments of any sort. She couldn't abide playbooks. Called them the devil's handiwork. My reading the *Dream* to Mam was our secret."

Scarfe frowned. "It seems an odd choice for a dying woman. Those on their last legs usually like psalms and sermons to ease them out of life. Why would your mother want a story about fairies and silly lovers running around the forest? I allow there is drollery in parts, but it's mostly foolishness."

I told him that foolishness is sometimes what we are most in need of, and then, as if I had known him all my life, I began to talk about my mother and her strange ways: her store of whimsy and odd beliefs in wood creatures and the spirit world, her pleasure in the company of an old woman who many accounted a witch; I told him of walking with Mam in the woods and how she talked to birds and flowers and didn't mind if I laughed at her. I spoke of her innocent nature and how she lay in the woods with a young man who couldn't speak, and for that was exiled to London. But I couldn't bring myself to tell Scarfe that Mam had met the poet Shakespeare when he was only an apprentice player, and that I was probably conceived not all that far from where we sat. It seemed too outlandish and I feared his disbelief and laughter.

Then, as though reading my very thoughts, he asked, "And how came you into the world, then? Were you born under a toadstool in those woods near your village?"

"No," I laughed. "Mam returned to Worsley and married a man named Wilkes, who died before I was born." So Wilkes proved more useful in death than ever he was in life, his character, more malleable now in my imagination, returning in my account not as the rogue he was, but as a poor honest fellow unlucky enough to be kicked by a horse while Mam was carrying me.

Scarfe had nearly finished the second bottle, and again he was at that bag. To my relief he didn't have another bottle, but drew from it a copy of *A Midsummer-Night's Dream* and handed it to me, saying, "Read me something from the forest and the fields. As you say, we often need foolishness in our lives." With that he lay on his back and closed his eyes. "Something now to put me in good spirit, Miss Ward. Your Mr. Shakespeare has a ready wit when he's a mind to use it. Read some of the lines he gave the mechanicals. One of them was a weaver, was he not? An idiot, but comical. As I remember, he plays Pyramus, who believes his beloved Thisbe has been devoured by a lion and so decides to join her in death. But he takes his time about it, does he not?"

I was a little heady myself from the wine, and on a whim leaned down and kissed him lightly on the lips. "I'll do better," I said. "I'll play the scene for you as though you were in a playhouse."

Opening his eyes, he sat up blinking. "Will you now, by God? A performance for me alone here on Finsbury's grass?"

"Yes," I said, grasping one of the empty bottles and getting to my feet. "And this will do for Bottom's dagger."

"That would serve better as truncheon," said Scarfe.

"It will have to do. It cannot be a truncheon, for Pyramus cannot hit himself upon the head. He must plunge the dagger into his breast. The scene demands it."

"Very well, then," said Scarfe, leaning back on his elbows. "A fat dagger, but yet a dagger. Play on. Let the commotion commence and continue. Declaim, child."

The wine fumes must surely have been in my head, for I cried loud enough to confound an elderly man who had stopped to watch. Beside him, a small dog began to bark, which seemed apt enough for my foolishness and anyway I didn't care.

> *Come, tears, confound!*
> *Out, sword, and wound*
> *The pap of Pyramus;*
> *Ay, that left pap,*
> *Where heart doth hop.*

How Scarfe laughed! Beside himself with mirth and perhaps I too had seldom been so happy. I could hear the distant church bells of London on a Sunday morning, and I was with a boy in Finsbury Fields and was making him laugh.

"I love that line," Scarfe said. "*Where heart doth hop. The weaver is an excellent clown.*"

"Be quiet," I said. "I haven't finished." The dog was barking frantically now and the old man looked merely baffled. Holding the bottle by its neck, I stabbed myself in the chest.

> *Thus die I, thus, thus, thus.*
> *Now am I dead;*
> *Now am I fled;*
> *My soul is in the sky:*
> *Tongue, lose thy light!*

"A tongue with eyes," Scarfe cried. "Jesu, I had forgot that."

"Moon, take thy flight!"

"Away, moon," said Scarfe.

"Now die, die, die, die, die."

Staggering back and beating the bottle against my chest, I collapsed finally to the grass while the maddened dog circled us barking. I lay there in laughter and tears, pleased that I had banished Scarfe's brooding humour, remembering too how Mam had so enjoyed that passage.

After a moment he said, "You're good company for your age, Miss Ward."

"Not all that younger than you," I said, wishing he would call me Aerlene, though he never did; I was always Miss Ward and he would always be Scarfe in the days ahead, and after a while I didn't mind. These were the roles we had cast for ourselves.

We parted that day by Crosby Hall, but before leaving he said he had been making inquiries of stationers and booksellers. "I was told Shakespeare lives over the river in Bankside near the new playhouse. They say he's a shareholder in Burbage's company, so he is doing well enough for himself, and you can see it in the cut of his clothes. That cloak of his would cost a barrister's fee and no mistake. You told me yesterday you wanted to see Finsbury and the playhouses. Well, you've seen the former, so now for the latter. I'll take you over the river next Wednesday afternoon if you can get free. Meet me by St. Magnus at one o'clock. Do you know it?"

"Yes, my uncle and I have walked to St. Magnus Corner."

The wine was wearing off, and I sensed that Scarfe was again growing sullen.

"I'm grateful to you for the day," I said.

"I enjoyed it myself," he muttered as he hurried away down Bishopsgate Street.

"I'll see you Wednesday, then," I called after him, but he didn't look back, only lifted an arm to acknowledge me.

When I returned to Threadneedle Street, it was mid-afternoon and I worried that my absence would be remarked upon with a flood of questions to follow. But it had not been noticed at all because there was drama enough in the family parlour with a quarrel involving mother, father and daughter. Jenny was listening at the door but when she saw me went quickly upstairs. At once I took her place, grateful for this timely distraction. Aunt Eliza's voice was raised in anger and I heard sobbing from Marion. The argument concerned a suitor who, it seemed, was not a boy in accord with Marion's age, but a man some eight years older—her dancing master, in fact, a Frenchman named Couric. For Aunt Eliza, the arrangement was unsuitable and must stop. Poor Marion pleaded on behalf of her heart.

"But I love him. Can't you understand?"

It was pitiful to hear, in a way.

From time to time I heard Boyer's voice, quieter and more reasonable, though he too was not in favour of his daughter's alliance with the dancing master. Good businessman that he was, his reason was more practical. Couric, he said, was known around town as a flagrant debtor.

"He owes money in half the shops at the Exchange," said Boyer, a hint of impatience in his voice. "You are only sixteen, Marion. You cannot align yourself to a man with such debts. I intend to speak to Couric."

Another burst of weeping from Marion.

I crept upstairs away from it all, wondering how her business with the dancing master had been discovered and whether Marion had already offered herself to him. What a nice predicament if she found herself with child! How would her sanctimonious mother deal with that? But it was an ill-bred thought and I chastened myself for its malice. Lying down, I began to count the hours until one o'clock on Wednesday, hoping that Scarfe would keep his word.

That Wednesday, I was early at St. Magnus Corner and stood watching the people as they crossed the bridge towards Southwark, some going, I guessed, to the playhouses or bear pits, others perhaps leaving London altogether, returning to towns and villages to start again, for a goodly number of them bore sacks or pushed small carts. I thought of Mam standing at that very corner waiting for Mary Pinder. I seemed to be following in her footsteps.

Scarfe was late by two quarter chimes of the St. Magnus bell, but appeared in a new doublet and hose, smelling of drink. I wondered if he had filched more books and resold them.

"And here is Miss Ward, waiting as I knew she would," he said. "And I am late again. I can only plead that I had business to attend. My apologies."

"Think nothing of it, Scarfe," I said. "I'm growing accustomed to your ways."

He took my arm. "We'll get away from this press and go by Old Swan stairs and get a wherry. It's only a few minutes."

I had been looking forward to crossing the bridge, but Scarfe was resolute and so we walked along Thames Street and followed others down an alley to the stairs. An overcast day, but mild; autumn was still lingering. A queue of sorts at the jetty with people waving for boats—playgoers fearful of being late, I imagined. The boatmen seemed to favour the well-dressed, and though Scarfe was in new clothes there was about him—I had to admit it myself—an unfinished look; despite the clothes he still had an air of the saucy apprentice, and his waving arm was overlooked until others had boarded. Finally a boat edged its way to the dock and we climbed in. Scarfe was clearly angered by the slighting he'd suffered, and as we were rowed across, he looked sulkily upriver muttering about the manners of watermen. I wished he would leave off, since I was enjoying the boatride.

The wherryman was amused by Scarfe's grumbling and said, "What's that you say, young master? Have you a complaint to lodge against our trade?"

Scarfe turned to look at the grinning man as he pulled on his oars. "Yes, I have," he said. "When trade is good, you fellows don't mind choosing your favourites. It's a matter of the gratuity, I suppose."

"It could well be, young master," said the wherryman.

Looking westward again Scarfe muttered, "It's not right. People shouldn't be kept waiting over their dress."

"What's that, young master?" said the man. "I didn't catch the words. I hope you're not being uncivil to my fellow watermen."

The man was used to all sorts of trade—that was clear enough—and he knew how to mock if the occasion demanded it. His even-tempered but insolent manner had put Scarfe off balance. After we docked on Bankside, the man was elaborate in his praise of the two pennies Scarfe gave him.

"Thank you, young master. We'll dine well tonight, me and the missus and all nine whelps."

Scarfe muttered, "Bastard," as we joined the crowd headed for the bear pits and playhouses. The word always rankled, but I was too busy looking at everything to care, watching the ladies on the arms of their gallants, apprentices taking the afternoon off, apple and hazelnut sellers—it was all there in front of me.

It was said that my father lived somewhere in this neighbourhood, and I was both surprised and disappointed; if he was now successful, why would he choose a place so crowded and noisome? When I said as much to Scarfe, he only shrugged.

"Close to his work, I suppose, or perhaps he likes the bawds. There's enough of them about. I need a drop of wine, and no mistake. That wherryman put me out of spirit."

In a tavern called the Antelope, he ordered wine, but I wanted nothing but a clear head. The wine soon improved Scarfe's outlook, however, and he said, "The performance will be on now at the new playhouse, so it will be quiet by the door. Let's see if anyone knows where your Mr. Shakespeare lives."

He was right. The performance had started at the Globe and we could hear laughter now and then. A hand-bill on a post announced the play, but since it was not by my father, I took no account of the author or title. A man in mouse-coloured livery stood by the entrance cleaning his nails with a penknife.

"A good day to you, sir," said Scarfe. The doorman nodded and went back to his nail cleaning. "I wonder," said Scarfe, "if you would be good enough to tell us where we might find Mr. Shakespeare?"

The man looked at us in an unfriendly manner. "Why would you want to find Mr. Shakespeare?" he asked.

"As it happens," said Scarfe, "this young lady is his cousin from Warwickshire. Just arrived in the city and staying with her aunt and uncle on Threadneedle Street at the sign of the yellow hat. Very fine premises indeed. She'd like to pass on good wishes to her cousin."

Scarfe's lie made me nervous, and the doorman's close examination of me didn't help. But perhaps he surmised that I *was* newly arrived and therefore ill at ease.

"Haven't seen him about lately," he said. "But he has lodgings at the Elephant on Clink Street by Horseshoe Alley. Down that way," he said, "where you came from."

"The Elephant, you say," said Scarfe. "I think I saw its board. Thank you, sir."

And off we went. "There now," he said to me, "we're on our way to finding the man. I wouldn't mind a word with him myself."

I couldn't believe how easily Scarfe had lied. And it worked, though I wasn't easy with the deception.

"I'll tell him how much I enjoyed his *Hamlet*," said Scarfe. "A very fine piece of work. Poets enjoy such praise."

At the bar in the nearly empty tavern, he told the same story to the tap man. I was Shakespeare's young cousin from the country, eager to make his acquaintance. The tap man didn't even bother to look at me, but spoke directly to Scarfe.

"You missed him by a few days," he said. "Saturday last, maybe Sunday, he left for lodgings in the city. Somewhere in Cripplegate, I was told. Too bad. A gentleman, Mr. Shakespeare, and a good customer."

Scarfe was pleased with the results of his inquiries. "I have missed my calling, Miss Ward," he said as we left the Elephant. "I might have done excellent service as a bailiff. I've tracked our man now to Cripplegate and I know that neighbourhood well. Why, Scriveners' Hall is on Noble Street, and when I was a boy, Pa used to take me to the Christmas revels there. I'll ask around."

I was grateful for Scarfe's help, but he made me nervous with his forward behaviour. I wondered what my father would make of him, and something within told me not much. But then, if it came to that, what would he make of me?

We had a quarrel that afternoon—Scarfe and I—by the Bankside dock. "Why don't we return along the bridge?" I asked. "You don't like wherrymen, and walking the bridge will cost nothing."

"We'll go by water," he said.

"But I'd like to go by the bridge and look at the shops. I'm told it's something to see. Even Uncle Philip says no city in Europe has a bridge to match London's."

Scarfe, however, looked grim and determined and repeated only that we would return by water. It put us both into a sulk, but by water we went, arriving again at Old Swan stairs.

When we parted at the corner of Gracechurch and Lombard streets, he told me to come by the bookstalls on Saturday afternoon. He might know more then and we could arrange for a visit to Cripplegate. We each felt ill used by the other as we parted, and it wasn't until later that it came to me—his telling of how his mother had leaped to her death from London Bridge. That would account for his shifting humours that afternoon, and I was sorry I hadn't remembered earlier. He had probably vowed never to place a foot on London Bridge, and who could blame him? Even crossing the river in a wherry might have proved an ordeal.

CHARLOTTE UNWELL THESE TWO days past and she took to her bed finally this afternoon with a mild quinsy. This damp weather has provoked coughs and fevers in many, but this evening the doctor came by and told Charlotte that her throat would soon improve and she was not to fret about her wedding, now two weeks off. Emily has been attending her with cold cloths to her brow and a soothing syrup for her throat. Mr. Thwaites looked in too and sat with her for a quarter hour, a calming presence to the poor girl, who can easily get into a state over something as uncomplicated as flowers in the church.

I too have not been well of late and fear the stone may be blocked, for this week past I have been making only a little water each day, and that with some difficulty. It is a true measure of my selfishness that with Charlotte now laid up I worried about finishing my story. Then, quite remarkably, as Mr. Thwaites was leaving, he asked if he might take down my words while Charlotte was recovering.

"She feels you may be worrying about your memoir, Miss Ward," he said, "so I told her that with your permission I would be only too happy to assist you for an hour or two each afternoon until Charlotte is well again."

When I asked if he was not occupied with his duties and his forthcoming marriage, he laughed and said that weddings were for women to fuss over. "I merely have to turn up at the church, Miss Ward."

I knew this was exaggerating; he has many accomplished friends in the university and ecclesiastical communities who are coming to his wedding, and Charlotte told me that he was arranging a dinner for them at the rectory the evening before the wedding day. Still, he is a man who remains unflustered by uncertainties; he will be an excellent husband for Charlotte.

I accepted his offer with thanks, though now it feels odd to imagine him taking down my words. Yet why not? Charlotte has read what's already there to him, and he has always expressed a keen interest in my father and his work.

THE DAY FOLLOWING MY Bankside visit with
Scarfe, Marion came to my room, a surprise
because she had virtually ignored my presence
in the house until then. But that day she sat upon my bed,
where I lay reading, and spoke of her unhappiness. There
had been yet another quarrel with her mother, and Marion's
eyes were red from weeping. Of course she didn't know that
I was aware of her situation, so she began to tell me all about
Alphonse Couric and what a good man he was, how they
had fallen in love and how she didn't care that he was eight
years older. It wasn't his age that bothered her parents; it was
the fact that he was not a merchant's son. He was not good
enough for the family.

Marion told me she had not slept for a week and I could
believe it, for her beautiful hair was lank and uncombed, her
pale face swollen. I had dismissed her merely as a spoiled
and headstrong girl. Yet now I could see that she was capable

of genuine distress and therefore pitiable. She loved this Couric, who might well have been worthless; Boyer was probably right about the dancing master with his good looks and charm, his considerable debts. Couric was not the right man for his daughter. But Marion loved him. She said they had talked of going to France, but where? They had no money and her father was intent only on hindering their happiness. She was wretched with grief.

She spoke as I imagined adults might speak of love, yet she was not much more than two years older than I was, and listening to her made me think my feelings for Scarfe were childish. I was taken with his youth and swagger, his careless good looks. Would I weep so at his loss? Could I ever feel so despondent over losing someone? Marion and Couric were like Romeo and Juliet, whereas I was more like Mercutio, who would never love another so ardently that he might risk heartbreak. Marion spoke that afternoon of loving another completely, and listening, I saw how I had misjudged her. To this day I regret my misjudgment, because Marion with her reddish golden hair, her long perfect feet and fingers, her slender neck would be in her grave within a year, as would Aunt Eliza and Jenny, and Prew and Corbet, all perishing in the plague that ravaged London the following summer.

We learned all this a year later from a letter sent by Boyer to my aunt and uncle in Worsley. Reading it then, I recalled how during one of our walks he told me of once being in Antwerp to buy lace goods, and there becoming infected with the pestilence. But the infection was mild and he survived, and somehow that saved him during later outbreaks, including the dire plague of 1603. I expect that he married again, but after that letter we never heard from him. He lived to the great age of eighty years, as I discovered in a letter from a London solicitor in 1633 informing me that I had been left five pounds in Philip Boyer's will. The bequest helped me to purchase the Folio that summer.

Yet all that lay in the future. As much as I listened with sympathy to Marion's plight that day, my mind was ever drifting to Scarfe and whether he could lead me to my father. The Saturday following, I went to St. Paul's yard, but Scarfe was not to be seen and I did not want to ask the red-headed boy, who clearly didn't like me. I kept well out of his sight and loitered about the stalls most of the afternoon, but Scarfe never appeared. Nor did I see him again over the next fortnight, though I went each day, once summoning the nerve to approach Parrot and his surly manner.

When I asked of Scarfe's whereabouts, he said only, "Robin doesn't work here now."

"And does he work elsewhere, then?" I asked.

He smirked. "Here, there, everywhere, that's our Robin." At the time, I guessed he had been caught stealing and was dismissed, and perhaps was even in prison. So it was a great surprise one December afternoon, a day of fog with drizzle and the smell of coal smoke in the air, when Jenny came to my room and said there was a boy to see me. My aunt had turned him away from the shop entrance and told him to use the alleyway door. When I went below stairs, there was Scarfe standing inside by the door shaking the rain from his cap and grinning. I could see Prew and Corbet sneaking glances at him while they worked at their benches. Corbet seemed especially irritated by Scarfe's presence, and Jenny stood apart, frowning with her arms crossed. Scarfe had been drinking. I could smell it on him. He swept the cap before him as he bowed.

"Your humble servant, Miss Ward."

I didn't know whether to laugh or cry at his unkempt look, his lopsided grin.

"Are you free?" he whispered loudly so all could hear. "Can I take you away awhile from all these bonnets and feathers?"

Grasping his arm, I quietly said, "They can hear you, Scarfe. And you're drunk."

"And why should I care if they listen?" he said. "Those two at their benches are rogues and want hanging from the look of them."

Corbet's face was reddening. "You hold your tongue, boy, or you'll find trouble."

"What's that?" asked Scarfe, settling the cap on his head. "Trouble? I'll give you trouble, bonnet maker, if you step out into the alleyway with me. I'll thrash you to within an inch of your life. Yes, and you can bring the runt with you."

Little Prew kept his eyes on the box of feathers before him.

I took Scarfe by the arm again. "What are you about? You'll have my aunt back here before long. You shouldn't have come here during work hours."

Scarfe whispered in my ear. "Today is my birth date, girl. We have new rooms and are going to celebrate. I want you to join us. I'll have you back before the Angelus bell."

Hushing him, I said he was carrying on like a drunken fool.

"Perhaps, but I have news which may interest you." He looked over my shoulder. "Stop your ears, you two," he called. "It's none of your affair." He glanced then at me. "Now it has stopped raining. Will you step out into the lane-way with me?"

In that alleyway dripping with water from the over-hanging roofs Scarfe said, "I have news of a certain poet known in this town."

"What news?" I asked.

"First you must come to our rooms and help me cele-brate my birth date." I must have looked uncertain, as he then said, "Fear not, for Pa will be there and later my good friend Parrot."

His excited cheerfulness was always hard to resist, but it could also mean trouble ahead.

"Listen," he said, "I have come into money. I have chinks in my purse and I am dying of thirst. And soon it will be raining again."

"How can I leave my aunt like this? Without a word?"

He shrugged. "An hour or two of merriment. You're good company. I told Pa about you and your Mr. Shakespeare. He'd like to make your acquaintance."

To go with him would be defiance and no doubt trouble. Where was Boyer that day? He was not at home. But it didn't matter anyway. I was going. Scarfe had news about my father, but he wouldn't tell me unless I went with him. I knew I wouldn't have it out of him until he felt like giving it.

"Why aren't you working anymore at Sharples?" I asked.

"A long and sorry tale," he said. "Far too cheerless for my birth date."

"Are you working elsewhere now? It can't be easy to change masters so quickly."

"Miss Ward, I have money in my pocket and wish to celebrate my birth date. Will you come along with me for two hours, or no?"

I remember running upstairs for my cloak and coming back down past the apprentices and out the door with Jenny's laughter behind me. A milky sun behind the clouds glimpsed between rooftops as we moved through the streets, and I hurrying as always to keep up with Scarfe's long legs, stepping around puddles and dog turds, horse buns, dodging the wheels of carts and wagons in Cornhill, passing by Leadenhall Market and onto Aldgate. I had walked this far eastward before, but as we went beyond the wall I was soon lost amid the alleys and laneways and shabby buildings of Whitechapel. I knew I could never find my way back on these streets among such rough-looking people.

I followed Scarfe into a tall, narrow house, one of many like it, and we climbed four floors to the topmost, where he knocked on the door and waited for the sound of the key turning. The door was opened by a frail elderly man with a shawl about his shoulders, for the room was cold and dank with no fire in the grate. It was Scarfe's father. I could see him in the face. But the old man's eyes were blank and I watched him feel his way towards a chair by the grate. The room was makeshift and dishevelled with boxes lying about unopened and a trunk by the only window. I wondered what had brought father and son to these dismal quarters; it struck me that it was a place not so much for living as for hiding.

The old man had found the chair and was seated. "There's someone else about, Robin," he said. "Is it the girl you spoke of?"

I hadn't made a sound since entering, but the blind can sense others without seeing them, as I myself now know.

"Yes, Pa," said Scarfe. "It's Miss Ward from the countryside. The young friend I told you about. A great admirer of Shakespeare and a fine reader of poetry."

He had found a bottle of wine, and after pouring some into a wooden cup, he took it to his father. Then he drank a cup himself and poured another. I told him I didn't want anything.

"A reader of poetry," said Scarfe's father. "Well now. Come over and introduce yourself, Miss Ward." He had reached out with his left hand. "I'm afraid my other hand is no longer useful," he said. "I am Robin's father, Martin Scarfe. Welcome to our new home. I'm sure there is untidiness about, as we've only just settled here."

Scarfe was refilling his cup. "All the comforts of home, Pa. I'll get us sorted out in time."

"As you can tell," said Martin Scarfe, "I no longer have my sight, and so may I ask your age, Miss Ward?"

"I am fourteen, sir," I said.

Scarfe was now rooting in the chest, and looking across at him, I realized how foolish I had been to come with him to this place. The rain was heavier now, and I watched it striking the window by Scarfe's head as he knelt at the chest. What did I know of him anyway? He was a drinker and a thief and a liar. And what would my uncle Jack think if he could see me in this meagre place? There must have been money in that chest because Scarfe had found what he was looking for and was putting on his cap. I asked him where he was going because I feared being left alone with the old blind man and his ruined hand. I shouldn't have been afraid of him, but I was, as he sat there leaning forward in the chair staring vacantly into the empty grate.

"I have to get provisions," Scarfe said. "There is not a rind of cheese in the larder, nor a drop of wine in this vessel. We want meat and drink in abundance and coal for the fire."

"Yes," the old man said. "These rooms are insalubrious and no mistake. A little fire would be welcome, Robin."

"And you shall have a fire soon, Pa. We also need candles. There's only a stub left in that holder above the mantel. Perhaps, Miss Ward, you could read something to Pa while I'm gone. There are books here in the chest. I won't be above an hour." And then he gave me the key. "Open the door to no one but me," he whispered as he left.

"Light the candle, Miss," said old Scarfe. "There are flints about, I believe. What are you called?"

"Aerlene, sir," I said. I found the flints by the candle-holder and with some difficulty lit a piece of paper and then the candle. Beyond the window the sky was dark with rain.

"And you're from Warwickshire, then?" he asked, and I said I was, for I might as well have been according to the Scarfe family. Martin Scarfe then asked me how I came to live in London and I told him about the circumstances that had brought me there and all of it was the truth except my invention of the shire I had come from.

"And how long have you known Robin?"

"Not long, sir. We talked mostly at the bookstall, but we spent a pleasant few hours together one Sunday in Finsbury Fields."

"Yes," he said, "Robin told me about your afternoon and gave you good report."

For several moments we said nothing and finally he asked, "Why did you come to this place, Miss? Why would you leave your uncle's on Threadneedle Street and come to these rooms? I know Threadneedle Street. It's a proper address. Why come here?"

"Your son said it was his birth date and he wished me to be at his celebration."

The old man was absently rubbing his palsied hand as if agitated. "Well, it is his birth date and that at least is no lie. He was born eighteen years ago this day. But I don't know what there is to celebrate beyond the bare fact of his coming into this world."

I was surprised that Scarfe was eighteen; I had thought he might be only sixteen. The old man was rubbing his hand again, and I found it troubling to watch, for he looked so bewildered and unhappy.

"I fear for him, Miss. I truly do," he said. "We came to these rooms early this morning. Trundling our goods in a carter's wagon through the streets at daybreak, fleeing the wrath of a landlord. It's beyond shameful."

He settled back in his chair as though grateful for someone to listen to his tale. I was no longer afraid of him.

"Robin hasn't told me, but I fear he has lost his position at Sharples. I got him the apprenticeship four years ago because Henry Sharples has been a friend for thirty years and he did it as a favour; it worked at first and Robin did well enough. He's clever and knows books and was personable in the trade. But within the year past he has changed. I don't know what has come over him, but the boy is not what he ought to be, Miss. You should know that now and I tell you as his father. He is not as he ought to be. I have done my best with him, but I have failed, and now I fear he is in some difficulty, either with the authorities or possibly with a money-lender. I'm sure he was stealing from Henry Sharples and the poor man simply ran out of patience. Who could blame him? Now Robin may be stealing from others. Or borrowing money from those who practise usury and have ruffians about who will do their bidding if the debtor doesn't pay. We travelled those streets this morning like fugitives. You sound like a good girl, Miss, decent and well raised. And you are very young. You should leave this place. I'll be all right alone."

"I am not afraid, sir," I said, though I was.

"Go out," he said, "and find your way back to Threadneedle Street before it grows too dark. I thought I heard a nearby clock striking three a while ago. It must be nearing four now. If you lose your way, ask someone, but don't inquire of the rougher sort or anyone in drink. I surmise we are in a poor neighbourhood. Ask a vendor. Be courteous."

I was tempted to do as the old man said, but I was even more fearful of being out on those streets by myself. "I think," I said, "I'll stay until your son returns. He promised to take me back to my uncle's by the six o'clock bell. He told me he had news of my fellow countryman, the poet Shakespeare, but he hasn't yet told me."

"Ah, Shakespeare the poet," he said, as though he'd quite forgotten his instructions to leave. "You know him, then?"

"No, sir, but we both come from Warwickshire."

"Yes, so you said. He's a fine playwright, Shakespeare. Robin took me to the Globe playhouse to see his *Hamlet*. It was in the early spring. After Eastertide. It had a good run, that play, and I enjoyed listening to it. I found the young Prince's mind quite astute with many fine distinctions in his thoughts. Have you seen the play, Miss?"

"I have not," I said. "I only arrived in early September."

"Ah. Well, perhaps it will be printed soon, for it was well received. An exemplary poet, Shakespeare. Does your family know the man?"

"Not exactly, sir," I said, but he might not have been listening.

"I was born in Canterbury," he said, "and that's where Marlowe too was born. My family knew the Marlowes. His father was a shoemaker, and when I came to London in 1568, I was wearing shoes made by Marlowe's father. I was just your age, Miss. Fourteen. And I walked to London for work on the recommendation of a family friend. I was apprenticed to a stationer named Robert Hill. Would you believe me, Miss, if I told you that over the years I became a prosperous and respected man in my trade, that I once gave a speech on legal language in Scriveners' Hall on Noble Street? Robin was there. A Christmas party for scriveners and their families. He was only six or seven and I could tell he was proud of me even if he didn't understand a word I said. There I was in front of all my fellow scribes, talking about the law and the words that define the laws. Now we trundle our few goods through the streets, ahead of the creditors. He is too fond of wine, Robin, and not to waste words, Miss, he is also a thief. He doesn't think I know it, but I do. I may have lost my sight, but I haven't yet lost my reason. I believe he is stealing from Henry Sharples, a good man who took him on as a favour to me. I think he's also stealing from other bookshops, and borrowing from rough people. He hasn't said as much, but that is surely why we are in these straightened circumstances, here in the suburbs of the city. It's shameful to me, Miss."

"Can I read something to you, sir?" I asked, but he seemed lost in his thoughts and anxious to tell his story.

"I can understand why you might want to meet your fellow countryman," he said. "In 1587 when Marlowe's *Tamburlaine* was playing at the Rose, I felt as you do now. Why, he came from the same town as I, and there he was with a great success in London and still only in his twenties. Everyone was talking about *Tamburlaine* that year. I would have liked to meet Marlowe and tell him how proud I was to be from the same city, but I was told he was prickly and difficult, and I was afraid. Robin told me that he met Shakespeare at the bookstall and said how moderate he is in temperament, so a different sort of man than Marlowe. I hope you meet him, Miss. But poor Marlowe. Had he lived longer, I do believe he might have proved a greater poet than your countryman. Do you know his work at all, Miss?"

"No, sir, I do not."

"Well, you are young. *Tamburlaine* was an entertainment, but the plays following: *The Jew of Malta, The Massacre at Paris* and *Dr. Faustus*. Oh, I loved those plays. *Faustus* I saw performed at least half a dozen times. I believe I could yet recite it all. I have spent my life among words, Miss, though not, alas, the words of poets. For my sins, the words of lawyers. The words that bind us to the laws of our land. I often wished I had been a joiner or a mason, but I had neither the strength nor the inclination. I was frail as a youth and fit only, it seemed, for taking down words. As your countryman Shakespeare has Hamlet say to the old fellow, the girl's father, 'words, words, words.' I have been fit only for the taking down of other people's words. Countless words. Over thirty years of writing words ten hours a day, six days a week. I can still recall writs and leases, bills of sale and conveyances, the entanglements of law, and behind all the words, stories—the bitterness of disinherited children; the disputes over everything from a childhood toy to five hundred acres and a fine house; the stories of lives enhanced or ruined by property and goods and money. Hope or despair in the words I took down. Shakespeare makes good sport of lawyers and the law near the end of *Hamlet*. Robin told me the Prince was staring at a jester's skull in the churchyard as he mocked the men of law."

Old Scarfe stopped for several moments and I didn't know what to say to him. Then he continued, "I often sit in this darkness imagining the thousands of reams of parchment, the thousands of quills, the hogsheads of ink used in my lifetime. My wife used to chide me for my stained fingers. Claimed she couldn't abide the smell of my right hand. She couldn't read a word herself, poor little thing, and never appeared to understand that my stained fingers paid for her bonnets and gowns. I fell in love with a pretty child, Miss, and have lived to regret it. She wasn't much of a wife to me, and soon took up with bad company. Did Robin ever speak of her to you?"

"He did, sir, yes."

"Yes. She leapt from London Bridge one night, did Kitty. Pursued by who knows? Demons? The henchmen of her creditors? A jealous lover? The boy was only three years and his mother not yet twenty. A sad tale indeed, but over and done with now these many years. You asked if you could read something to me and I would enjoy that, Miss. It's been some time since I've heard good words. Words of comfort or understanding. When he was younger, Robin used to read to me, but he no longer cares for Scripture. I fear he has lost his Christian beliefs, and much as I admire Marlowe's work, I think his influence on Robin was harmful since Marlowe made no secret of his disbelief. A dangerous mind, and his wild thoughts and reckless behaviour, honey to the young. I am now forty-eight years of age and must seem ancient to you. I hardly saw the sun in my lifetime, and breathed the dust of generations in my searching through old court scrolls. But I admire the talent of men like Shakespeare and Marlowe. I still believe in God and his Son, the everlasting Christ, and my greatest regret is that I am no longer able to read Scripture."

"What would you like to hear, sir?" I asked.

"You could read a psalm to me," he said. "The forty-sixth has always refreshed my spirit. I believe you will find a Bible in that chest."

And I did, though I might have easily recited the words by heart, since I remembered them well enough from the Geneva Bible on the sideboard in the dining room of the house in Worsley, with Aunt Sarah at her embroidery, listening with prim satisfaction as I read.

When I finished the psalm, we sat in silence. I had thought Martin Scarfe an old man of at least sixty, but he was only forty-eight. How strange it all was to me there in that shabby room in Whitechapel, listening to the rain in the dwindling light, having just read a psalm to a blind man. But what must have scored my imagination that December afternoon so long ago—for over the years the Scarfes, both father and son, have returned to me in dreams—was the depth of that old man's misery: a life of toil at a trade he despised, an unfaithful wife and a wayward son, blindness and a palsied hand and penury towards the end. Job himself had scarcely endured more. And looking at Martin Scarfe in our silence together, I remember wondering how I could avoid such unhappiness. Such thoughts are apt to trouble us most in the hours of a sleepless night, and then with daybreak vanish like the mist across a meadow. But I have carried such thoughts from that room in Whitechapel over all these years and with them attendant questions. How may we find some measure of contentment in this life? Or should we look instead to whatever lies beyond the grave? And if we fail the test, as preachers are so fond of prophesying? What then? Damnation?

Old Scarfe seemed on the verge of sleep when I heard footsteps on the stairs, a light knocking on the door and

Scarfe's voice. I opened the door to see him dripping with rain, his arms filled with parcels and bottles, a satchel of charcoal.

"Is that Robin back?" called his father.

"Yes, Pa, and I'm laden with good things," he said, stepping past me into the room, glancing at the Bible I was still holding. "Reading Scripture to the old fellow, were you?" he whispered. "Thank you."

In his quick, nervous fashion he laid out the wine and foodstuffs upon a worn deal table. "Could you start a fire, Miss Ward? It's damp enough in here and no mistake."

I knew how to work a grate, and so found paper and crushed a small basket for kindling, and with the charcoal soon had a proper blaze.

Scarfe, still shivering from the cold and wet, addressed the fire as he held both his hands before it. "Oh, warm us, we beseech you. Have pity on us poor, suffering mortals. We are in your debt."

"A fine fire now, Robin," said his father. "Miss Ward has done the job. I can feel the heat now."

"Are you close enough to it, Pa?"

"Yes, I don't want a spark to light upon me. I don't want to perish in fire."

Scarfe laughed. "No fear now, Pa. Our little friend from Warwickshire will keep an eye on you—won't you, Miss Ward?"

"I will," I said.

Scarfe abruptly clapped his hands. "Now, we'll celebrate. Giddy should be with us soon."

"Where is he, then?" I asked.

"Where is he?" said Scarfe, looking around in mock alarm. "Why, he's selling books for Mr. Sharples, I hope. Someone has to earn a living in this household. Now, some wine to warm our innards."

And soon he was filling the wooden cups again. I took a little, but had no great taste for it. Scarfe had bread and cheese and mustard and sausages. He found a toasting fork and set me to cooking the meat. There were also pippins and medlar tarts and plenty of wine. The meal was ready when Gideon Parrot came in, sodden from the rain and in ill temper. Scarfe fussed over the boy with wine and a cloth to wipe his face and hair, but Parrot was not easily placated, complaining of the long walk from St. Paul's with bawds and louts in the streets.

"It makes no never mind, Giddy darling," said Scarfe. "You are home safe and sound now, so partake."

Parrot nibbled at a piece of cheese and sulkily drank his wine. "There were people today looking for you," he said to Scarfe. "Old Sharples was not happy to have such fellows on the premises."

Scarfe smiled. "It is to be hoped, Giddy, that you didn't lead them to our door."

"I'm not such a fool as that," he said. "Anyway that was this morning. They left hours ago."

"But perhaps," said Scarfe with a hint of mischief in his voice, "you didn't notice the one who may have lurked unseen, waiting for you to lead him here."

"So what was I to do, Robin? Tell me that. Look behind me every minute? There are plenty enough on the streets around here who could do me in."

"True enough, old son," said Scarfe. "Have another cup of wine and don't give those fellows a thought. I'll deal with them in good time."

"You'll deal with them," Parrot sneered. "That I would have to see."

"Now, now, it's my birth date, so be of good cheer. Try one of these little pies. They're tasty, and no mistake. Then we'll have a song and perhaps a reading or recitation. Pa likes to hear such things, don't you, Pa?"

"I do, Robin," said old Scarfe. "What did Gideon say about the bookshop?"

"Nothing of import, Pa. Now, let us be merry. Will no one wish me well?"

To which Parrot said, "How could anyone be wished well in such a hovel as this?"

To my surprise and without thinking I replied, "I expect it's the best he could do in his circumstances. We're out of the weather, at least."

"Well said, Miss Ward," Scarfe cried. "You speak the truth."

"The girl from the countryside, is it?" said Parrot with a smirk. "I didn't see you there crouched by the fire with your sausages."

"Now, now, no soreness of heart on this, my night. Full cups all around," said Scarfe, and he went about the room filling our cups, though I had scarcely touched mine. As he bent down by the fire, he kissed the top of my head. "Thank you for your thoughts on my behalf, Miss Ward."

The afternoon had got away from me and now it was evening, and I knew I was not going back to my aunt and uncle's until morning; there was nothing I could do but wait until then, and it came to me that I should take what I could from this singular experience. Old Scarfe recited a passage from *Dr. Faustus* and Scarfe himself some lines from *Tamburlaine*, and I, heartened perhaps by a few sips of wine, declaimed Prince Harry's lecture to Falstaff, the foretelling of the likable old rogue's downfall. Even Parrot was impressed and all three applauded. Gideon Parrot then sang a love song and I was surprised at how moved I was by the sweetness of his voice.

The wine finished, Scarfe's father went to bed in one of the two small rooms at the back. The two boys sat talking together for a time and then Parrot went to the other room. Scarfe had drunk a great deal of wine, but he was steady enough and helped me arrange a blanket before the fire, where I would sleep wrapped in my cloak. It didn't bother me not to have a bed, though he apologized, sitting on the floor beside me and saying that he was sorry too he had not returned me to my uncle's by the Angelus bell.

"First thing in the morning," he promised, "and no mistake." Then he said, "I should tell you that I have made inquiries about your father and now know where he is lodged."

Startled by his use of the word? I surely was. Startled and apprehensive.

"What do you mean, my 'father'?" I asked. We were talking in low whispers.

Scarfe grinned. "I know he is your father, Miss Ward. I can see him in you. Don't fret. I have told no one and never will. Why should I? It's your business alone. You will find him in Silver Street. In St. Giles Cripplegate in the house of a Frenchman named Mountjoy, who has a shop on the premises. His trade is in women's headdress. Perhaps your uncle knows him. Another Frenchy."

"My uncle knows nothing of this," I whispered angrily. "No one does, except you."

"And you worry that if others know you will be ridiculed?"

"There is that, yes," I said, "but there is also my father to think on. I do not want it known in the city that he sired a bastard. I don't want that report made of him, Scarfe."

"Nor shall it be. Your secret is safe, Miss Ward."

I asked him when he had first suspected it.

"Why, from that first day at the bookstall. Had you been merely passing, I might not have taken note of the resemblance. But when you stopped and were so intent on seeking his work, I studied your features. At first I thought you might well be a niece or cousin. I still believed as much on our day at Finsbury. But on our visit to Bankside, when I told the doorman at the playhouse that you were Shakespeare's cousin, I saw you flinch at the word, and I could tell you didn't like it, and I said to myself, 'Robin, old son, this girl is not his cousin; she's his daughter.'"

For several moments we sat gazing into the fire, as people will in conversation when some point has been arrived at and a truth revealed. At length I said, "What will you do, Scarfe? What will become of you?"

"Become of me?" He laughed softly. "Why, who knows what will become of anyone? We are all at the behest of Fortune, the wicked old bitch!"

"But you make matters worse by putting yourself in harm's way with your thieving and borrowing."

Scarfe kissed me lightly on the cheek and whispered, "All shall be well, Miss Ward. And as I've said, your secret will be safe with me. Now we must sleep and early tomorrow I will get you back where you belong."

That night I slept but fitfully, once hearing a drunken tenant from a floor below singing, and later the cries and sighs of lovemaking from Scarfe's room. I wasn't particularly surprised, for I could see behind Scarfe's banter and Gideon Parrot's scoffing the affection between them. Maybe I loved Scarfe too, in my own way. I loved his generous heart and spirit, perhaps the legacy of his young mother, and his subtle intelligence and fondness for poetry, the gifts of his gentle old father.

Scarfe awakened me at daybreak. It had stopped raining and under a pale, cold sky we hurried through the mostly empty streets as far as Leadenhall Market, where the vendors were opening their stalls. I told Scarfe I could make my way from there, and we wished each other well and parted. I didn't look back, and I doubted I would ever see him again, though the thought saddened me as I hurried westward along Cornhill. Yet now I knew where my father lived, and I remember saying the sentence aloud because I liked the sound of it. *He lives in a house on Silver Street.* I would make myself known to him and then I would leave the city; London was not for me, and over those weeks of late autumn, I had begun to long for Worsley. I missed Uncle Jack and even my stern and rigid aunt. I wanted to walk again in the meadows and woods near the village, even in winter. I was of age and would have to find employment in service, but I was now prepared to do that.

Jenny admitted me that morning and Boyer, always an early riser, was already at his breakfast. I was glad, at least, that Aunt Eliza was still asleep. Boyer was composed as he listened to my story, amended to suit my purpose, though not straying altogether from truth: I laid emphasis on the friendship I had formed with the young apprentice bookseller and the celebration of his birthday, his father's blindness and frailty, the presence of Scarfe's red-headed friend who also worked in the book trade; I omitted Scarfe's drunkenness and dishonesty, the squalid condition of his quarters and any mention of my father. I said I was sorry that I had overstayed my time and caused concern for him and Aunt Eliza, but the streets were too perilous to walk by dark and so I had accepted shelter for the night.

Boyer listened while at his bidding Jenny served me a slice of bread and a cup of chocolate. When I finished, Boyer remarked on what he had heard from the apprentices about Scarfe's behaviour, and I replied lamely that he was easily provoked, but certainly no ruffian. Boyer told me that Aunt Eliza intended to write my uncle that very day to report my truancy and request that he take me back, as she no longer wanted the responsibility.

"You must understand, Aerlene," he said, "that we already have enough to concern us in the household. We cannot take on more, and so I have agreed with your aunt that you must leave. We will await your uncle's reply, and then I will see about transport for you."

I told him I understood and would do as he and my aunt wished, but I wanted to make clear that I had done nothing improper on my night away. He said he believed me and would report as much to Aunt Eliza when she arose. He said I looked tired and should go to bed. I was grateful to him for understanding and happy enough that it was not the ordeal I had imagined.

In my room, I lay on the bed whispering the sentence, enjoying its graceful sibilance, *He lives in a house on Silver Street.*

YESTERDAY CHARLOTTE and Mr. Thwaites were married in St. Cuthbert's, the service conducted by an old university friend of the groom. Mr. Thwaites's parents are long dead and Charlotte told me some time ago that he was raised by his mother's sister and her husband in Bath. His widowed aunt attended the service. Mr. Walter gave Charlotte to the bridegroom at the altar and Charlotte's friend Annabelle was her maid of honour. The church was filled with friends, mostly from Oxford, though a few had made the journey from London.

We had a wedding dinner for twenty-five at Easton House, and Mrs. Sproule and Emily were assisted by three servants on loan from a neighbouring manor. Charlotte's wedding day was overcast but dry. When she came down the aisle with her husband, she looked quite lovely as she smiled at me. Mr. Thwaites too looked kindly upon me and

I was happy beyond measure for both of them, glad that I had made the effort to attend, as I have been far from well of late, this damnable stone tormenting me day and night. Last Friday, Mr. Thwaites asked me if I would consent to being seen by a lithotomist in Oxford, a man of notable regard. I said I had no memory of acquainting him with my ailment and he replied, "But I can see you are in some discomfort this morning, Miss Ward. Charlotte has told me of your difficult time. Pray don't be angry with me. We have only your well-being in mind."

"Charlotte," I said, "is very free with information about my personal problems, Mr. Thwaites, and though I'm grateful for your concern, I want no fussing over my difficulties. And I certainly have no wish to see your man from Oxford. Nature will take her course, for good or ill."

"Sometimes," he said quietly, "science can lend a hand to nature, Miss Ward—"

I interrupted him by asking where I had left off. He looked rueful, weary perhaps of trying to cheer an irritable old woman. "You were describing your feelings towards the boy Scarfe, who I must say is a complicated youth."

"What are the last words on your page, Mr. Thwaites?" I asked.

He looked down at the book and read, "'. . . his subtle intelligence and fondness for poetry, the gifts of his gentle old father.'"

When Mr. Thwaites left that morning, I looked through my glass at his writing. He has an excellent hand, but the letters are smaller and closer together than Charlotte's, so I can scarcely read them. It makes no matter; the words are on the page and my story will soon be finished. I shall have to wait, however, because the bride and groom left for Oxford today, to return on Wednesday. They had originally planned a fortnight's holiday visiting friends in Bristol and Bath, but Charlotte was not at ease with the thought of being away so long from Easton House, citing my poor health. I tried to dissuade her from changing their plans, but to no avail, and perhaps my entreaties struck Charlotte—who knows me better than I had thought—as only half-hearted, for indeed I fear they were. It is selfish of me, but I am glad that they have gone not too far, nor for too long.

AUNT ELIZA TOLD ME that I was not to leave the house for longer than two hours on Saturday and Sunday afternoons; during the week I was to assist the apprentices in the workshop and, if there were no tasks to perform, return to my room. She had written to Uncle Jack and Aunt Sarah. Marion was both curious and fascinated by my adventure and confessed that she had never considered me the sort to attract a boy. Overlooking her pejorative observation, I hastened to say that in my case the particular boy was of no consequence; it had been a mere dalliance between two childish hearts and certainly nothing as serious-minded and profound as what was taking place between her and Monsieur Couric. Poor Marion may have been capable of genuine love, but she was still a vain girl, and easily flattered. But it did win me an ally in the household. Over the years, I have sometimes regretted my tendency to tell people what I think they want to hear, though it has proved useful in managing those who live and work together under the same roof.

My concern was to find my father before the arrival of Uncle Jack's reply to my aunt's letter. I knew that despite what happened, my uncle would take me back, and as soon as this was confirmed, the Boyers would have me on my way. It was important therefore to use my Saturday and Sunday afternoons to good purpose, since I could not be certain how many I would have left.

In the workshop, Jenny and the apprentices were reticent in speech and manner, but I didn't care; I did what I was told and kept to myself. I was waiting for the carters, and when one arrived, I stepped into the laneway to greet him. He said he missed my banter—and where had I been? I told him I'd been ill, then asked him where Silver Street might be.

"Cripplegate," he said. "Not far, Missy. Not above half a mile from here. Just take Poultry to Cheapside and go as far as Wood Street and turn right. Go up Wood and just beyond the Bell Inn on your left is Silver Street."

On Saturday afternoon, I set out despite a cold drizzle, walking up Wood Street past the great carrier inns with their travellers and bustle and the smell of stabled horses. I saw the Castle Inn, where Philip Boyer had put Mam up the night before she left in the company of the Tuttle family with all their belongings in two wagons drawn by oxen.

That was fifteen years ago and I was then in her womb. Beyond the Bell, I turned at Silver Street, where I asked a man if he knew the Mountjoy house. "The tiremaker, you mean?" He pointed down the street. "Across from the church at the corner."

This was nothing like Bankside, but a prosperous neighbourhood with many fine houses and, near the end of the street, a great property with a walled garden. But now that I was on the very street where he lived, I was overcome with nerves, and to compose myself I went into the churchyard across from the house and lingered there for fifteen or twenty minutes, reading the names on the tombstones and from time to time glancing across the street. I saw two well-dressed women go into the house, and all this time I was nervous with a fast-beating heart, as I didn't know how to approach him. What would I say? How would I begin? Would it not be an unpleasant surprise to have a fourteen-year-old girl tell you that she is your daughter? Would such an assertion not unsettle anyone? What if he denied everything? Rebuffed me? He had his own family, and when all was said and done, it was a long time ago when he knew Mam. He was young then and newly arrived in London. The city was filled with young women, and he was making his way in the theatre world. Mam could have been just one of many and now quite forgotten.

Such questions assailed me as I stood in the rain in

St. Olave's churchyard that Saturday afternoon watching the two women come out the front door of the house. And all those questions made me so fearful that I lost whatever resolve I might have had and left the churchyard and walked back to Threadneedle Street.

Awaiting me there was a parcel from Uncle Jack and an accompanying letter addressed to the Boyers. This was sheer coincidence, having nothing whatsoever to do with Aunt Eliza's letter, which would not yet have reached Worsley. Uncle Jack wrote of a position available with a Miss Nash, an elderly woman in Woodstock, whose maidservant was soon leaving for marriage. Uncle Jack had spoken to Miss Nash about me, and she appeared interested, but I must try to get back as soon as possible for an interview. He asked the Boyers to arrange my way; in the parcel was a handsome new cloak for the journey and money enough for a horse and lodgings. Aunt Eliza could not have been happier had I said I was walking to Worsley that very afternoon.

When Philip Boyer looked in on me later, he remarked on how provident it was that I might soon find work in a good house. He was only sorry that the parcel had not arrived a few days earlier, for it would then have been unnecessary for his wife to have written. Still, he was confident that my aunt and uncle would welcome my return. Meanwhile, he had arranged for the rental of a horse with a pack train leaving for Oxford early in the week—Monday or Tuesday, if the weather improved. I suggested that he and his wife were keen enough to be rid of me and he offered only a thin smile.

"Aerlene, if you read your uncle's letter carefully, you will see that the position is not yours until you talk to this Miss Nash and see if she finds you acceptable. There may well be others applying, so it is important that I get you back to Woodstock as quickly as possible. It is all in your best interests. I shall take you to the Castle Inn myself and see you safely on your way."

"My mother told me that you put her up at the Castle Inn when she left London fifteen years ago," I said, "so I am following in her footsteps, am I not?"

"I do not think the circumstances are quite the same," he said. "At least I hope I am correct in thinking that."

"Well, Uncle," I said, "you are correct."

"You don't seem altogether pleased by this news."

"I am fine with it, Uncle."

"We can only hope this rain lets up. They like a dry road, these fellows."

But *I* could only hope I would see my father the next day, and much of that night I lay awake willing the bad weather to continue.

It was still raining lightly on Sunday when I knocked on the door of the house on Silver Street dressed as a girl might for church in my best skirt and smock and my new cloak. A maidservant, not much older than I was, opened the door, and when I asked if Mr. Shakespeare lodged in the house, I sensed her appraising me and my country accent.

"He does," she said.

"I wonder if he might be at home?"

"You might wonder," she said, "but I can tell you he is not."

The pertness of her reply may have unstrung me a little, and I said I was from Mr. Shakespeare's part of the country, newly arrived in London and looking to pass on good wishes to him. I immediately regretted the lie, but didn't really know what else to say.

"Mr. Shakespeare went out some time ago," the girl said. "But I shall tell him you called when he returns. What name shall I give?"

"Ward," I said. "Aerlene Ward. What might be the best time to find him in?"

"Difficult to say," she said. "He is often at the play-house across the river, though he has been working in his rooms of late. When he is here, he goes out to his dinner at one o'clock. You might try tomorrow at that time. I shall tell him you called."

"I'll come by tomorrow, then," I said.

I had said it without thinking because the next day would be Monday. Yet as I walked away, I decided that

Aunt Eliza and her curfew could go to the devil. If the rain held, the carriers would not set out, and I would try again to meet my father.

As it happened, the rain did stop that Monday, but not until late morning, when a strong northerly wind scattered clouds across the sky, the sun emerging to cast the streets into vivid light, then just as quickly darkening them as the sun went into hiding. The wind met me full in the face as I walked towards Cripplegate. When I turned in to Silver Street, the St. Olave's bell pealed a single chime. I was halfway down the street when I saw a man in a dark cloak leave the house at the corner and begin to walk towards me holding a hat to his head in the gusty, bright air. He stopped and, taking off the hat, looked down as if inspecting it for something. Loosening threads? A rent, perhaps? It was only a few moments, but time enough for me to observe the wide brow and balding head. Then he settled the hat again and, with a hand upon it against the wind, began to walk towards me, looking downward as if his mind were occupied elsewhere.

As he approached, however, he glanced up at me, and I said, "Excuse me, sir, but are you Mr. Shakespeare?"

Stopping, he regarded me severely with hazel eyes that were very like my own. "I am," he said, "and you would be the girl who asked after me yesterday."

"I am, sir, yes."

"I saw you from my window on Saturday in the church-yard. What is it you wish of me?"

I remember how disappointed I felt at his guarded air, the note of mild exasperation in his voice.

"You told the maidservant you were from Warwick-shire," he said, "but your accent is most certainly not War-wickshire. Where is your birthplace?"

"Oxfordshire, sir," I said. "Worsley under Woodstock."

"I know it," he said abruptly. "Your name is Ward?"

"Yes, sir. Aerlene Ward."

"So what brings you to my door, Miss Ward? And why that lurking in the churchyard?"

The buffeting wind kept his hand on the big hat, and my hair was now loose and disordered and I could have wept at the circumstances of our meeting: the unruly air, my father's curtness, my own labouring to explain my presence before him. I spoke quickly, imagining my words flying through the wind unheard.

"I believe you knew my mother, sir," I said.

"Did I?" he asked. "And when was that?"

"It would have been some fifteen years ago, sir. When you first came to London and lived in Shoreditch. My mother told me you were an apprentice player at the time. One Sunday she said you went walking together in Fins-bury Fields and you were nearly struck by an arrow. People had been out all night revelling and one young man was showing a girl how to use a bow, and her shot misfired and the arrow passed carelessly by you and my mother. You remarked then on how easily chance can overtake us in this life. She never forgot that."

He looked away and I wondered if he remembered that morning in Finsbury Fields.

"It's a poor day to be standing in the street," he said. "It's cold when that sun goes behind the clouds, and I'm tired of holding this hat on my head. Let us walk along. I'm going for my dinner. Have you eaten?"

"I have not, sir," I said.

"Well, come along. I'm going to the Mitre. It's not far."

We walked and he asked what had brought me to London, and I told him of the fire that destroyed our house and how I came to live with my aunt and uncle, who was a milliner in Threadneedle Street. I hastened also to tell him that I was soon returning to Oxfordshire since I had just learned by letter there might be work for me in service at Woodstock. He nodded as though this news was agreeable, inferring perhaps that at least I was not there to pester him and would soon be gone. And truthfully, I wanted him to have that impression.

"And how did you find me?" he asked. "I have only moved within the month."

"A friend told me, sir. He works in a bookshop at St.

Paul's and knows your plays well. He made inquiries of friends in the trade."

He smiled. "Well, this city is rich enough in wagging tongues."

From the weary amusement in his voice, I sensed he now felt better disposed towards me.

The Mitre was spacious and noisy, the taproom filled and a fire blazing in the enormous hearth. My father nodded to several while the landlord escorted us past the benches and tables to a small room at the back with its own fire. As my father busied himself ordering our meal, I wondered what I could next say to him. He was hungry, he said, and the meal was bountiful with oysters and cutlets, a dressed rabbit and a minced pie. Stewed apples. It may not have been precisely that, but something very like it. He enjoyed his food, my father, and I could see from the tightness of his doublet that he was growing a little stout in his middle years. He urged me to eat, though I had no appetite. He said he no longer had much stomach for ale and now drank only wine. As we ate, we listened to the voices and laughter from the taproom; he was studying my features and I think he knew I was his daughter. Yet I found him circumspect by nature. Not a man to welcome complication into his life. I thought of how my mother had seen him as a prudent and watchful young man fifteen years before, and now I too saw those qualities in his disposition.

"So," he asked finally, "you are now about fourteen?"

"I am, sir," I said. "I was fourteen on Lammas Eve. The same age as Juliet."

He smiled wryly. "Did I mention her birth date in that play?"

"You did, sir. Early on the nurse reminds Lady Capulet, *On Lammas Eve at night shall she be fourteen*."

"You have seen the play enacted? Where? In Oxford?"

"I have seen none of your plays performed, sir, but I have read them many times."

"You can read?" He looked both surprised and pleased, and I could not help myself and told him of all the plays that I had read.

Finishing his glass of wine, he stared at the pitcher for a long moment before pouring another. "And your mother," he asked, "did she perish in the fire?"

"No, sir. My mother died of a lingering illness a year ago last January. She never married and I was raised by my uncle and aunt, who were not in the house when it burned."

"So," he said, "the aunt and uncle in Threadneedle Street are looking after you in the meantime."

"Yes, but now my uncle in Worsley has written of this position in Woodstock, so I shall likely return this week coming. We got his letter only two days ago."

"Your mother's dying was prolonged?"

"Yes, sir."

"And painful?"

"Yes. Over those last months I read *A Midsummer-Night's Dream* to her. It was her favourite, and she was happy that you have done so well with your writing. I read the *Dream* to her six times in that last year, though she died before the end of the last reading. It was our secret, Mam's and mine, for my aunt in Worsley is a Puritan and thinks that plays are fit only for the wicked. I hid all your playbooks beneath the rafters in my bedroom, but all were lost in the fire and now I am trying to replenish them."

A boy came into the room and we watched him clear away the plates and cutlery and put more coal on the fire. After he left, my father said, "And you are called Aerlene?"

"Yes, sir. Mam got the name from an old book of Saxon tales. She said that when I was born I looked like an elf, and *Aerlene* means 'elf' in the Saxon tongue."

Smiling he said, "I remember your mother. Her name was Elizabeth."

"It was, sir."

"A gentle-natured soul. She was new to London, and she missed the countryside and so did I. We often talked of the woods and streams and meadows of our childhoods." He finished his wine. "I remember that day by the archery butts in Finsbury." He stared at me for another long moment before saying, "What do you want of me? Do you know I have a family in Stratford?"

"I have been told so, yes."

"My younger daughter is only three years older than you and our first-born, Susanna, is now a woman of nineteen. It's hardly believable to me at times."

"I want nothing from you, sir," I said. "I wanted only to meet you. To tell you how happy my mother was at your doing so well. She lived her life as she found it without regretting anything, raising me with help from her brother, my uncle Jack, who is a good, honest draper in Woodstock. I have met you now, and you were good enough to see me and have me to dinner. That is enough."

Silence fell between us again as we listened to the clamour of the taproom beyond the door. I asked him if he would be going home for the Christmas season to see his family.

"No," he said, "our company has been summoned to perform before the Queen at Whitehall on St. Stephen's Day night."

"What will you present to her?"

He looked at the fire. "They want a comedy. Something to lighten her spirit, as she is in poor health. We shall probably enact *What You Will*. She may be amused by the Puritan steward in his yellow stockings."

"I have been told that your *Hamlet* was well received, sir. My friend accounts it your best work yet."

He was silent for several moments. "Perhaps, but my last play was not so well regarded. An old and honest acquaintance told me it was too bleak. 'Bitter as gall,' he said. 'As full of bile as an egg is full of meat. Who wants to lay out pennies to hear such stuff?'" He told me this with another of his wry smiles. "As I say, an old and honest acquaintance and ever forthcoming in opinion."

"And are you working now on something else?" I asked.

Perhaps it was the wine, but he looked genuinely amused by me now. "You *are* interested in my work, are you not?"

"I am, sir, yes."

"And appear to study it."

"I do."

"I am writing about a Moor."

"A Moor, sir?"

"Yes," he said, staring away again at the fire. "I am half-way finished, or thereabouts."

"What will the play be called, sir?" I asked.

"I don't yet know."

"I'm sure it will be a triumph."

Turning his face from the fire, he looked at me intently. "Perhaps, perhaps not. I must be getting back now."

"Of course, and thank you for the meal."

"You are leaving the city this week?"

"I am, sir," I said. "My uncle is arranging transport for me."

When the boy opened the door again, my father asked for the reckoning and then said to me, "It's as well you go before more rain makes the roads too mucky. This northerly wind will bring fair weather for a few days, but you should dress warmly, as it will be cold on the highway this time of year."

After counting out the coins for dinner, he stood up and fastened his cloak with a handsome pin. "There has been plague all summer in the Low Countries," he said. "I was told a Dutch ship was stayed by the authorities at Gravesend in August, and already there have been plague deaths in Yarmouth. It's coming this way and in all likelihood we'll see it by spring. It's one reason I moved up here. It's crowded in Southwark and the pestilence readily thrives there. But I'll leave the city too when times demand it. They'll close the playhouses, and anyway, London is no place to abide the plague. You are well to be off to the countryside. Now, let us do battle with that stubborn northerly, and mind it doesn't blow you down the street. You're not very big."

"I'll be fine, sir. I'm stronger than I appear."

"I well believe it," he said, "and it seems you have a good mind too."

On the street the signs over shops and taverns were creaking in the turbulent air, but the bursts of sunlight between the clouds were pleasing and I felt excited and joyful at having met and talked to my father at last, each syllable of his compliment resounding in my ears.

Standing in front of the Mitre he said, "Your mother was a woman of sweet temperament, and I am sorry she was taken from you so early in your life. I lost my son six years ago this August past, and I mourn him yet."

He put on the tall hat again and held it firmly in place with one hand. Looking fully at me one more time he said, "It appears you are well tended by your relatives. I wish you a good and long life, child, and I am glad we met."

Turning then, he walked away and I called after him, "And long life to you, sir, as well. I hope your play about the Moor is well attended." But already he was hurrying up Milk Street holding his hat, the black cloak flapping in the wind.

Looking back across all the years, I wonder now if I was as joyful as I have described, for not once had he acknowledged our kinship. Not once had he called me his daughter, though I could tell he knew I was, and perhaps that is enough.

I went by St. Paul's yard one last time. I didn't expect to see Scarfe there and he wasn't. Gideon Parrot was busy carrying armfuls of books from the tables into the shop. There were few customers about and when he returned I asked him how matters stood, and what of Scarfe and his father? Were they all still in Whitechapel? I told him that if he thought I was prying, it would be the last time, because I was leaving the city in a day or two.

Parrot looked tired and worried and told me he hadn't seen Robin in over a fortnight. "He has no sense at all," whispered Parrot. "He owes to many and has so freely stolen here and in Paternoster too that he dare not show his face. He is either in hiding or in the river. When I return to that horrid place in the evenings, his father is sitting there wringing his bad hand and weeping. I do what I can for him, and my master is trying to find a place for the old man in one of the almshouses for the winter. It's not good for him in that room all day. He can't make a fire and we've been visited too by rough people. One took me by the throat the other night and might have put an end to me had the other not restrained him. They want to know of Robin's whereabouts, but I said I could tell them nothing in God's truth, and they went away. But they will return, I have no doubt. I may tell you, girl, that I fear every day for my life." He looked back towards the shop. "You'd best be going now. I have work to do and I can't afford to lose my position."

Walking back to Threadneedle Street I thought of how people enter our lives and then vanish to leave us wondering: I thought of Margaret Brown and the hunted look of her as she stood by the blacksmith's wife that day in August before fleeing into the night and that storm. Where was she now? Or was she anywhere but in a grave?

And what of Scarfe? Now wandering or hiding in the great muddle of humanity around me that was London. Perhaps as she left the city Mam too wondered what would become of her friend Mary Pinder, lying ill in a trugging-house in Shoreditch. These were all unfinished stories in our lives.

A day or two later, I left London riding in the company of a half-dozen carriers with their packhorses. So miserable had been my first experience that I had thought never to ride a horse again, but I had no choice and this time the journey proved uneventful. The weather stayed fair but cold, and my new cloak kept me warm. I also wore one of Boyer's school caps, and some men in the company thought me a boy, which I didn't bother to dispute. I shared a room with three of them at an inn at Wycombe, sleeping in my cloak, which fell below my skirt and apron. Their snoring and farting kept me awake most of the night, but lying there I didn't mind; it was only one night in my life, and I had met my father and would soon see my uncle.

After reaching Oxford in the afternoon of the second day, I walked the eight miles to Woodstock, arriving at my uncle's shop as darkness was falling and he was closing for the day. He was as overjoyed to see me as I was him, and as in former days, we walked together down the hill towards Worsley and our new house, now roofed and habitable though not entirely finished within. My aunt Sarah received me civilly enough, but she looked unwell, and Uncle Jack told me she wasn't yet in full spirits; the destruction of her home had mortified her will. She was, he said, in many ways easier to live with, but not the woman she was, and he missed that part of her.

My interview with Miss Nash was successful and the week following I was in her employ as maidservant and companion. She was old and frail, the only daughter of an Oxford clergyman, quiet and moderately tempered. She ate the same meal twice a day, at seven o'clock in the morning and at seven o'clock in the evening, a bowl of wheaten porridge boiled in goat's milk to which I added a cup of Malmsey. Each Saturday evening I bathed her, for she wished to be clean-smelling at Sunday service.

Miss Nash was a tiny creature with soft, wrinkled skin, and as winter came on with its dampness and cold, she asked me to share her bed for warmth. We lay together, youth and age, listening to the wind, feeling the house cool as we waited for sleep; sometimes she talked of her life in Oxford fifty years before, during the reign of Queen Mary, the Papist. Her father had witnessed the burning of the Protestant martyrs Ridley and Latimer, and Miss Nash recalled how shaken he was upon returning home that day to tell her about it. I had read about their deaths in Foxe's book as a child, and found it passing strange to be listening to someone whose father had been there to witness it.

Each Saturday at noon Miss Nash gave me two shillings for my week's work and out of that I had to buy my food. On

Sunday afternoons, I was free to visit my aunt and uncle, who always provided me with an extra loaf, a plate of cold meat, a pudding, or a few apples to supplement my meals. It was, I suppose, a tolerable life, though I can't say that I thought much about whether it was or not; it was just life as I imagined I was supposed to live it. It ended one February morning when I heard a thump and, coming from the pantry saw Miss Nash on the floor where she had toppled from her stool chair. There was still breath rattling in her, and I ran at once to my uncle's shop, and he returned with me, but the old woman was dead.

For several weeks, I stayed in the new house in Worsley and then one evening in March, Uncle Jack came home to say he had been talking with Mrs. Easton about me. She was expecting her first-born by lambing time, and so was in need of a nursemaid. Already she was conducting interviews with local girls. My uncle said he had spoken to her about my service with Miss Nash, but more importantly about my reading, which greatly interested Mrs. Easton, since reading was uncommon among servants.

I came to Easton House for my interview on Lady Day, 25 March 1603. The day before, the old Queen had died and all churches throughout the land, it was said, were tolling knells. As my uncle and I walked down the avenue of elm trees that spring morning, we could hear the solemn note of St. Cuthbert's bell. It was raining, and I worried about my hair being tousled, but if it was, Mrs. Easton took little notice, putting me at ease at once by asking gently about my experience with Miss Nash and my duties in her house. I told her what I had done, confessing to no skill whatsoever in needlework, which made her laugh in praise of my forthrightness. She asked if I had any experience in the care of children and would I enjoy looking after them. She told me she wanted her children to be surrounded by books at an early age. She would have much to do running the household and needed a reliable guide to help with their education. Did I understand that? I said I did and told her I had yet little experience with children, but I would learn their humours and inclinations and prove a good nursemaid to them. I loved reading stories aloud, and when the children got older I would teach them their letters and tell them stories to nourish their imaginations. I liked Mrs. Easton so much and wanted so badly to work for her that when she chose a passage from the Bible for me to read, I began but haltingly; yet as I read, the words themselves appeared to calm me and soon I was reading with such a confident air that Mrs. Easton laughed and raised a palm.

"That will do nicely, Aerlene. Thank you," she said.

I waited then outside the hall while she conferred with my uncle, and when he opened the door, I saw from his smile that my life at Easton House was about to begin.

THIS MORNING WHEN I finished and Charlotte had written the last words, she came to my chair and embraced me. As she knelt, I breathed in her fresh, clean smell, but I can no longer mark her features; like everything else now, they float before me in this watery grey light. But I could detect a sadness in her. I know she has been worrying about me this week past, for I have been dropsical and feverish, my legs now badly swollen. Emily helps me up the stairs and undresses me as she would a child. Charlotte holds my hand at bedtime.

Last evening I fell asleep early and have now awakened from a dream of Nicky. We were in the light carriage, returning from the auction at Harrington Hall. My copy of the Folio was covered in cloth and safely in my lap. A summer evening and Nicholas was only eighteen. As his switch deftly touched the little mare, she quickened her pace and we moved briskly along the road. I was telling Nicky a story and he was laughing at its foolery and we

ENVOIE

Miss Ward passed beyond all earthly cares during the night of 30 September, and after funeral observances at St. Cuthbert's she was buried in the churchyard within the Easton family plot. Miss Ward was loved more than ever she imagined by Charlotte, her brother Walter and those who served with her in the household. Charlotte has written to her sisters in America, and I doubt not but that our loss will likewise be duly mourned across the sea by Catherine and Mary.

I once asked Miss Ward which of her father's plays was her favourite, and without hesitation she told me it was Hamlet. *It is perhaps fitting therefore to end her story with Horatio's farewell to the Prince:*

And flights of angels sing thee to thy rest.

The Reverend Simon Thwaites
The Rectory of St. Cuthbert's
Worsley under Woodstock
Oxon

5 October 1658

AUTHOR'S NOTE

Among the many estimable biographies of Shakespeare available, I found Stephen Greenblatt's *Will in the World* [USA, 2004] and Michael Wood's *Shakespeare* [USA, 2003] not only refreshingly concise, but also engaging and informative. To help navigate the streets of old London, I referred to John Stow's magisterial *A Survey of London Written in the Year* 1598 [UK, 2005]. For a guide to how life might have been lived on those streets, Lisa Picard's *Elizabeth's London* [UK, 2004] was both helpful and entertaining. *The Diary of Ralph Josselin*, 1616–1683, edited by Alan Macfarlane [UK, 1976], provided interesting glimpses into rural life in seventeenth-century England.